Didn't I Say to Make My Abilities *Average* in the Next Life?!

VOLUME 2

Didn't I Say to Make My Abilities *Average* in the Next Life?!

FUNA

ILLUSTRATED BY

Itsuki Akata

Seven Seas

Seven Seas Entertainment

DIDN'T I SAY TO MAKE MY ABILITIES AVERAGE
IN THE NEXT LIFE?! VOLUME 2

© FUNA / Itsuki Akata 2016

Originally published in Japan in 2016 by EARTH STAR
Entertainment, Tokyo. English translation rights arranged
with EARTH STAR Entertainment, Tokyo, through TOHAN
CORPORATION, Tokyo.

Seven Seas books may be purchased in bulk for promotional,
educational, or business use. Please contact your local
bookseller or the Macmillan Corporate and Premium Sales
Department at 1-800-221-7945, extension 5442, or by
e-mail at MacmillanSpecialMarkets@macmillan.com.

Follow Seven Seas Entertainment online at
sevenseasentertainment.com.

TRANSLATION: Diana Taylor
ADAPTATION: Maggie Cooper
COVER DESIGN: Nicky Lim
INTERIOR LAYOUT & DESIGN: Clay Gardner
PROOFREADER: Jade Gardner, Stephanie Cohen
ASSISTANT EDITOR: Jenn Grunigen
LIGHT NOVEL EDITOR: Nibedita Sen
DIGITAL MANAGER: CK Russell
PRODUCTION DESIGNER: Lissa Pattillo
EDITOR-IN-CHIEF: Adam Arnold
PUBLISHER: Jason DeAngelis

ISBN:978-1-626928-71-8
Printed in Canada
First Printing: June 2018
10 9 8 7 6 5 4 3 2 1

God bless me?

CONTENTS

The Kingdom of Tils ----- *C-Rank Party "The Crimson Vow"*

Mile

A girl who was granted "average" abilities in this fantasy world.

Reina

A rookie hunter. Specializes in combat magic.

Pauline

A rookie hunter. A timid girl, however...

Mavis

A knight. Leader of the up-and-coming party, the Crimson Vow.

Eckland Academy

The Kingdom of Brandel

Marcela

Adele's friend. A magic user of noble birth.

Morena

The king's third daughter. Intrigued by Adele.

Monika

Adele's friend. A merchant's second daughter.

Aureana

Adele's friend. A peasant girl.

Previously

When Adele von Ascham, the eldest daughter of Viscount Ascham, was ten years old, she was struck with a terrible headache and just like that, remembered everything.

She remembered how, in her previous life, she was an eighteen-year-old Japanese girl named Kurihara Misato who died while trying to save a young girl, and that she met God...

Misato had exceptional abilities, and the expectations of the people around her were high. As a result, she could never live her life the way she wanted. So when she met God, she made an impassioned plea:

"In my next life, please make my abilities average!"

Yet somehow, it all went awry.

In her new life, she can talk to nanomachines and, although her magical powers are technically average, it is the average between a human's and an elder dragon's...6,800 times that of a sorcerer!

At the first academy she attended, she made friends and rescued a little boy as well as a princess. She registered at the Hunters' Prep School under the name of Mile, and at the graduation exam went head-to-head with an A-rank hunter.

A lot has happened, but now Mile is going to live a normal life as a rookie hunter with her allies by her side.

Because she is a perfectly normal, *average* girl!

CHAPTER 10

Wonderful, Miraculous, Magical Girls

"**Y**OU COULDN'T FIND HER?"

"No. I am truly sorry..."

Bergl, the guard captain, stood in the king's office and gave his shame-faced report to a grim-looking king and the third princess, Morena.

Nearly a month had passed since the young daughter of Viscount Ascham—no, actually, the true head of the Ascham family, Adele—had gone missing.

"She's only a young girl. We thought that with half a day's lead, we could catch up easily. But our search parties have scoured the roads and every town and hamlet in between, and turned up nothing...

"We even sent several people ahead to places that neither a young girl's legs nor a carriage could carry her. Still we found nothing. Perhaps she's been forging her way through the forests or mountains away from towns and roads—or, heaven forbid, a young girl all alone—she's already been snatched up by bandits..."

"That's impossible. If she were to fall victim to an attack, surely that *thing* would intervene."

"Well."

The king was quite bold, referring to a goddess as a *"thing."*

"And then, of course, there's the message that she wrote to her friends: 'I'm going to live a happy life somewhere in the country, so please don't worry.' But we combed a number of towns and villages throughout the countryside and still could not find her.

"She may be living alone in the forest or the mountains somewhere, or perhaps she's already managed to make it beyond our borders..."

If she had left the country it would be difficult for soldiers to continue the search or even spread word in another land. Even if they found her, trying to bring her back by force could be a nightmare for international relations. Quietly abducting her was also out of the question. If they angered the goddess again, she would surely lay their country to ruin.

"The girl ran away because she had no idea that the problems with her family have been taken care of, didn't she?" asked the princess. "If we let her know the facts, she might change her mind. We could issue a proclamation. Tell her that the bad people have been apprehended, and it's safe for her to come back."

The king and Bergl grimaced.

"It's impossible," said the king. "This incident shames our entire country. We can't stop the rumors from spreading, but we can't do anything to expressly acknowledge the matter, either."

Bergl continued his report, "We've already inquired with a

number of the girl's classmates at the academy in the hope that we might find out where she's heading. However, the results were..."

"Were what?"

"Well...here is the transcript of what they told us."

The princess took the report that Bergl pulled from his breast pocket and looked it over.

"That girl could make it anywhere!"

"Her special skills? *Breaking boys' hearts, you mean?"*

"Somewhere she could live? As a guest in Heaven, or an overseer in Hell..."

"I want to know!"

"But I was supposed to be looking after her!"

"She finally found her freedom. Would you expect a bird to return to a cage of its own free will?"

"She's long gone—you're never gonna catch her."

"She could blend in perfectly with commoners. I wonder if she really was a noble..."

"Wh-what is this?"

"Just what kind of girl is she?"

The king and his daughter were dumbfounded.

"I want to meet with her close friends!" the princess exclaimed. "I want to ask them what kind of person she is. I want to ask them all sorts of things!"

"Hmm..." the king said after thinking for a while. "Perhaps that is a good idea. It might help us to find her, and perhaps Morena may get something out of the experience as well."

Bergl nodded silently.

✧◈✧

Three days later, eleven figures sat around a table in a small room at the palace.

In truth, the room was only small in comparison to the rest of the palace. Otherwise, it was a gorgeously furnished chamber, with splendid chairs and décor, and a table overflowing with sweets, fruits, and teacups.

Among the assembled parties were four members of the royal family: the king; the first prince, Adalbert, age sixteen; the third princess, Morena, age fifteen; and Morena's younger brother the second prince, Vince, age thirteen. Along with them were the prime minister; the captain of the guard, Bergl; and Count Bornham and his wife, who had been specially invited.

The presence of the Bornhams showed foresight on the king's part. Count Bornham had played a large role in the king's fateful audience with Adele's family. And the count's wife, a former classmate of Adele's mother, knew much about the Ascham family. Both of them wanted to know about Adele, the orphan child of their dear friend.

The last three invitees were the ones who knew the most about Adele: the girls known as the Wonder, Miracle, or Magic Trio.

"U-um, th-thank you most k-kindly for your..."

"Don't worry," said the king. "This is just an informal tea party. Please don't bother yourself over formalities. Just think of me as a father who's sitting in on his daughter's first meeting with some friends."

"A-all right..." stammered Marcela, attempting to offer an appropriate greeting on behalf of the three. Although she was of low rank, she was still a noble.

Monika and Aureana, who were both commoners, could not muster up a single word.

However, their nerves were not the only reason that Monika and Aureana did not speak.

Three days earlier, after the departure of the palace messenger extending a tea party invitation from the princess, Marcela had been the first to speak.

"They must be looking for information. We can't betray Adele's secrets!"

Monika and Aureana nodded.

"Adele might be blessed with many talents, but she's still a normal girl. She doesn't use weird magic, and she doesn't tell absurd stories. She's completely average. Just like she always said... Of course, a *truly* normal girl wouldn't go out of her way to point that out every single day, but let's put that aside for now."

The girls nodded again.

"We need to get our story straight. Decide what we can and can't talk about. For the sake of simplicity, if they ask us any questions, I'll answer. The more we all talk, the more contradictions will arise, and the more we might slip up and mention something that we shouldn't. Does that sound like a plan?"

Monika and Aureana nodded emphatically.

And so the day of the party arrived.

They were to leave the questions to Marcela, while Monika

and Aureana only offered acknowledgments and brief, carefully-prepared statements.

Around the table, the king and the other adults sat a small distance away from the children, establishing the pretense that they could talk on their own. Marcela and the other girls, the princess and the princes, all faced one another.

Ostensibly, the princes were present because it would be difficult for the princess to speak to three girls on her own, but naturally the adults had an ulterior motive. They hoped the two princes would find out more about Adele indirectly, in case she should ever be found.

The fact that both princes were in attendance made the plan fairly obvious.

"Um, I am Morena, the third princess..."

"I'm Adalbert, the first prince."

"And I'm Vince, the second prince."

Marcela and the other girls introduced themselves after the royals.

"I am Marcela, a second-year at Eckland Academy."

Although she was a member of a noble family, they had made the decision to introduce themselves as academy students and give only their first names.

"I'm Monika, and likewise."

"And I am Aureana."

A hush fell over the group. Since the adults were there only as observers, they neither introduced themselves nor intervened. At least, no more than necessary.

"Um, the reason we invited you here today was to ask you some things about Miss Adele..."

There it is!

Of course the three girls already knew this, so they weren't really surprised. They couldn't think of any other reason why they would have been invited to the palace, and someone here had obviously been carrying out a relentless investigation into the disappearance of their classmate. First there were whispers that the palace was searching for someone, and then of course, the rumor of a scandal surrounding a certain viscount...

Although Eckland Academy was considered the lesser of the city's two schools, there were still members of many noble families there. If something was happening, the rumors were sure to work their way through the school. More than that, the girls had some hint from Bergl when he returned Adele's letter to them, and the borrowing of the letter in the first place came with the promise of an explanation.

So far, they'd only heard about the turmoil surrounding the Ascham family, with the details about Adele's possession by the goddess carefully left out. But, given that aligned fairly well with what Adele told them herself, the girls had a pretty accurate grasp of the situation. On top of that, Marcela knew of other rumors—nonsensical stories about how Her Highness, the third princess, met a servant of a goddess. By this point, Marcela had heard about it from several different sources. Apparently, it happened on a rest day, around the time when Adele was returning home from work at the bakery, and on the same road that she would have taken home. Then there was the mention of a young girl with silver hair, this divine messenger.

Yes, this was most definitely Adele's doing. Marcela realized it the moment she heard the story. She knew it was only a matter of time before this day would come.

Honestly, what's the point of telling others to keep quiet if you run around doing that sort of thing yourself?

Right from the outset, Morena didn't hold back in her questioning. "Could you tell me what sort of person Miss Adele is? What sorts of things she talked about?"

As a princess, Morena had a diverse education, so while she appeared relatively straightforward at first glance, she was by no means stupid. Although speaking to girls who were three or four years her junior, she maintained the level of politeness she'd offer an equal, taking care not to belittle them. Perhaps this was only because she thought of them not as academy students, but as "that girl's dear friends." Still, it made a difference.

Seeing Morena's serious expression and sparkling eyes, Marcela thought, *We must protect Miss Adele's secrets! I will do everything in my power to give the third princess a good impression of Adele.*

Marcela's body ceased its subtle trembling, and her usual confidence returned.

Okay, third princess Morena, she thought, *let the battle begin!*

Morena cut right to the chase.

It was only natural. There was nothing else she was interested in asking the girls and no other shared topics of conversation.

Marcela, too, was fully aware of this. She'd already decided to present a pre-prepared story.

First, they'd speak of Adele during her time in the Ascham household, offering guesses based on the stories Adele had told them and the contents of her letter.

However, they could only go so far with that. Adele never spoke very much about her time at home, so there wasn't much to go on.

"It seems that at the start, she lived a very normal life with her parents and maternal grandfather. Then, when she was eight, her mother and grandfather were both killed by bandits. There are a number of mysteries surrounding that attack, but I believe an investigation has already been carried out about the circumstances.

"After that, Adele was all but under house arrest on the grounds of the Ascham mansion. She was neglected and bullied by her father and his mistress, whom he brought to live with them along with her child. At the age of ten, Adele was banished to Eckland Academy without a copper and forbidden to carry even her own surname so that her father's stepdaughter could take her place as the heir to the Ascham line...

"She received nothing from the Ascham family—no allowance, not even a letter. Impoverished, she worked at a bakery on her days off so that she could earn a living.

"That is the extent of her relationship with the household."

The king, the prime minister, Bergl, and Count Bornham already knew this much and wore grave expressions, but the eyes of Morena, the two princes, and the Countess Bornham were wide with shock.

The countess choked back tears. "N-no...her only daughter... went through such horrid things... why wasn't I more attentive?"

For their three years at Ardleigh Academy, and even after graduation, Mable, the only daughter of Viscount Ascham, was the countess's closest friend. When she heard the truth about Mable's untimely demise, the countess was filled with rage, sorrow, and a sad sense of inevitability.

Of course, it gave her some satisfaction to know that the former viscount and his new wife, who'd orchestrated this foul deed, were imprisoned. But to think that Mable's daughter endured such tragedy while the countess sat by...

She hadn't known, but there were still not enough words to apologize to Mable in heaven. She knew that if their roles were reversed, Mable would have done everything in her power to help the countess's children.

When her husband said, "We're going to go hear about her daughter," the countess overflowed with emotions she could not hold back. Her eyes sparkled with tears of apology and regret.

The princes and princess remained silent, their faces dark. At length, Marcela began her tale of the day that they first saw Adele.

"We met on the day of the entrance ceremony..."

She told them all sorts of amusing stories: Adele's introduction and the tale of how they confronted her for hogging their classmates' attention. She made sure to omit the details of Adele's peculiarities, wanting to give the impression of Adele as a fine, interesting girl.

"...and then, she offered to make *me* a pair of the underpants like the ones she'd made for herself, but that was..."

"Ah ha ha ha ha ha ha ha!"

The princess let out a peal of laughter, and none of the adults even bothered to scold her. The first prince, Adalbert, remained impassive, but the second prince, Vince, looked away, red-faced.

Wiping the tears of laughter from her eyes, the princess asked, "So, I suppose she granted you divine magical protection, too? Just like she tried to grant you underwear?"

"Huh...?"

The Wonder Trio were speechless. The princes and adults whispered to one another.

"Well, you all suddenly knew how to use magic one day, didn't you? Or were improved in it? All three of you, close friends, all at the same time. Can you believe the coincidence? Isn't it natural to wonder if it was the doing of one particular person?

"Of course, you helped Miss Adele out of sympathy at first, but you very quickly grew close to her and covered for her in a number of ways, far beyond mere sympathy. It was almost like you were returning a favor...

"You all know Miss Adele's secret, don't you?"

From the stories she'd just heard and the reports she had read beforehand, the princess reached a far too accurate conclusion.

"Wait!"

Just then, the king's panicked voice resounded through the room.

"You must all leave!"

"Huh?"

The prime minister, the Bornhams, and the princes all raised their voices, surprised at the king's sudden order.

"B-but..."

"Go!"

With a wave of his hand, the king dismissed all five of them: the protesting prime minister, the bewildered Bornhams, and the princes, annoyed to be chased out just when the conversation was getting good.

"How careless can you be, Morena?! You were told to *never* discuss this matter."

"Ah..."

The princess blanched, suddenly aware that the only people left in the room were the ones already aware.

"What's already been said cannot be helped. Thankfully, you did not touch at the core of the matter. However, you *must* be more careful in the future!"

"I understand."

Having narrowly missed throwing the kingdom into ruin, the princess looked back to the girls, still pale.

"So, you do know it, don't you? Miss Adele's secret..."

Th-this girl! She has such a soft face but an iron fist! Marcela feigned calm, even as she broke into a cold sweat.

Monika and Aureana entrusted the full burden of this conversation to Marcela and sat silent as stones. Marcela tried desperately to come up with an excuse that might hide the truth of Adele's abilities.

"You know, don't you? About the goddess residing within Miss Adele?"

"Wh..."

With that spectacular piece of self-sabotage, the princess continued. "As reward for hiding the fact that Adele is an avatar of the goddess, for aiding her and covering for her, she gave you the divine blessings of magic, isn't that right? You can tell the truth. Everyone here already knows about the goddess..."

What in the world is she talking about?

Marcela thought hard.

This had to be the result of a ruse Miss Adele concocted after overdoing it in front of the princess. There was no doubt in Marcela's mind. But, just what would she...

She probably let herself be seen using some kind of impossible magic. *If I were her, how would I try to cover that up?*

If Marcela lowered her general knowledge to Adele's level, and matched her lack of common sense and her inability to read people, then multiplied her carelessness by five, and tried to imagine what Adele could have been thinking...

Marcela had become quite adept at deciphering Adele's actions thanks to this Adele Simulator, which allowed her to emulate her friend's thought process.

Marcela was able to sense—sometimes right in the middle of conversation—"Oh no, she's about to say something weird." And she would clamp a hand over Adele's mouth or grab her by the arm, just before Adele could make a move, thus preventing in the nick of time an undue tragedy...or comedy. Now, once again, the "Adele Simulator" was running at full tilt.

All the rumors I've heard up until now were about...the descent of a goddess, or the servant of a goddess. And now, there's this talk. An avatar of the goddess? What might Adele have said to lead them astray?

She was surrounded by people making unreasonable demands, so to protect herself... What could she have decided with that tricky brain of hers?

That's it!

"What?!" Marcela exclaimed. "You all know all about the goddess too?!"

"I knew it..." At Marcela's cry, the princess nodded, satisfied to have her own suspicions confirmed.

"Then," Marcela continued, "you should also know that it's forbidden to meddle in her affairs..."

"We are not meddling! I merely want to be her friend—and properly thank the girl who put herself in danger to protect my

reputation. Where is the harm in that? It has nothing to do with the goddess. Don't tell me the goddess ordered Miss Adele not to make friends!"

There was a triumphant ring to the princess's voice.

This girl! She doesn't really want to make friends. She just wants Miss Adele all to herself!

Marcela glanced the king's way, but he and Bergl merely nodded in agreement.

Are they all in on this?!

Inside, Marcela was grinding her teeth, but she would never show such feelings in front of the royal family. But if she said nothing, she wouldn't be able to contain her anger.

"But if you can't find Miss Adele, there's nothing you can do about it, is there?!"

"Grngh..."

"I-In that case—" The king interjected as the circumstances looked grim. "Do you have any idea as to Adele... as to the Viscountess Ascham's whereabouts?"

"WE DON'T KNOW ANYTHING!"

The three girls answered in unison. Just as they had practiced, many times before.

After that, they were asked many things: if the names of any towns or countries had come up in their conversations with Adele, or whether she mentioned any acquaintances. These were all things that the girls truly knew nothing about, so they answered straightforwardly.

Then, after quite some time had passed, the Wonder Trio were finally released.

No matter how good their magic had become, they were

nothing without Adele. Therefore, as things stood, Marcela and
the other girls were of no value to the palace.

They had not accomplished their plan to win the princess
over and someday open a useful avenue for their friend, but
at the very least they had managed not to hand over a single
detail about Adele beyond the incorrect reports the palace already had.

I'd rank that quite a good performance, thought Marcela, as
she, Monika, and Aureana stood to leave. Just then, a voice called
to her from behind.

"Um. Could I trouble you for another talk sometime?"

"O-of course! I would be happy to..."

There was no way that the third daughter of a poor noble
could possibly refuse a request from the princess.

Several days later, Marcela was in her dorm, chatting with
Monika and Aureana, when suddenly there came a knock at the
door.

"Miss Marcela, your father is here to see you!"

"Oh! All right, I'm coming!"

Marcela scrambled from her seat and opened the door to find
the dormitory supervisor and her father, who appeared flustered
and out of breath.

"What's the hurry, Fath—"

"M-Marcela! I-Is it true that you were called to the palace?!"

"Ah, yes! That is true..."

"Wh-why did they summon you?! What's going on?!"

Her father's panic was understandable. If his daughter had been summoned to the palace and the visit went well, it would mean a magnificent fortune, but if it went poorly, or she had been impolite, then woe betide their family's legacy.

Paying no mind to the presence of her friends, Marcela continued. "Well...it seems Her Highness the third princess was very interested in becoming my friend..."

"Wh-what?! Wait. If that's true, that's an enormous blessing—but, why? Why someone like you, without connections?"

"Who knows?"

"Wh-who knows, my foot..."

"If you really want to know, then perhaps you should ask the princess herself."

Marcela pointed, and her father's gaze followed her finger to...

"I am Morena, the third princess. Please, pardon the intrusion."

There stood a girl of around fifteen years old, bowing her head politely.

Didn't I Say to Make My Abilities *Average* in the Next Life?!

CHAPTER 11

Completely Normal C-Rank Hunters

"THIS IS A HISTORIC MOMENT! It's time for us to take on our first ever job as C-rank hunters!" Reina announced as they stood proudly in front of the posting board at the hunters' guild. "What shall we choose?"

"Goblin hunting, definitely!"

"Huh?"

Mile's proposal didn't appeal to the others.

"Why, after all this time, would we bother with goblins?! The extermination reward is low, goblins carry nothing you can sell, and you can't even eat their meat. They're only good for D-rankers to get pocket change and target practice!"

"No!" Mile was not prepared to back down. "A hunter's job starts out with gathering herbs and ends with hunting goblins. Definitely! Hunting goblins is the first hurdle you face as an E-rank hunter, after rising from a rookie F-rank who can't do anything but harvest herbs and hunt jackalopes. It's a job that symbolizes our growth! Besides, what will happen when we have to guide those who come after us if we don't know a goblin's behaviors and weaknesses?!"

"Huh? Isn't a goblin's weak point its neck? I'm pretty sure if you cut off their heads they'll die, so..."

At Mavis's interjection, Mile let out an uncharacteristic yell. "Even a dragon would die if you cut off its head! That's not a weakness!

"Anyway, we may be C-rank hunters, but we've only ever hunted goblins once, during our training at the prep school, and that was in a secure location, with everything set up ahead of time so we could just wave weapons around and blast some spells. That can't possibly be considered a *real* goblin hunt.

"Reina, you were an E-rank, so perhaps you have some experience already, but Mavis, Pauline, and I only hunted goblins that once. Even if we fell a direwolf or an ogre, you can't be a full-fledged hunter if you haven't done the basics. Skipping too far ahead might get us in trouble someday. Honestly, we should probably start with herb gathering, but we already did that so much on our days off that the thought makes me feel sick..."

Though Reina still appeared dissatisfied, she understood that Mile had a point and, for the sake of the other three, she agreed.

Certainly, it wouldn't just be a bit of pruning for pocket change. When the request for goblin extermination came from a small village, the battling wasn't even the important part. What mattered was the preliminary investigations, planning, and preparing the surroundings so that not a single goblin escaped.

If even a few of them managed to slip away, they would just multiply again and return to harm the townspeople. So, you demolished the goblins' dwellings as swiftly as possible, leaving not one male, female, or child. Besides, the females and young were weak and could be hunted for their soft flesh.

"Very well. I suppose that's what we'll do then. Mavis and Pauline, what do you say?"

"Roger that!"

"No problems here."

After hearing Mile's explanation, both were wholly in favor of the plan.

The surrounding hunters were moved by the girls' exchange, too.

"Impressive. They're so young, but they've got good heads on their shoulders. Normally, you'd think brand-new, inexperienced C-rank hunters, just out of school, would get themselves into some established parties to gain more experience. Instead, they've formed a party of rookies. You'd expect them to overstep—act on their whims and get themselves killed—but it looks like they might surprise us and live long, healthy lives."

"Yes, siree! Those rookies are already legendary! That training school sure did a good job this year..."

"Oh, of course. I heard those Roaring Mithril fellows were contracted for the graduation exam and lost on purpose to give those kids some confidence. But still, they seem pretty promising... Ha ha ha! Maybe it was just a special service for cuties!"

"Uh..."

The other hunters cast shocked looks at the man who'd spoken. He clearly hadn't attended the exam himself but heard only the most twisted of rumors.

"There's nothing..." Mile slumped in front of the board, disappointed.

There was not a single goblin extermination request to be seen, only fetch quests and culling tasks. Apparently, there currently weren't many goblins in the area around the capital.

To make matters worse, there were very few other nearby postings that could be completed before nightfall. On their very first day, they weren't inclined to take any jobs that required a significant amount of travel, and they weren't prepared to make camp.

"Well then, why don't we just go kill some orcs for the daily requests? There are a lot of food-related requests in there, so we can hunt anything else as we go... we *did* hunt orcs during our training. That should be fine, right?"

Mile nodded agreeably at Mavis's suggestion, while Reina and Pauline looked a little relieved. While they saw the sense in Mile's idea, they didn't really look forward to hunting goblins.

The smell of burning goblins is disgusting... orcs don't smell nearly as bad on fire, thought Reina, the fire magic specialist.

Certainly, the smell of roasting boar was far more enticing.

✧ ◈ ✧

"We can't catch them..."

Reina collapsed in a disappointed heap, hands planted on the ground.

This is a familiar sight, thought Mile, though she didn't say it out loud. She was finally learning to read the room.

This forest was unlike the places they had visited during their time at the prep school— the hunting areas used by E and F-rank hunters. These were genuine hunters' stomping grounds, used by those of C and D-ranks.

In fact, this was one of the *primary* grounds for their fellow C and D-ranks, so there was a lot of competition. It would have been surprising to find much prey left in the thinner parts of the woods. Small animals like jackalopes and birds scampered here and there, but the girls hadn't made it all the way to C-rank just to spend their first day pursuing the same critters they'd hunted before.

"We have to go deeper!"

The other three nodded. That was something they could all agree on. Together, they pressed deeper into the forest.

Bwoosh!

Mile suddenly shot off a pebble and then hurried forward a short way, returning with a jackalope in hand.

As much as they wanted to track down bigger prey, there was a chance that they might not catch any. Besides, even if they did catch bigger creatures, they couldn't let quarry slip away before their eyes, no matter how small or humble. Even with just two additional silver, dinner for the four of them would be that much more luxurious. And since they had an unlimited carrying capacity, there was no need for the Crimson Vow to be choosy about their prey.

"That magic really is handy, you know..." said Reina a bit jealously, glancing at Mile's finger gun for the hundredth time.

"But what if you lost your fingers?"

"Grngh..." Reina grumbled in frustration.

When Reina first pressed Mile to teach her magic, Mile discouraged her by showing her how she could bend a copper coin with just her fingers. In order to use magic, she said, she

underwent special training from a young age, lest she lose her
fingers when a spell went off.

In truth, it wasn't magic, but raw finger strength—something
she couldn't have taught Reina even if she wanted to.

Whoosh!

Snap!

As they traveled, they gathered enough prey to guarantee a
decent payout, but it was all just from Mile shooting pebbles. The
other three grew bored.

They'd already traveled quite deep into the forest when, after
walking for some time, Mavis stopped and held up her hand in a
silent signal. Prey was near.

Mavis was at the front. She was the broadest and tallest, and
could spot prey quickly. Besides, if anyone else was in the lead,
clearing grass and undergrowth out of the way, Mavis's height
meant she still had to avoid the higher branches. But the number
one reason for Mavis's position was that she was the party's only
forward guard. Reina and Pauline were in rear guard, while Mile
covered forward, middle, and rear.

At Mavis's signal, everyone stood still, peering ahead.

There it was.

As they'd not taken on any special requests and only gone for
prey with a standing order, they couldn't really call it fate, but
nonetheless, it was an orc. Exactly what they had been aiming for.
Three orcs, actually—adults, by the looks of them.

"Mile, you've caught plenty today. Leave them to us!"

Mile nodded at Reina's whisper and took advantage of the
opportunity to sit back and observe.

"I can take one of them out for sure. Pauline, see if you can wound the other two. And Mavis, the moment the magic hits them, you launch a surprise attack and strike the final blows."

The other girls nodded.

Reina and Pauline began casting in soft voices, releasing their spells simultaneously at Reina's signal.

"Icicle Javelin!"

"Water Blade!"

Though she was a powerful mage, ice and water magic were not Reina's specialty. All the same, she poured all her strength into one powerful ice attack while Pauline, whose strength was her quick thinking, let off two rounds simultaneously.

The ice attack went splendidly, striking one of the orcs straight through the gut, while the two rounds of water struck the other two.

Crystals spread through the orc struck by the ice and it fell, but while Pauline's water attacks left cuts in the gut and shoulder of the other two, the blows were not fatal. After a moment's faltering, both orcs were ready to jump back into the fray, searching for a glimpse of their opponents.

By that point Mavis, who leapt out the moment the magic struck, was already in front of them, brandishing her sword with a flourish.

Before the orcs realized, she was bringing down her blade. With one diagonal slash, the first orc was mincemeat. There was a horrid scream as it fell forward and collapsed, blood gushing from its body.

Mavis stepped aside, drawing her blade back and bringing it down on the other orc in a diagonal arc.

This orc was already doubled over from the magical wound to its gut. The tip of Mavis's blade struck it in the throat, and it fell down into the dirt.

"W-we did it..."

Having felled an orc for the first time with her own two hands, Mavis stood in a daze of surprise, satisfaction, and adrenaline.

"Behind youuu!!" Reina screamed, and Mavis whipped around to look. The orc which had been struck by the ice spell—and should have been vanquished—was on its feet again, barreling toward Mavis.

"Ahh!"

There was no time to raise her sword, so Mavis tried an upward cut from below.

Mile had no intention of interfering, planning to stand by and watch her friends achieve victory with their own hands. Luckily, Mavis's practice adjusting to Mile's speed allowed her to strike the orc in the nick of time.

Even a second later and—

Cutting the orc through from below, Mavis safely avoided being flattened.

However...

Snap!

"Oh..."

It broke.

No, not Mavis's heart. Her sword.

There was a particular formula that could be applied to this event:

$$E_k = \frac{1}{2}mv^2$$
$$Kinetic\ Energy = 1/2 \times mass \times velocity^2$$

Thanks to her special training with Mile, Mavis was incredibly strong. The speed of her blade was even more remarkable.

Naturally, this amplified her power. However, it also amplified the stress on her sword.

The sword had been almost at its limit, and Mavis thrust it into the orc at a rather unfortunate angle, which further increased the pressure on its blade.

And so, it broke.

There was nothing to be done about it.

"I'm hopeless..."

Mavis was crestfallen. She knew better than anyone how the amateurishness of her final strike had contributed to it. Looking upon her sullen face and her broken weapon, there was nothing for the other three to say but...

"Let's go home."

A cold wind blew, whisking fallen leaves around the Crimson Vow as they trudged along, shoulders drooping.

It was a picturesque sight. One that, in a painting, would take first at any exhibition.

The title, naturally, would be "Hard Times."

That evening, the four girls made their way to a weapons shop.

It was their first day as rookie hunters, and they'd done well enough to receive the praise and blessing of the other hunters when they exchanged their spoils at the guildhall.

Despite this victory, however, the girls looked gloomy. Puzzled, the other hunters asked them what happened. Mavis drew her sword with a self-deprecating smile.

"Oh jeez..."

Swords were by no means cheap.

No matter how much they'd earned, this would put them into the red.

The other hunters recommended this shop, which was said to stock decent, relatively cheap swords.

"The dilemma here is whether to buy an okay sword with the funds we have on hand or to buy a cheap one now and save up for a better one. What to do...?" Reina pondered. "Tell us what you think, Mavis. We want to do whatever will be best for the party, after all. That sword was on the verge of breaking as it was, and we already knew that we'd have to replace it. Really, it's my fault for being so insistent about landing the kill. If the sword broke even a second sooner, you might have been killed. I'm so sorry..."

Having a sword break in the midst of battle was a one-way ticket to the grave. Buying an unreliable weapon just for the price tag was out of the question.

"Okay. I'll try to make the best decision for all of us. What we need is..."

"A cheap one!" Mile interjected suddenly.

"Huh?!"

"Go on, Mavis. Just pick one with a grip that feels good, that's about the right length. From the duds in the bargain bin."

"M-Mile!!!"

CHAPTER 12 |

New Gear

AND SO, Mavis's new (used) sword was purchased.

That night, in their room at the inn, Mile turned to the others. "Why don't we take a day off tomorrow?"

"What are you talking about? We've only done a single day's work! If we carry on like this we'll never save up any money!"

"C-calm down..." Pauline attempted to pacify Reina, who bristled at Mile's suggestion.

"Well," Mavis jumped in, trying to help. "If Mile is suggesting this, there must be a reason, right? After all, she's always so sure of herself."

"S-sure of myself...?"

Contrary to Mavis's intention, Mile looked wounded, her posture crumbling as she folded her hands on the table.

"What? Is something wrong?" asked Mavis, perplexed.

"N-nothing. It's fine... even though that's really not..." Mile stood again, mumbling her final words. "Um, anyway. I was hoping to go out with just Mavis tomorrow..."

"Huh???"

The other three exclaimed as one.

"M-Mile, don't tell me..."

"N-no way!"

"That's fine with me," Mavis said. "But what for? You want to go shopping or something?"

It was hard to know exactly what she was imagining.

The following day, somewhere in the woods...

"What are you two doing here?!"

Somehow, Mile and Mavis weren't alone in the forest. Reina and Pauline were there, too.

"I was concerned about what the two of you might be doing all alone!"

"She dragged me along against my will..."

"In that case," said Mile. "Why didn't you just say something? Why did you have to follow us in secret?!"

"If I'd told you, then I'd never be able to find out what the two of you were doing!"

"Gah!!" Mile struggled to collect herself. "Whatever! We may as well do what we planned anyway, Mavis."

"Okay. What should I do?"

"Just lend me your sword a minute."

"Sure. Here." Mavis unhooked the sword from her waist and handed it over.

Mile removed the sword from the sheath, then stabbed it into the sandy ground with ease, plunging the blade deep. The sword slid into the hard ground until all but the hilt was buried, show-ing no resistance.

"Wh...?"

Even though the ground was sandy, this wasn't a desert. It wasn't normal to drive a sword so deep into the ground with so little effort.

"So Mavis, how much would you like this sword to weigh?"

"A-ah, well, my sword style is focused on speed, so if it was a little lighter I could swing it a little faster. But...that would de-crease its power. Also, if I always used a lighter sword, I would never hone my strength, and if I had to use something else, then I would get in trouble. I think a normal weight is best."

"Of course! Normal is best after all!"

Mavis drew slightly away, put off both by the ease with which Mile had plunged the sword into the ground and her strange enthusiasm for this. Then again, Mavis was used to Mile's strange-ness by now. Perhaps she didn't need to be so concerned.

She was more interested in what was going on with her sword.

"Um, Mile, my sword...?"

"Ah! Just a little longer."

With these words, Mile sank deep into thought, her eyes go-ing unfocused.

After a short while, she blinked once and gripped the hilt of the sword, yanking it from the ground. She used wind magic to clean the excess dirt from the blade, returned the sword to the sheath, and handed it back to Mavis.

"All done!"

"Ah, thanks..."

Mavis took the sword and hung it back at her waist, then drew the blade to inspect it.

It didn't really *look* all that different, but...

"Why don't you try it out? You wouldn't want to test a new sword for the first time in a real battle."

"You're right. It's better to give it a whirl ahead of time. I need to get a good sense of the sharpness and weight."

"Yes. And I have something that I'd like to try out as well, so perhaps we can do some hunting togeth—"

"Hold it right there!" Reina, who'd been watching quietly this whole time, finally interjected. "Going out to handle some sword matters on your own on a day off is one thing, but hunting is another matter! We're your party, and we're coming, too!"

"Huh? That's fine if you really want to, but we're mostly just going out to test our weapons. We aren't going to be catching all that much. Are you okay with that?"

"It doesn't matter. A party hunts *together*! And that's all I have to say on the matter," declared Reina, standing firmly with her arms akimbo. It was a familiar pose.

"In any case, why don't you take a few practice swings, Mavis? To make sure that the weight and balance are to your liking."

Mavis swung her sword around for a short while, then answered, sounding satisfied. "No problems here. It's got a good feel, sits nicely in my hand..."

Mile pointed to a nearby tree, grinning.

"Well, then. Why don't you try chopping down that tree?"

"Wh...?"

The girls looked at the tree. It was as thick as an adult's arms could grasp.

"How could I possibly cut through that?! If I even tried it, the sword would be damaged, and we *just* bought it! This blade is much cheaper than the one I had before."

Mavis's previous sword was taken from her family's personal armory and had been of a fairly decent make. The blade was strong, but Mavis, lacking the technique to match the weapon, had shortened its lifespan considerably with her amateurish attacks...

The cheap sword they obtained yesterday was certainly not capable of the sort of thing that Mile was suggesting...was it?

Despite Mavis's objections, Mile urged her on. "It's fine! I used earth magic to strengthen the blade for this very reason. You can swing it as hard as you like, and it won't even chip!"

"........."

Mavis stared silently, her face sour.

Mile didn't realize that, in trying to reassure her friend, she'd implied that Mavis's swings were less than impressive.

"Fine. I'll cut it. But whatever happens next is not my fault!"

"Of course. If your sword gets damaged, I'll just fix it. It's no problem!"

Yet a sword wasn't something you could just reshape, Mavis thought. No matter how cheap, a sword was still a sword. It wasn't the same as a metal plate.

Ignoring Mile's foolish words, Mavis prepared her sword and swung it.

Ka-shunk!

With a dull ring, the blade sunk into the tree, about one-fourth of the way through.

The sword didn't break. It didn't even show any sign of bending.

"Uh..."

The three girls were shocked, which was quite understandable. There was no way that a normal sword—which wasn't an axe, and shouldn't function like one—should have been able to cut through a tree.

If every blade were capable of power like this, then lumberjacks around the world would toss their axes away and become swordsmen.

"Wh...?"

Mavis stared down at the completely normal-looking blade, lost for words.

Thanks to her training in the past half a year, her strength could rival even the strongest of men. There was no doubt that, if the sword had gone so far into the tree, she had put her full strength behind it. But even though a tree was wood, not metal, a sword in these circumstances should break, or at least bend.

In a match against another person, you didn't use your full force in every swing. You used only a certain percentage of your power. Yet here she'd swung with full force and, because the blade did not cut all the way through, the sword had absorbed most of that power. Even so, it had not been bent, broken, or even warped. This might be expected of a magic sword or heavenly blade, but this had been simply a cheap, used...

Don't tell me—did some amazing, high-quality blade end up in the bargain bin by mistake?

Reina and Pauline's eyes glittered at the thought of this unbelievable steal.

Or...is this because of Mile's strengthening magic?

"Now, could you try cutting through that for me?"

Mile, who didn't seem surprised at all, pointed to a spot about seven or eight meters from the tree. To a great boulder, about two meters in diameter.

"M-Mile...?"

This time, as Mavis stared, slack-jawed, Reina stepped forward, snarling.

"That is absolutely, one-hundred percent impossible! What on earth do you think you're doing with the sword we just spent all that money on?!"

Even Pauline could not keep silent. Her money had been involved too, and she nodded wildly in agreement.

But, after a few fraught moments of uncertainty, Mavis readied her blade a second time.

"Mavis!"

"D-don't do it!!"

Reina and Pauline protested, but Mavis's resolve was firm.

"When I cut into that tree, I felt a *response*. Almost as if the sword were speaking back to me. Besides—everything we have now is thanks to Mile, so... no, wait. What I mean to say is, if we can't have faith in our friends, then what can we have faith in?"

"........"

Reina and Pauline fell silent.

"Fine," said Reina, "Do as you like! But if that sword breaks, there will be no more days off until we've saved up enough to buy another one!"

Pauline gasped, but Mavis only grinned.

"You guys...!"

Even shy Pauline could not help but protest at the thought of so much money, but it was not enough to stop Mavis.

She stood before the boulder, gathered all her strength, and swung down into the rock with one fell swoop.

Snap.

...The blade broke.

"MIIIIILEE!!!"

"I-I'm sorryyyy!!!"

Mavis collapsed to the ground, while Reina leapt for Mile, and Pauline, still thinking of the party's finances, stared with a hollow gaze.

"M-Mile, you little..."

"W-wait! Just let me explain!"

"What is there to explain?! I believed in you, and you made a fool of me!"

✧◈✧

After a few minutes, Reina finally calmed down and Mavis picked herself up off the ground, while Pauline still sat, mentally recalculating their budget.

Mile stood before them and explained. "I'm sorry. I thought that my earth magic would be able to strengthen it, but apparently it wasn't enough..."

"........."

Mile had done so much for them, and there was no way the others could be truly angry with their teammate. However, this was quite a blow to their finances.

It couldn't be helped that Mavis's previous sword had broken. It was nearing the end of its life, and they had already planned to set aside money to replace it. But it hurt badly to lose a brand

new sword which they'd bought with the majority of their funds. Each of the girls wore dark expressions—even more so than the day before. That is, except for Mile.

Her bright voice rung out cheerfully. "Well then, I'll go ahead and fix it!"

"Huh...?"

"H-hang on, even if you *say* you can fix it, you can't just patch a sword back together with glue!" Mavis protested, looking distraught. "Even if you stick it together with earth magic, the moment it strikes something, it'll snap again, and that could be fatal! I absolutely *refuse* to wield a sword like that!"

"Weapons," added Reina, "aren't nearly as simple as you seem to think. When a sword is broken, there's nothing to be done but melt it down to reuse the raw metal. Have you ever heard of someone using a sword that was merely stuck back together?"

Pauline nodded as well, but Mile appeared calm and confident.

"Please. Wait until you see the results before you pass judgment!"

"Your results are already rolling away!"

Sure enough, the broken sword was tumbling down the hill and away.

"Sorry about the wait. Here's your new-and-improved sword. It's tough, unbreakable, unchippable, unbendable, low-maintenance, and will never lose its cutting edge. And, it carries the Mile Company quality assurance guarantee!"

Mile drew the sword from its sheath in a single motion.

Mavis received it wordlessly.

"Is it really fixed...?"

Reina and Pauline eyed the blade suspiciously.

"Don't be rude! It's fine this time! Last time, I was just holding back. When I put my whole heart into it, then surely..."

"Maybe you should put your whole heart into it from the start!"

"...Yes, ma'am."

In order to restore their confidence in her, Mile worked hard. For the sake of the party, Mavis, and herself, she couldn't afford to conjure up a sword that was *too* efficient. Therefore, the first time around, she'd aimed to give the sword only the minimum necessary improvements.

However, if the sword broke, there was a chance that Mavis could lose her life, which would put the rest of the party in danger, too. Even if they did make it out safely, having to purchase yet another sword would be a considerable drain on their savings.

And so, Mile had poured her energy into creating a sword that was merely sturdy, but possessed no other special properties, conjuring up the image of carbon fibers, titanium, and high-tensile steel— materials that were thought to be among the strongest on Earth.

She had assumed that this would give Mavis's blade the necessary strength, and yet the boulder had proved too much for it.

Now, Mile was indignant.

On Earth, were there not blades that could cut rock and iron? Should hers not have been able to slice through that boulder? How could she restore her own credibility?

Failing again was not an option. If she failed this time, there was no way that Mavis would ever trust her life to a sword that Mile had tampered with.

She had to do it. There was no other option.

This time, Mile told herself, *don't worry about the range of techniques that exist in this world! Instead, make an absolutely unbreakable blade, by any means necessary.*

A useful sword with an unchippable blade that never rusts and never needs maintenance! The edge should be the fifth sharpest in this world. However, the weight and shape should be the same as before. It would still look exactly like a cheap, normal weapon.

Let's gooooo!!!

Mile packed the dirt with her feet, then thrust the broken blade into the ground, driving it deep, and channeled her magic into the hilt.

This was the sword she presented to Mavis.

"All right! *Now*, please try cutting that boulder!"

Mavis was hesitant, but if she didn't do it, then she would never know how much confidence she could have in this sword. And anyway, the blade had already broken once. If she didn't test it, how could she know it wouldn't snap again? A weapon she couldn't trust was not one she was willing to fight with.

Mavis readied herself and swung the blade up, bringing it down onto the boulder.

Crack!

As was to be expected, the blade did not slice through the boulder. However, seeing how far the blade *had* sunk into the rock, Mavis, Reina, and Pauline's eyes grew round.

"This..."

Mavis inspected the blade in disbelief, finding that it had not even chipped. As she did, Mile quietly pulled a short sword from storage and presented it to her teammate.

Though the blade was shorter than average, it was not knife-sized, but rather about half a meter in length.

"Wait. That's..."

"Yep, it's the sword you broke yesterday. I fixed the part of the blade that was left and shaped it into this. I figured you could use it as a spare, in case your main sword broke. In a pinch, it might be enough to protect yourself..."

Mavis took the short sword and held it to her chest, overjoyed that her old weapon might still be of some use.

"Miley," Pauline called. For some reason, she sounded rather displeased.

"Yes?" Mile answered.

"If you could always fix up Mavis's sword, then we didn't need to buy a new one, did we?"

"Ah..."

Everyone's gaze fixed on Mile.

"Well, she still needs a backup weapon, doesn't she?"

"Even if her main sword is absolutely unbreakable?"

"......"

"N-no, but she might have it knocked away, or drop it, or something else! R-right?"

As she babbled, Mile looked to Mavis for support, but the other girl looked doubtful.

In truth, of the two blades, Mile had pulled out all the stops in order to strengthen the short sword.

Since most people wouldn't see it and it would only be used if Mavis's main sword was lost, it made sense to put more power into it.

Mavis cleared her throat. "Well, now that we've confirmed the sword's abilities, why don't we test it out on some real prey?"

"Yes, of course," Mile said. "But first, I thought I might try out my weapon..."

"Your weapon?" asked the other three.

"Yes. Remember how I said I have something that I'd like to try out as well?"

Mile pulled a peculiar-looking item out of storage.

"What *is* that?"

"It's called a slingshot. You can use it to hunt birds and other small animals."

"Hmm..."

Reina studied it doubtfully. She wasn't particularly impressed by this thing, which looked nothing like a proper weapon.

Nevertheless, Mile drew a pebble from storage and loaded it into the pouch of the slingshot. In truth, this pouch had a special gimmick—it held a magnetic charge. It could be loaded with a number of small metal balls, and fire them like buckshot. Though *that* was a trick Mile would save for later.

She pulled back on the rubber strap and aimed for a tree branch a short distance away.

The slingshot was based on a product that Mile had seen in a magazine, long ago in her previous life. It was the sort of make-shift thing that would horrify the tool's original designer.

In her version, Mile had barely considered balance and completely overlooked adding something to maintain its attack strength, or a wrist piece to help with stability. It was an incredibly basic slingshot.

But this wasn't a problem as long as Mile was using it. Her drawing method was appropriate, and the slingshot was durable enough to withstand being pulled back with immense strength.

The body of the slingshot was made of a mysterious metal which far surpassed the strength of titanium. The rubber strap was carbon nanotubes, and though they had a limited elasticity, that was no matter in the hands of a near-god.

This was the slingshot that Mile held in her hands, although the way she held it would have made enthusiasts cry out in dismay and horror.

First of all, her stance was lopsided, and she didn't draw it using the entire upper half of her body, but only with her arms thrust out before her. Her left hand held the slingshot, while her right grasped the pouch, drawn back to her shoulder. Even the strap was only stretched to half the distance that it should have been.

And then, she let the pebble fly.

Crack!

It smacked dead into the intended branch and snapped it off the tree.

Mile gave thanks for the nanomachines' course correction.

"Whoa..."

The other girls were stunned.

"Th-this is just like your wind magic..."

"Yes, though the basic principle is completely different. I'm not using magic at all. But it's a similar method of hunting.

"From here on, I'd rather not face as much scrutiny about the number of prey we bring in, or the methods we hunt with.

Besides, if I use wind magic, there's a chance that I might forget to hold back and make my target explode! That would be bad enough if I was aiming at a bird, but if it was a human..."

"........."

The other three were silent. It was clear from their faces that they were thinking unpleasant thoughts.

"Speaking of which, I'm hoping to use this weapon to draw attention away from my wind magic. If anyone wanted to get their hands on that magic, it would be an enormous bother—"

"L-Let me borrow it! I want to use pseudo-wind magic, too!"

Reina didn't want to get her hands on the wind magic, which Mile had claimed would blow her fingers off, but she did want the slingshot.

"I can lend it to you, but I don't think it'll work..."

"What are you talking about?! If I practice, then I should be able to use it just as well!"

With a peculiar expression, Mile handed the slingshot to Reina.

"G-grrrrrngh... I-I can't pull it!"

Reina tugged on the strap, which she had thought was rubber, but was actually carbon nanotube. Finally, she stopped, red in the face.

"Like I said..."

The slingshot's power was all a result of kinetic energy, and that energy had to come from somewhere. Pulling the strap required an absurd amount of strength.

The strange way that Mile had fired it before was not because she didn't know the proper method, but because she *wanted* to fire it that way. Using this technique, her shots had the power of a .22 caliber pistol—just enough for hunting birds and other small critters.

If she were to use proper form—that is to say, pull the strap nearly twice as far—the slingshot would surpass the power of a Magnum hunting rifle. Mile would never use that kind of strength unless she had no other choice. Her sword or magic should be enough for hunting larger prey. This was her secret weapon.

After their exchange, Mavis and Mile hunted for a little while, gaining skill and confidence with their weapons.

Reina, still peeved that she was unable to use the "optimal weapon for hunting small animals in the forest," fired off water and ice spells all over the place. They weren't her specialty and made a mess of the hunting grounds.

In the end, though they had meant to take a day off, the girls yet again took home enough prey for a decent wage.

And they all lived happily ever after...

Didn't I Say
to Make My Abilities
Average in the
Next Life?!

CHAPTER 13 |

Pushing the Limits

"WHAT A FORMIDABLE FOE!"

"This isn't fair!"

"I don't think we can beat them..."

"Should we retreat?"

Rookie C-rank hunting party, the Crimson Vow, was embroiled in a fierce battle. Their enemies were a horde of kobolds, about twenty of them in total. These were not strong creatures at all. However...

"Meeew"

"Cooo cooooo..."

They were adorable. Incredibly so.

On Earth, Mile thought, *kobolds are hideous and evil spirits! Why are these so endearing?!*

The creatures were roughly the size of a human child, with dog-like heads, and all the cuteness of a puppy. Still...

Slash!

"You jerks!!"

They had a strong attack instinct, turning them into monsters.

And, although it was true they weren't particularly strong, this was only from the perspective of Mile and her party of C-rank hunters. It would be dangerous for the women and children of the village to take on one of these creatures one-on-one, and an adult man, or even a group of people, could be in a lot of trouble when surrounded by a horde.

And so the Crimson Vow had taken on the job of clearing the kobold dwellings near this village. And yet...

"We can't stop! This isn't a standing order—it's a real job. If we give up now, we are admitting failure on behalf of the dispatch office. We will have to pay the fine, and our reputation will suffer!"

Indeed, in order to prevent parties from failing to complete jobs for which they were not well suited—or to avoid a single party taking a number of jobs at once and leaving them unfinished—parties taking a job were required to pay a bond that was generally about 10 to 30 percent of their promised pay.

This rate varied from job to job. In the case of monster culling, or other matters that were not time-sensitive, the bond was cheap. But for jobs with a tight deadline, or ones that might cause harm to the client if left unfinished, the fee might even exceed 30 percent.

If victory was impossible, that would be one thing. However, if they abandoned a job on the basis that kobolds are too cute to kill, what would they say to the parents of children these kobolds might murder?

They were all well aware of their circumstances.

"We gotta do it! We're C-rank hunters now—this isn't play-time. It's a job! People's lives are at stake!"

At Reina's words, the others felt a pang in their chests.

She was right. Their duty was one of life and death.

It was not only their own lives at stake, but those of all the villagers, as well as any travelers passing by.

"O raging flames of the deep, burn my enemies to the bone!"

This was not the forest, but a cliffside beside a highway. Thrilled to finally be able to use fire magic after so long, Reina let off her trademark spell.

The goal of today's job was extermination, and none of them would have had the heart to skin the kobolds, even if their pelts were worth something. Fortunately, kobold skins weren't particularly valuable, so it didn't matter if they were burnt to a crisp.

Reina's fire ripped through the spot where the kobolds were gathered, and when they tried to escape in a panic, Pauline cut them off with a Fire Wall. Mavis's blade dealt with the rest, while Mile sniped any bolder souls with her slingshot.

On top of the ten Reina took out with her initial attack, more and more kobolds fell victim to pursuing girls, their movements slowed by the burns they'd suffered. One by one, they were eliminated.

✧ ◈ ✧

"Now then, let's have our daily review..."

The discussion was started, as always, by Reina. It wasn't the usual private conference in their room, but rather an informal chat over dinner in the inn's dining room. Their food was already laid out on the table.

"First of all, what was with that battle today? We got serious in the end, but early on, we were pretty messed up by the cuteness. We can't be making a mockery of our profession!"

At Reina's words, Mavis and Pauline hung their heads, poking at the food on their plates.

"Um, but...weren't you the one who was the most taken, Re—"

"Don't you finish that sentence!"

Reina slapped her hands down on the table to cut Mile off, a bit red in the face.

"Anyway, I think that we have a considerable amount of ability as a party. The problem lies with our resolve. I mean, we're still young and inexperienced, so maybe it's to be expected, but I'm worried people might think that we're soft. Or that we don't take things seriously..."

Wow, Reina really is thinking hard about this...

Mile was moved. She had been considering the same thing.

At first, Mile had been ignorant of the ways of the world. She'd thought that she could rely on her powers if something went wrong. But, even with her limited self-awareness, she had the presence of mind not to say that out loud.

The problem was that Mavis and Pauline—unlike Reina— had almost no experience. All they had under their belts was their field training, and the F-rank jobs they'd taken on their days off at the prep school.

As a hunter, so long as you earned a living with your work, you managed. Even if you were unwell, you'd still put your life on the line to earn your keep. But Pauline and Mavis didn't have that sense of urgency and resolve yet.

Thanks to Mile, they were blessed with combat prowess

superior to that of an average rookie C-rank hunter. However, that meant nothing when compared to the strong will and experience of a veteran.

The battle against the Roaring Mithrils had not been a real fight; it hadn't even been a game. No matter how you looked at it, it was a *test*. There was no sign that the Roaring Mithrils even recognized it as a real match.

They were just doing their job—carefully holding back their power and creating opportunities for the newbies to shine, drawing out their full strength. They had merely let a little of that strength slip through the chinks in their armor. If the Roaring Mithrils had really meant to fight, they'd had more than enough chances.

"So, I've been thinking. What if, just once, we faced a formidable foe that wasn't concerned about status?"

"Huh...?"

The other three were surprised, but Reina explained.

"If we only keep hunting the low-ranking monsters that D and C-rank hunters take on, and only accept jobs of that level, it'll be too easy. There's no challenge. Won't that end up dulling our senses? If that happens, then one day we'll slip up, and someone is going to end up dead—or at least seriously injured—because of it."

"......"

Mavis and Pauline were silent. Mile already knew her own mind, so she hung back, watching.

"Now, I'm not saying that we should do reckless things all the time. All the lives in the world wouldn't be enough for that. But just once we should do a job where we can barely scrape by unscathed so that we know our own limits. From then on, we can choose our jobs based on that knowledge. I'd say that the jobs we choose on a daily basis should be at about 70 percent of our reasonable limit."

"All right. Let's do it!"

"I'm in too!"

After thinking on it a while, Mavis finally agreed. Pauline nodded.

It seemed that both of them were unsatisfied with the current state of things as well.

"All right then!" Reina said. "Tomorrow, let's take a good look at the job postings at the guild and make all the necessary arrangements. The day after tomorrow, our real career begins."

"Okay."

"Got it."

"Hey, um, I didn't get to voice my opinion yet..." Mile said.

"But, you do agree, don't you?"

"W-well, I suppose I do, but..."

"Then it's fine!"

"Sure. I guess." Somehow, Mile was still a bit dissatisfied.

The girls chattered on. "If we use this as a chance to take on higher level jobs, our earnings will increase immensely. Then we can move to an inn with a bath, not a cheap old place like this! Once we graduate from this dive, we'll be in the big time! I mean, we never meant to remain at a cheap place like this in the first p—"

"Will you stop calling us cheap?! This inn *isn't* a 'cheap place.' We made it cheaper for you!" Lenny shouted from the other side of the reception desk.

Indeed, this was the same inn that Mile had stayed at for her first six days in the capital, before she moved into the prep school dorms.

"Wasn't it you who came to *us*, begging, 'Oh, we've just

graduated and we've got no money, could you give us a cheaper rate until we're earning a steady wage'?! So we gave you the *unprecedented* rate of three gold a month for a four-person room, regardless of whether or not you came back every night! We hoped that you'd give us the image of being a safe, comfortable inn that young girls could be happy to come home to...but here you are, shouting 'cheap hotel, cheap hotel!'

"Whenever you're in town, please eat your meals here! That's the profit we need! And since being known as a safe inn to stay at is great for drumming up business, please don't stay in your room all the time! Come down to the first floor and mingle with the other guests! Was that not the agreement we made when we negotiated the rate?!"

Little Lenny, the innkeeper's daughter, was only ten years old. And already, she had all the presence of a matriarch.

"Please forgive uuuuusss!!!"

✧◈✧

After that, the Crimson Vow did their part—wandering around the first floor to make conversation with guests when they didn't have anything else to do.

It was Lenny who had persuaded the master and mistress of the inn to give them a discount in the first place, talking about their "marketing potential." Whether or not other fledgling female hunters would receive a discount in the future hinged directly on the girls' performance.

For the sake of all the female hunters that came after them, they had to prove their worth, even if it killed them.

"H-hello mister, is this seat free?"

With a tray full of food in hand, red-faced and trembling, Mile smiled at the man.

"You don't have to do all that, Miss..."

Lenny watched in disbelief, while Mavis, Reina, and Pauline went utterly pale, realizing that they might be next.

✧ ◈ ✧

A bit before noon the day after, the four girls made their way to the Hunters' Guild.

Because the hall was crowded in the early morning and they were looking for jobs that started the following day, they decided to hang back until things quietened down.

Besides, if people saw still-green Crimson Vow looking to take on a high-level job, the other hunters would rush over to stop them. That was a hassle they would rather not deal with. No matter how good people's intentions, they weren't interested in being lectured over something they had already set their minds on.

"Ugh, there's nothing good here..."

Reina looked over the job board, pouting.

It looked like the day would be a wash. They had no choice but to take a low-stakes job—one that would not cause trouble for the client or anyone else if they failed. That is to say, the Crimson Vow could not possibly be linked to a loss of life or the loss of a great sum of money.

"Orcs are too easy, but the four of us aren't strong enough to take down a rock golem. The wyvern hunting job is too far away, and worms and spiders are super gross..."

One might think that Reina was being too picky, but with their lives and their futures at stake, it was good to be cautious. Mavis, Pauline, and Mile studied the job board with serious expressions.

"Oh, hey! What about this one...?"

The rest of them turned to look at the posting Mile was pointing at:

Rock Lizard Harvesting. Reward: 15 half-gold apiece, up to 5. Dependent on condition of returned parts.

Rock lizard meat was edible, and their livers were prized for their medicinal value. The hides could also be used to make armor and the like. The way the request was written, it was clear that they were primarily after the meat, but also likely that they wanted to extract the livers and use them for gourmet cuisine, or sell them off to an apothecary. The hide would go to an armorer or workshop.

There was a reason Mile's eyes had fixed on this posting.

First of all, rock lizards were not particularly strong. Yet despite their sluggish appearance, they were fairly fast, with rock-hard scales, and could make sweeping strikes with their powerful tails. Even so, a group of even just two or three C-rank hunters could probably manage to defeat one.

The issue lay in the location. Unlike a rock golem, a rock lizard's body was not actually made of stone. Instead, they earned their name from living on rock faces deep in the mountains, where stronger monsters such as rock serpents, rock golems, or sometimes even iron golems might appear.

"Rock lizards, huh? The reward is pretty good..."

Reina did not appear especially interested. They would have

to bring back the bodies, so she couldn't use her fire magic and, even if they encountered golem-type monsters along the way, her sort of magic wouldn't be much help with them, either.

Plus, it was a two-day journey each way. At minimum, this venture would take them five days and four nights—longer if things proved difficult.

Still, there were also advantages.

First, because the hunting ground was distant and perilous and the quarry itself was such a difficult foe, the reward was substantial. Netting just three lizards would be enough to cover the party's minimum food and lodging expenses for a month. Part of the reward was probably compensation for carrying a bulky and easily bruised creature such a very long way, but for the Crimson Vow, who had Mile and her absurd abilities with storage magic, that wasn't a big deal.

Plus, there was plenty of time before the deadline, and the penalty for non-completion was low—only two half-gold. At most, they could get five rock lizards, but given the dangers and the difficulty involved in transport, they were only expected to get one at a time.

It was also incredibly convenient: rock lizards were not a strong monster that would serve as their trial of strength. So as long as they bagged at least one, they could retreat whenever they liked.

"We have a lot of freedom here and not much to lose. What do you think?"

"I have no objections."

"I don't either."

"Me neither!"

Mile quickly tacked on her agreement after Mavis and Pauline. "Well, then. Let's do this! The Crimson Vow will give it our all!"

"Yeah!!!"

"I would really advise against this..."

As expected, the guild clerk tried to stop them.

"I *am* aware that you all fought bravely against the Roaring Mithrils. However, this is a completely different matter. I cannot stand idly by and watch as you recklessly take on jobs that may be the death of you."

Ah, she didn't say "won," just "fought bravely"... I guess that's how they saw it.

Mile understood that this was probably what others thought of their mock battle at the graduation exam.

"We already know that! But we're not asking to do this kind of job all the time—just this once. If the going gets tough, we'll retreat. It will be fine. This is a trial that we of the Crimson Vow must overcome!"

"W-well..."

While the receptionist could advise them on their best course of action, she did not have the authority to refuse a job assignment request from C-rank hunters. As long as the applicants themselves fulfilled the basic requirements, the guild had no choice but to honor that request, as long as it did not violate a mandate from the guild master.

"Please!!!" begged Mavis, Pauline, and Mile.

The receptionist reluctantly processed the request.

"Please, if you do find yourselves in danger, run away as quickly as you can."

"We will! Of course. We value our lives, and we aren't the kind of fools who would get injured just to protect our own pride!"

With the fretful eyes of the receptionist, the guild officials, and the other hunters watching over them, the four girls left the guildhall.

"All right. It's time to get our equipment in order! We'll need cooking tools and bedding, food, rain gear, toiletries, and a few other things. And since we'll be using all of these for the foreseeable future, we had better find some good stuff."

Because of their considerable magical abilities, the Crimson Vow could easily take care of things like water, flint, kindling, and medicine. Indeed, it was a huge advantage over parties without magic users. Furthermore, thanks to Mile's storage skills, they could journey unburdened by even their minimal amount of luggage. Honestly, it hardly seemed fair.

Mavis and Pauline nodded at Reina, but Mile shook her head.

"Oh, I'm fine. I've slept outside plenty of times, so I'll just use the gear I already have."

"Oh yeah? And where in the world are you keeping all of... w-wait, don't tell me..."

"Ah, yes. It's in storage!"

"........."

They looked at Mile with utter weariness.

"Fine. But you're still coming shopping with us! We need to help Mavis and Pauline pick out what they need, and we still need your input on purchases that affect the whole party!"

"Oh."

Naturally. This was not an "every man for himself" sort of situation. They *were* a party of four.

Not having realized that, Mile was a bit crestfallen.

Reina patted her on the head. "C'mon, let's go!"

"O-okay!"

They made their rounds at the used clothing shop, the general store, the grocer and the like, purchasing cloaks, saucepans, cooking tools, preserved food, and other accessories before returning to the inn.

At dinner, they notified the mistress at the inn of their upcoming absence and requested that their lunchtime meal for the following day be left in a box at breakfast time. Then they retreated to their room on the second floor.

Tomorrow was a big day, and they had no time to play hostess to the other guests.

"All right, we want to get an early start tomorrow, so let's eat breakfast as soon as we get up. And let's all try and get a good night's sleep."

In spite of Reina's words, she was the most restless of all of them—far from ready to fall asleep. There was still plenty of time before the night's second bell at 9 PM, and so they sat up and talked. The night ended with Reina raging at Mile—who was telling a story called "The Weeping Red Ogre" from her Altered Japanese Fable series.

"Why would you tell us a story like that right before we go kill monsters?!" Reina cried.

✦◈✦

The next day, after finishing their breakfast and washing up, the Crimson Vow departed the inn. By all appearances, they were nearly empty-handed. Except for their weapons, armor, and water skins, everything—including the boxed lunches they had received—had been stowed away with Mile's storage magic.

In truth, Mile only pretended to use storage magic, instead stashing their lunches away in the time-frozen world of her loot box where they wouldn't spoil.

"That sure is handy," said Reina, worrying what would happen if they grew too used to it.

Their destination was two days' walk.

Normally, the number of days a trip would take was calculated according to the pace of an average adult male. That was nothing for Mavis and Mile, but Reina and Pauline would have taken longer if not for the benefit of the storage magic.

It was no question that between full-grown men wearing weapons and armor, carrying water, food, and tons of other equipment on their backs, and women carrying nothing but armor and weapons, the latter would move much quicker—*especially* if said women were hunters. No matter how much slower the rear guard might be, their weapons were light staves and rods, which nearly made up for the difference.

The Crimson Vow left quite early that morning, planning to stop only one night along the way. They should be able to reach the foothills by the evening of the following day.

After they arrived, they would camp and spend the next day

hunting. Then they would camp for one more night and set off home the morning after.

If all went well, the trip should last five days and four nights— perhaps a day or two longer if they were delayed. They hadn't packed very much food, but that wasn't a problem; there was plenty to gather along the way. With their magic, they didn't have to worry about water, either. Finally, although the other girls didn't think they'd brought much food, Mile stashed plenty away in her loot box.

They took a nice long rest at noon and dined on their boxed lunches. Then the Crimson Vow proceeded down the highway where, suddenly, they noticed two wagons following behind them.

A wagon should move quicker than someone on foot. Even Mile and her company, who were reasonably quick, would be a little slower. But, for some reason, the wagons never tried to pass, always keeping a fixed distance behind.

When they stopped for a rest, the wagons stopped as well.

When they started moving again, so did the wagons.

"Looks like we've got a parasite," Reina said, peevishly.

"A parasite?" asked Mile, clueless as usual.

Reina replied, "Ah, I guess they never brought it up at school. 'Parasites' are merchants who are too cheap to pay for an escort, but think they can just shadow hunters or other parties traveling the same route and get free protection. If they're near enough, the chance of them being attacked falls significantly, and even if they are targeted, it's unlikely that the hunters will just ignore them. The merchants are compatriots for the time being, after all. Just standing by would leave a bad taste.

"The problem is that when you allow this sort of thing, it means fewer job requests for small escorts and more unpaid work for hunters. It's a huge nuisance for the merchants who pay for an escort like they're supposed to, as well as the hunters who put their lives on the line for someone that isn't their employer."

While it would be clear to anyone that these four young women were novices, they were obviously still hunters. Besides, to be traveling this far they must be D-ranks at least, and their positioning indicated they had two advance guards and two magic users. That would be sufficient to fight off several orcs, and lesser parties of bandits would think twice before ambushing them. Even if the bandits thought they could win, they wouldn't want to chance serious injury. If even a few of them were injured, a small group could be wiped out entirely.

"Parasites, huh? Well, what do we do?"

"We don't do anything. Or rather, we can't. Even if we go yell at them, they'll just shrug and say, 'We've got business in this direction, too,'" Reina replied.

"I guess you're right..." said Mile, understanding.

Well, it was an underhanded thing to do, but at least they weren't interfering with them directly. At least for now.

When the sun starting going down, the girls moved into the woods near the highway and set up camp.

No one would stay outside cover where bandits and other travelers could see you. Since the starlight couldn't get through the treetops, the forest got dark fast.

Reina had the most experience, so she gave directions and the members of the Crimson Vow scurried about, preparing an efficient sleeping shelter and a nice bonfire, and making ready for dinner.

But just then...

"Hey there! Good evening!"

They were greeted by a rather portly, grinning, middle-aged man, flanked by two guards—most likely, the merchant parasite.

There was only one guard for each wagon, but it seemed this caravan did have escorts after all. Perhaps they were the man's personal bodyguards. That was only sensible—even if the wagons were lost along with his wares, if a merchant worked hard, he could earn that money back again. His life was not so easily recovered.

Presumably there were also drivers, who had probably been left at the campsite.

"Allow me to introduce myself. My name is Dewberry. I'm a merchant from the capital. We've made camp just over there, and I saw your bonfire, so I thought I would come and say hello."

He was a parasite after all. It was a bald-faced lie, but there was no use in calling him out.

"Ah, that's courteous of you. We are the C-rank hunting party, the Crimson Vow. I am Mavis, our leader."

Normally Reina would take the helm, but when it came to formal exchanges, Mavis—the official leader—was in charge. Even Reina knew that her abrasive manners could be misconstrued and that her appearance gave a certain kind of impression. However, her face still twisted at Mavis, who'd slipped up by announcing their rank to a total stranger with unclear intentions. Mavis didn't seem to notice.

"Perhaps you girls would like to dine with us?"

The merchant smiled, but there was no mistaking he was

planning something. No typical merchant would share his precious food with strangers he'd just stumbled upon. He'd surely packed only enough for himself and his staff.

He was underestimating them, planning to take advantage of their inexperience—or perhaps his intentions were more sinister...

Whichever it was, Reina was certain that nothing good could come from the man's invitation. She gave a sign to the other three—one of the many hand signals they had devised—which meant, *Let's show them how much stronger we are.* Being underestimated or swept up into something weird meant trouble, and the others agreed immediately.

"As far as I can tell, you don't appear to have any food. My own supplies may not be sufficient, but if you come along with us we'd happily share our stores."

"Actually, we have plenty of food." Reina responded. "In fact, if you don't have enough, then I suggest you share some of ours."

And so the merchant's invitation was rejected in a single blow.

"Huh? I don't see any—"

"Mile, please bring out the food!" Reina cried, cutting the merchant off.

"Yes, ma'am!"

Mile reached into her loot box and pulled out a number of ingredients.

Vegetables, fruit, and even meat, which had been magically "kept on ice" (that is to say, stored inside the loot box), so it was not dried, but raw.

"Wh..."

The merchant and his two guards were completely lost for words.

"S-so you have storage magic, then..."

"And you're C-ranks..."

Glancing at the stunned merchant and his guards, Mavis quickly sliced the meat with her short sword and Reina roasted it over the bonfire. Pauline used magic to funnel boiling water into a pot. Watching them, Mile thought fondly of the night of their field trip.

And secretly, the nanomachines wept to see the short sword they'd worked so hard to craft make its debut as a cooking knife...

Reina used the bonfire instead of her fire magic to cook the meat. While flash-roasting it with her spells would only blacken the outside and leave the inside raw, food cooked over a normal fire was much tastier.

"So, as you can see, there's no need to worry about us," said Reina.

The merchant retreated, dejected.

"So what d'you think?" asked Mavis, her cheeks stuffed with roasted meat.

Reina's mouth was downturned.

"Well, I don't think they'll try anything funny, but if they're attacked by bandits or monsters they'll definitely come running with their tails between their legs."

"That's still unpleasant. It's one thing to come across some merchants who are under attack and give them a hand, but to be used by penny-pinching strangers..."

It was a way of forcing hunters to work for free, something they were not especially interested in doing. Pauline was particularly offended.

"Well then, let's just ignore them!"

"Huh???"

Mile's words startled the others.

"We aren't actually working for them—or even traveling with them, right? We just happen to be traveling in the same direction? It would be uncomfortable to watch them get attacked by beasts or bandits right before our eyes, so we just have to *not see it.*" Mile grinned. "If some strangers *somewhere* get hurt... well, that's none of our business!"

✧◈✧

"We're under attack! A horde of orcs is coming this way! I can't tell how many!"

Late that night, the merchant, the drivers, and the guard who'd just completed the first watch were startled awake by a cry from the other guard.

"Dammit! We should've been fine around here! We've got no choice!"

"Got it!"

The guards had been hired to handle this sort of situation. The merchant listened, then followed their commands.

The plan, as always, was to drive the attackers ahead towards their "hosts." In this case, that meant four young and seemingly inexperienced women, but they *were* C-ranks, and they even had storage magic, so they must be at least somewhat capable. And rookies were always soft, their hearts filled with thoughts of justice. They wouldn't easily abandon someone in need, even a complete stranger. It was a stupid way to live, but quite convenient for the merchant and his crew.

They called out to the party of young women. They hadn't been able to convince the girls to camp with them, but at least they had managed to change from "total strangers" to "passing acquaintances."

The wagons were empty and the horses were lashed to trees, so the orcs would attack the humans first before they ran away. All they had to do was draw the orcs toward the girls' campsite. After that, they'd probably be drawn into the fight.

Veteran hunters asked for payment afterward, but if you charmed a bunch of young ladies, you could probably get by without giving them a single coin. Sure, if the girls lived, there was a chance you might run into them again, but they could cross that bridge when they came to it.

For now, the young women would fight desperately, and the merchant's party would cry out something valiant like, "We'll attack from the rear!" Then make a detour back to their campsite, escaping with the wagons. They would make their getaway, leaving the hunters to deal with the orcs.

Indeed, it was fortuitous that the hunters were all young girls and that the enemies were orcs. Given the proclivities of those creatures, the orcs were much more likely to be interested in the young women.

But then again, thought the guards, *why have the orcs attacked us first, instead of heading towards girls and the smell of cooking meat? Don't tell me the orcs already ransacked the other camp? That's not possible... even if they're only C-ranks, they couldn't have been annihilated without a sound...*

Yet as the guards arrived at the spot where the hunters had camped, all they found were marks of a dismantled campsite and the ash of an extinguished fire.

"They...got away...?"

Orcs preyed on women. Four girls should have easily attracted them. The merchant's party should be running back to the wagons to make their escape, but now...

The guards stood there, dumbfounded. The distant cries of the approaching orcs rang in their ears.

✧◈✧

The Crimson Vow walked the night road, starlight their only guide.

Yet, as long as they stuck to the main highway, they were relatively unhindered.

"Reina, orcs and goblins are carnivores, right?"

"They're omnivores. Didn't they teach us that in school?"

"Huh. Did they...?" Mile asked, sounding concerned.

Reina poked her in the head. "Why are you asking about this all of a sudden?"

"Well, we were cooking a lot of meat over there, weren't we? I figured the smell would reach pretty far, but we didn't seem to attract any monsters, did we?"

"What are you saying?"

Reina looked stunned. Mile shrank back timidly.

"Of course we did."

"Wh..." Mile's face twitched.

"Huh?" said Pauline, surprised, "You didn't realize, Miley? From the moment we started cooking meat we..."

"Huh?"

"Huh?"

"............"

"We have to be realistic about this. If monsters follow the smell of burning meat, they're sure to notice the smell of horses, people's voices, and other noises, too. But without that smell, the chance of them noticing is much slimmer. When you're cooking meat, if you're attacked then you're attacked, and if you aren't then you aren't. It just depends on your luck.

"Of course, in our case, luck wasn't much of a factor. Those guys should have known this better than us. In spite of the fact that we had cooked meat, they chose not to relocate their campsite. They prioritized leeching off of us over their basic safety. So really, it's none of our business. We simply took a nice break to eat our meal, then packed up and started moving again. That's all," Reina explained, seeing Mile's strained expression.

This put Mile a little more at ease.

"You really do know a lot of things, Reina," Mile teased. "I can't believe you were only an E-rank when you started at the prep school!"

"And you *don't* know a lot of things?" Reina asked flatly, her expression suddenly blank.

Oops. I feel like I just stepped on a landmine...

Even Mile could see that Reina was clearly in a bad mood.

Things didn't look up until they had traveled far enough from the merchant to settle on a new campsite and set up for the night.

✧◈✧

The next morning, the Crimson Vow woke up bright and early so that the merchant party, whom they had long outstripped, couldn't find them.

They didn't know if the other party had set out late or if they were looking for the girls. But when noon came and there was still no sign, the girls finally breathed a sigh of relief. They came off the main road, onto a small path that led to the rocky mountains. During the night, Reina's foul mood resolved itself, and she was back to her usual self.

To pass the time as they walked, Mile told another of her Altered Japanese Fables, "Gon, the Little Kobold," and Reina asked again, "*Why* would you tell us a story like that *right before* we go monster hunting?"

They trundled along, eventually reaching the foothills. With sunset already fast approaching, they made camp as they'd planned. It would have been nice to track down some smaller animals for dinner, but hunting at sunset in an unfamiliar place could prove dangerous—plus, they could hardly risk the smell of cooking meat again. And so the girls resigned themselves to a quiet meal of preserved food. Another part of life as a hunter.

Preserved meals could be quickly prepared—especially for the Crimson Vow, who could summon hot water in an instant.

They had already talked through tomorrow's hunting plans at length along the road, so there was no need to go over them again. Now it was too early for sleep, but there was nothing else to do.

At times like this, a particular scene often unfolded:

"How about another from my World Tales series: 'The Three Little Orcs'! Followed by 'Kobold in Breeches'!"

"Stop iiiiiit!!!" Reina screamed, a vein protruding from her forehead.

Mile tilted her head, wondering if Reina's mood had righted itself after all.

"Say, Mile, this has been bothering me for a while," Mavis asked. "Where exactly did you hear all of those stories?"

"I've been curious about that, too," said Pauline. "I've never heard any of these tales before, but they're all so interesting! I bet they'd fetch a pretty good price if you sold them to a minstrel troupe."

"It's a family secret!" Mile replied smugly.

Before the sun had fully risen, and after a simple breakfast of hardtack and soup (or rather, ingredients for soup boiled in hot water), the girls set out again. They planned to get an early start and hunt all the way until lunchtime.

Depending how well things went, they'd either start back tomorrow or the day after. During daylight, they wouldn't waste their time on cooking. If they wanted, they could take a leisurely meal late in the evening, when it was too dark to hunt.

The rock lizards lived a bit higher up, so the girls ascended the mountains, keeping a close watch on their surroundings.

They hunted rock rabbits and any other creatures they came across, which doubled as practice for Pauline and Reina. Mile stored their prey in her loot box, pretending to use storage magic.

They reserved most of their strength for the real deal. To avoid sapping their magical power, they used only the weakest spells and quickly recovered their energy.

"Mavis, ahead to your left! There's a rock wolf!"

"On it!"

Rock wolves rarely hunted in packs. When the solitary figure appeared, Mavis heard Mile's cry and leapt out, cleaving the wolf in half with one stroke of her sword.

"Uh..."

"Mavis! Didn't I tell you that rock wolf pelts sell for good money?! If you cut 'em up like that the price goes way down!" wailed Pauline, whose forcefulness always emerged when talking about their finances.

"S-sorry. Th-the edge on this sword really is something... it reminds me of when I used to watch my big brother practicing..." Mavis muttered, feeling blood rush to her face.

There was a strange sort of sultriness to her voice, the sort of tone a young woman would take when she'd fallen head over heels...

"M-Mavis, stop that! The sharpness is only there to compensate for your current lack of strength! If you rely on the blade's power, you'll fool yourself into thinking that it's your own!" Mile said in a flustered voice. She had also been bewitched by the blade's motion.

"I know, I know. And if I'm weak without this sword, then I have no value as a knight. Power is meaningless if I don't possess it myself. I know that. Don't worry."

Mile breathed a sigh of relief. Mavis was still Mavis, after all.

"Reina, can I ask you something?"

"What's that?"

"Rock rabbits, and rock wolves, and rock snakes, et cetera— why do they have such uncreative names?"

"*How should I know?!?!*"

Reina always seems to be shouting these days, thought Mile.

"There it is."

Mavis, both tallest and walking at the front of the party, was first to spot their prey.

Everyone followed her gaze to see the massive lump of a single rock lizard. It looked as though it was sleeping peacefully—perhaps sunning itself, as it was early in the morning and the air was not yet warm.

"About three meters long... that's small, but a lizard's a lizard. If we can get it, then we don't have to go back empty-handed. Let's do it."

The other three nodded.

Even though it was small for a lizard, three meters was about twice as long as Mile was tall. It probably weighed ten times as much as she did and would be impossible to carry without a cart. Even with storage magic, you'd be lucky to accommodate just one such creature.

But one lizard still wouldn't earn enough when you took account of their numbers, the time they'd spent, and the distance that they'd traveled. Without Mile's absurd storage abilities, this job wouldn't be worth the time. No surprise that the job was still there when the Crimson Vow found it.

Calling a rock lizard a "lizard" didn't give a particular impression of strength, but it was basically a land crocodile.

It had a thick hide and a huge mouth full of sharp teeth. It could easily be outpaced by a human running at full speed, but proved quite agile when it came to battle—with its quick bites and the snappy whip of its tail.

Even the strongest adult hunter couldn't withstand a lizard's crushing jaws, and if you took a whack from that tail, not even leather armor would protect you from shattered bones.

Particularly troubling was the phrasing of the job request.

Harvesting Parts

As the name suggested, rock lizards lived in stony places, so extermination requests were slim to none. The bulk of the jobs—like this one—were for harvesting.

Rock lizard meat was edible, and their livers could be used medicinally. Their claws and teeth were used to make weapons and craft tools. Their hide could be used for armor, boots, and more. It was essential to avoid damaging the lizard in the hunt, so hanging back and blasting magic was out of the question.

"Mavis, you got this?"

"Yep! Leave it to me!"

Though Mavis tried to act normal, her heart was already whipped into a frenzy. With her beloved sword—which would not break, bend, or chip no matter how hard she swung it—her time to shine finally at hand, how could she not feel the adrenaline?

"...Maximum Freeze!"

Pauline had started her incantation ahead of time and released her spell with these final words.

Because it wasn't the flashy sort of spell that sent a projectile flying toward the enemy, the rock lizard failed to realize it was under attack. But it did shift its weight, uncomfortable at the sudden drop in temperature.

"Icicle Javelin!"

Reina let off her attack. It wasn't her specialty, but that couldn't be helped. Burning the lizard would cause the price to plummet.

The ice spell flew towards the creature's neck where, even if it damaged the body, it would not greatly affect their returns. The conjured icicle bounced right off of the lizard's thick hide.

"What the...?"

Even if it was not her strength, Reina had a decent command of ice magic. Coupled with her usual power and accuracy, the attack should do considerable damage. She was taken aback. But, as she considered the matter, she realized it was to be expected. It would be unthinkable for a hide used to make armor to be pierced so easily. Reina prepared her next spell. Pauline was in the middle of her second incantation.

"Now!" shouted Mavis.

"On it!" Mile shouted back, leaping toward the lizard.

This time, Mile would fight as a swordswoman as well.

If she used her magic, the lizard would probably end up worthless. That was the majority opinion—and given that this had been the "majority" of a four-person group, it meant that everyone except Mile had agreed.

The lizard, lazing in the sun, was aware of its opponents the moment the icicle struck. It assumed a battle stance. Seeing Mile and Mavis advancing with swords drawn, the lizard began to move, but its progress was slow and awkward.

Rock lizards were not speedy outside their attacks, but this one seemed especially sluggish.

Is Mile's plan working? Mavis wondered as she dashed forward.

"Rather than launching a direct attack, we should chill it in order to cripple its movements." Honestly, how did Mile come up with these things?

Reina and Pauline kept their focus on their spell casting, but surely the thought flashed through the back of their minds.

Mavis aimed for the neck to avoid damaging the body as much as possible. As long as they focused on the neck, legs, or tail, that wouldn't be much of an issue. However, striking anywhere but the neck would only make it struggle more violently. Its neck was the only viable target.

Mavis lifted her sword to strike, when suddenly she was caught by the lizard's tail, moving much more quickly than she'd anticipated.

"Argh!!"

In a panic, Mavis tried to block it with her sword, but it wasn't enough. The powerful blow sent her flying.

The others couldn't worry about Mavis yet. That would have to wait until the final blow was struck.

"You jerk!!!"

Mile aimed for the lizard's neck, and the tail came flying at her, too.

This should be no big—

If she truly had half the strength of an elder dragon, Mile should have been able to stop the rock lizard's tail with one hand—but when she tried to do just that, she went flying spectacularly into the air. Just as Mavis had.

"...Huh?"

"MIIILE!!!"

Reina screamed. Mile was thrown into a cliff face nearly ten meters away. Unlike Mavis, who was just tossed onto the ground, Mile seemed to have taken a lot of damage.

Reina dashed forward—not toward Mile, but the rock lizard.

The moment that Mavis was thrown to the ground, Pauline moved to offer her healing magic. Now, she ran toward Mile.

No!! I can't lose a friend already! No no no no no no no no nooooo!!!

Reina recited a spell, tears streaming down her face.

"O raging flames of the deep! Consume my enemy and burn them to the ground!"

A deep crimson flame whipped up, enveloping the lizard.

"Mile!!!"

Ignoring the lizard thrashing in the flames, Reina rushed to Mile's side, only to find her grinning bashfully and Pauline standing beside her, gaping.

"H-how...?"

Reina was utterly stunned. Mile seemed to be completely unharmed.

Mavis hobbled over, rubbing her side where the lizard struck her. Somehow, by deflecting the tail with her sword, she'd avoided being killed. And, because she flew back the moment she was struck, she hadn't broken any bones, either. Thanks to Pauline's healing spell, it appeared that she was already recovering.

"...Family secret?"

"YOU LIAAAAAAAAR!!!"

Naturally, not one of them bought Mile's explanation.

Behind them, the rock lizard burned to a crisp.

✧◈✧

"All right, emergency meeting!"

As usual, it was Reina who kicked things off. She had already wiped the tears from her face.

Initially, they'd thought not to cook anything until dinner. However, they needed rest after the battle, and right in front of them sat a great big lizard, roasted to perfection.

"First off, we need to discuss the failings of Mile's plan," said

Reina. "The 'lizards move slower when they're cold' plan. While it certainly appeared to have some sort of effect, the explosive force of the tail wasn't affected."

Mile shrank back. "I-I'm sorry. That's *supposed* to be how reptiles work..."

"There's no need to apologize," Reina continued. "We knew from the start that if that plan *did* work, it would be a godsend. It's possible that maybe we just didn't chill it enough. Anyway, let's skip that bit next time. Pauline, you should use a different spell."

"Sure thing!" Pauline agreed, nodding.

"The problem is how to take one of those things down without damaging the body, but also while dodging the tail attacks— which are a lot faster and stronger than we thought."

Simply defeating the creature would be a small feat for the Crimson Vow, but the issue was how to kill it without damaging the hide or meat.

Thanks to the previous lizard's fiery end, its value was now almost nothing, so the girls made the decision not to even try to sell it. Instead, they'd eat it themselves.

Reina, who had cast the decisive spell, couldn't be blamed for this. And there were still plenty of lizards to hunt, so no one worried over it.

"Um... So, wouldn't it be best for us to just cut the tail off first?"

"Unfortunately it's not that simple..."

"I'll do it!" Mile volunteered.

"Wha...?"

Reina was dubious.

"No matter how fast and strong you are...is it really safe?"

"Yes. Probably."

"........."

"Very well. Let's start with that next time. However, if it starts looking dangerous, pull back *immediately*. It's not like we don't have other options... come to think of it, Mile, you still owe us an explanation. Why didn't you get hurt?"

"F-family secret?"

"WILL YOU LAY OFF WITH THAT ALREADY?!"

In the end, Mile explained that her sword cut some of the power from the lizard's blow and that she'd flown back of her own accord. She was fairly light, and since the tail hadn't broken bones, when she landed she was able to use wind magic to cushion her impact.

Thankfully Mavis, who had been nearest, had been preoccupied with her own concerns, so she hadn't watched Mile closely.

Mile had already worked out why she was thrown back so easily, against her own expectations. No matter how strong she was, there was no way that a girl weighing 40 kilograms could absorb so much kinetic energy and hold her ground.

If the blow came down from above, she might be able to withstand it. However, if it came from the side, or from below, no amount of physical strength could prevent her from going flying, even if she wasn't hurt.

"Even if we did poorly," said Reina, "the two of you managed to avoid grave injury while facing a rock lizard, a creature that an average party of C-rank hunters couldn't take down unscathed. Perhaps we got a little carried away with minimizing injuries to the lizard..."

The other three nodded meekly.

Having covered all there was to discuss, the girls set to work handling the heap of lizard meat.

Thanks to its time inside the maelstrom of Reina's fiercest fire magic, the outside of the lizard was in a piteous state, black and ashen. However, the intense heat hadn't made it all the way through, so once the outer parts were removed there was plenty of meat that was barely cooked at all. Now that they had the chance, they took some of the more delicate cuts of meat and roasted them over a gentle flame.

Mile decided to eat hers rare, as she generally did. In truth, though Mile's mother in her past life was not a particularly bad cook, she was the sort of person who always cooked meat well done. She came from an old family and likely inherited the technique from when it was dangerous to eat rare meat. Regardless, no matter how high quality the meat was, she always overcooked it until every last piece ended up rubbery and dry.

Because Misato, Mile's previous self, had eaten that way all her life, she just assumed that was how it was meant to be. Coming to this world and experiencing the delectable tenderness of a rare cut of meat had opened her eyes.

Although the food preservation in this world was far inferior to Earth, the time between slaughter and table was also far shorter. More than that, Mile was aware of her body's strength and unconcerned with such trivialities as food poisoning. Eating rare meat brought out the most flavor, so that's what she was partial to.

Even if she did eat something bad, as long as she had healing magic, she could get by. Of course, she still kept an eye out for anything still pale or blue—that was just raw meat. But rock lizard, cooked rare, often looked like this.

At first glance, it seemed that only the outside was cooked and the inside was still raw. However—somewhat like seared tuna—the heat did get through, warming the meat and allowing the fat to melt on your tongue, leaving a lingering savory taste. The only seasoning here was rock salt, sprinkled on just before roasting. It wasn't like when you went to a strange shop in Japan and asked for rare meat, only to receive something that was raw, still cold, and dripping blood and juices.

Mile cut off a bite-sized piece of meat and placed it gently into her mouth, chewing.

"D-delicious!" she exclaimed.

If you took really high-quality chicken and made it a little firmer... Yes, it had the same toothsome quality as a chicken breast, with almost the same neutral flavor. Yet just a hint of the sharpness of rock salt brought out a truly delicious, indescribable taste.

Most of a meat's flavor came from its fat composition, but although the rock lizard didn't have any obvious fat—such as a beefsteak's marbling—it still melted on your tongue. And with such flavor... No wonder it was such valuable prey, from its rich, leathery hide all the way down to its meat.

"This is delicious."

"Yeah, it's pretty good..."

One would think Mavis would be accustomed to eating delicious foods, but, like most nobles, Mavis's family would never serve monster at their dinner table. All the same, as far as Mavis was concerned, there was no better spice than killing something with your own hands and enjoying it with friends.

In the end, the four of them decided to take some more out of storage and roast up seconds. After that, they settled on a new plan and the magic Pauline would use next. Then they set off again.

Their expressions were resolute. The talking, eating, and subsequent break had prepared them to hunt again.

They continued their search, catching rock rabbits along the way.

"There it is."

Yet again, Mavis was the first to spot the rock lizard. This one was larger than the first, just under four meters long.

"Let's do it."

Reina and Pauline began incanting their spells.

Mile and Mavis drew their swords and readied themselves to attack.

"Condensation!"

"Freeze!"

As they spoke the last words, the spells went flying.

Reina caused water droplets to appear all around the lizard, drenching the creature's body and the air around it. Pauline's magic caused that same water to freeze.

"Now!"

This time, at Mile's command, both Mile and Mavis jumped forth.

The lizard whipped its tail at Mile, who ran towards it, brandishing her blade.

The water froze, and a thin layer of ice clung to the lizard's body, but of course this only affected the hide. Since the cooling didn't reach any deeper, the speed of its tail wasn't greatly slowed.

However, that was not the point of the plan.

Swoosh!

As the rock lizard launched the tail attack, its feet slipped.

Rather than losing its balance, the beast flailed its tail power-lessly in one direction and then another. Mile swung her sword down with all her might.

From her previous experience, Mile understood that, no matter how strong she was, without the weight to withstand an attack, she couldn't land a decisive blow. As she could not increase the weight of her own body or her sword, she decided that she would attempt to compensate with speed. Yes, once again, it was the law of $\frac{1}{2}mv^2$.

The moment the sword struck, she drew it back toward herself.

Unlike Japanese swords, western-style swords weren't used for clean cutting, but for hacking with weight and power. But Mile's sword also possessed a sharp and sturdy blade. Even though there was no curve to it, it could be used like a katana.

Snap!

Like a hot knife through butter, the rock lizard's tail was detached from its body in a single blow.

The rock lizard did not appear to be in much pain. Instead, it looked around nervously, perhaps distraught to be robbed of both its greatest weapon and its source of balance. Whipping its head away from the girls, the lizard prepared to run.

But—it was too late. Mavis was already leaping toward it, swinging her sword.

Slash!

Naturally, a single blow was not enough to cut clear through the thick protective hide of the neck, but the blow Mavis delivered was more than enough to end its life. With that, the rock lizard perished.

"We did it!"

"We did!!"

Though Mile accomplished the most difficult task in cutting off the tail, Mavis beamed with pride as well. She had felled a rock lizard in a single blow. What's more, they hadn't laid a hand on the lizard's torso, so they'd be able to collect the full reward.

Reina and Pauline walked over looking satisfied. This time all had gone according to plan, and both the magic and the melee squads had worked together splendidly.

"Well, while we're in the swing of things, let's keep at it!"

"Yeah!!!"

Their hunting proceeded splendidly. They bagged one rock lizard after another, snagging plenty of rock rabbits, rock wolves, rock snakes, rock tanuki, and even rock candy along the way.

Sometimes they swapped responsibilities: Mavis taking on the tail and Mile the neck. Sometimes they even slipped and fell on the frozen ground. But they bagged a massive amount, surpassing even the five-lizard maximum stated in the posting. Even if the client didn't want to purchase the extras, the guild would probably pay. There was no such thing as too many rock lizards.

Besides, if it came down to it, Mile could always tell her companions that the meat in her storage space would never go bad. Then they could store it until the next time there was a rock lizard request and pretend they'd hunted it when they were outside the capital for some other job.

The next morning, they decided they'd depart for the journey back home. They would spend the rest of the day hunting leisurely, until it grew dark. Everyone was in high spirits.

However, after their fearsome fight with the rock lizards, they'd forgotten something.

That *something* being the entire reason they had taken this job and traveled all this way.

That *something*, which materialized, quite suddenly, before them.

"It's a r-r-rock golem…" Reina stammered, staring at the beast.

They'd chosen the rock lizard job partly to earn some money and cover their living expenses. But the real reason they selected this particular job was to test their skills and determine their own limits.

While the first battle had been tough, once the Crimson Vow got into the groove of things, they'd focused all their attention on hunting rock lizards, and the possibility of fighting stronger monsters completely vanished from their minds.

Now, whether they liked it or not, they happened upon just such a monster—one of many that called these mountains home.

A rock golem.

Unlike other beasts of the "rock" type, rock golems didn't get their name from their rocky habitat. They were called rock golems because they were made of rock. Since they also dwelled in rocky places, they could have been called "rocky rock golems," but somewhere along the line, someone had probably decided that was too unwieldy. Besides, you never heard about "sand rock golems" in the desert or "earth rock golems" underground.

The minimum requirements for felling a rock golem without injury were: 2 or 3 B-rank hunters; 4 or 5 C-rank hunters if they were skilled; or 6 or more C-rank hunters if they were less so.

That didn't mean a smaller party couldn't defeat one of these creatures, only that the chances of making it out unscathed were greatly diminished. They *could* do it—assuming they were not opposed to the idea of grave injuries or death.

From the beginning, Reina had vastly overestimated their strength—having annihilated the Roaring Mithrils, a top-class B-rank party under the direction of an A-rank hunter, she had assumed that toppling a rock golem would be a breeze.

Now, having slogged through battle after battle with the lizards, she realized that perhaps she'd been a little bit prideful.

"We have to retreat!"

"Huh? But isn't this what we came here for?" asked Mavis, looking perplexed.

Reina's mind was made up. "Please, just shut up and do as I say!"

"Got it."

Seeing the serious look on Reina's face, Mavis shut her mouth and obeyed.

There was no time to shoot the breeze, and Reina was the most experienced in their group, so in times of battle, she was the most reliable commander.

But things weren't resolved quite so easily.

"I don't think we can..."

When they turned to look at Pauline, they saw yet another rock golem approaching from the rear.

"We're surrounded!"

"It doesn't look like we'll be able to get away without a fight," said Mavis.

"This can't be..." Reina murmured, her voice far weaker than usual.

The others couldn't understand why Reina was shrinking away from a battle they'd all meant to fight from the start. But, because of her experience, they figured she must have her reasons.

Mile, for her part, had never even seen a rock golem outside of pictures.

It truly had a body made of stone, massive and almost four meters tall. It had a tiny head and spherical joints.

That's right—it had ball joints!

You might expect Mile to remember the jointed doll exhibition she'd attended with her mother and her younger sister, back in her previous life. Instead, what came to mind were the giant, ball-jointed robots from the midnight creature features she watched with her father.

"Their weak points are probably their joints or their narrow legs..."

At least, she recalled learning something like that.

"It looks like we've got no choice but to fight! We're not looking to defeat them, just to clear an escape route! Prioritize protecting yourself from injury, not damaging them!" Reina issued snappy directions, her manner changing completely.

"Got it!!!"

"Pauline," Reina continued, "hold back the golem in front! Mavis and Mile, attack the rear golem's legs! Slice them horizontally through the gaps!"

They didn't reply this time, but nodded as Pauline began her spell. Mavis and Mile both readied their blades. Reina took to the rear, directing a spell at the golem blocking their way out.

There's something strange here, Mile thought.

She recalled something that had puzzled her during their lessons at the prep school.

Goblins, kobolds, orcs, ogres?

Yes, well, of course those kinds of creatures existed. This was a fantasy world, after all.

Wyverns, land dragons, elder dragons?

Yes, well, those weren't so strange either...

But, rock golems? Iron golems?

What were they? Were they alive? Were they artificial life-forms? Did they have a consciousness?

Weren't they rather implausible in an environment filled with carbon-based life? Had they been specially made by the gods?

No matter how much she thought about it, her imagination only stretched so far.

Surely, if she asked, the nanomachines would have an answer for her. But where was the fun in that? This was a riddle she would have to solve for herself.

Yes, some mysteries just have to remain mysteries, Mile decided. And yet...she was still so curious about them.

I really want to take one apart!!!

"Green Mist!"

Pauline used water magic to conjure a haze, obscuring the golems' vision.

As always when she heard this spell, Mile wanted to protest that the incantation should be "fog," but that was probably not something that anyone in this world would understand.

After Pauline, Reina released her spell.

"Flame Orb!"

This was a type of fire spell that exploded on impact. It was a higher-level magic than fireballs, which were simply moving balls of flame. However, since the people of this world had little familiarity with explosions caused by something like gunpowder, their idea of an explosion was only a small thing, lacking in destructive force. Half of the damage came from enveloping flames that erupted after impact, which meant this spell had little effect on monsters such as golems.

Nevertheless, it was more than enough to distract them.

"Now!"

Mile leapt forth at Reina's command.

Four meters might not sound like that much, but in reality, the golem was more than twice Mile's height. Even Mavis could not reach its head with her sword.

A slashing attack would have little effect on the creatures' sturdy torsos and arms, and any normal sword would be shattered if it came into contact with their rocky bodies. There was no logical place to strike besides at the joints.

If I recall correctly, the spheres of the joints themselves will probably be hard. But if I can damage the area around the spheres, where the rock is thinner, that should make it hard for the spheres to move...

Mile reviewed her strategy, then slashed at the golem's left knee.

At the same time, Mavis struck the golem's right knee.

If they'd struck at its hip joints, they'd be able to impair its movements much more, but those were higher up and it would be difficult to inflict enough damage in one blow. And the golem's hips appeared much sturdier than its knees.

This should be fine. Just damaging the knees would impede its movement and create an opening for them to escape.

Ka-thunk!

Ker-snap!

"...Huh?"

Mile and Mavis said simultaneously.

The golem's left knee was blown away, and its right knee crumbled as the sphere rolled right out of its joint. It made a spectacular sound as it toppled onto the ground face first.

Having felled a rock golem much more easily than they had imagined, Mavis and Mile were momentarily stunned. They looked down at the swords in their hands.

No matter how sturdy the blades were, just flinging them should not have produced enough power to destroy anything. Destroying objects required specialized power and skill. No one could just simply smash a copper sword with a steel one...besides Mile.

Before the girls could be thrilled with their results, which far surpassed what they were expecting, they were stunned again by the power of their own weapons. Even Mile, the swordsmith, was taken aback.

They hadn't even swung at full strength, yet they'd smashed through the solid joints of a rock golem in a single blow.

These were nothing less than the legendary blades of a mythical hero...

"Mavis!"

Mavis had been drowning in the sea of her own thoughts, but she snapped back at Reina's shout, rushing toward the golem she and Mile had felled. From behind, they slashed, pierced, and twisted the hip and shoulder joints away.

Snap!

Rumble rumble...

One after another, they demolished the joints until the rock golem couldn't move. None of this should have been so easily accomplished with a normal sword—no matter how sturdy.

Reina watched, slack-jawed, before snapping to attention. Hastily, she issued another command. "Change of plans! Forget running. Let's take down the other one! Pauline, blast the head with fire! Mile and Mavis, that one's done—come take care of this guy!"

Reina fired off a quick fireball spell at the other golem, creating a diversion. A moment later, Pauline's Fire Wall obstructed its vision. Mavis and Mile ran toward the blinded golem at a dash, brandishing their swords.

Thunk!

Snap!

Rumble...

"......"

The rock golem's knees broke, and it toppled to the ground. Mile and Mavis shared a momentary glance, then silently destroyed the other joints.

As they pierced the rock golem's head, it ceased to move, seemingly devoid of any further function. Just in case, they returned to pierce the skull of the first golem as well.

Though this was easy enough, no normal sword would be able to pass through the skull of a rock golem. At best, the blade would break. It was just common sense. When striking a golem's weak points, you aimed at the frail joints. The head was strong and difficult to reach.

"Are we just...super strong?"

"Assuming that the golems weren't weak, then...I guess so." Mile muttered doubtfully.

"......"

Reina and Pauline appeared equally perplexed.

"A-anyway, we should see what we can harvest. I think we can call quits on the hunting for now, so after this we'll go back to camp..."

Reina spoke quietly, all the pep gone out of her, and the other three nodded silently.

It seemed like there was a lot on her mind.

As it turned out, the only things that were worth gathering from a rock golem were the spheres of its joints. Mile puzzled over what these could possibly be used for, but Reina explained that if you sorted them by size, they could be used for some sort of tool.

I guess there's not much use in taking the body home. You can't eat it, it doesn't have the size or shape to be useful as building material, and it's not even especially durable...

However, the spheres were fairly large and heavy. Furthermore, there were several of them on each body. If they didn't have storage magic, carrying them would be quite a hassle.

At least there was no worry of them rotting or getting damaged as time went on. If they had a cart or wagon, they could leisurely drag them back home.

It would be great if these fetch a high price, Mile thought, but she was not especially hopeful.

The members of the Crimson Vow returned to their campsite and began preparing dinner.

They'd finished hunting a little earlier than planned, but had plenty of prey.

The roasted rock lizard from earlier would serve as their main dish, accompanied by the fruits, vegetables, and dehydrated soup blocks they'd purchased in the capital. It was fairly luxurious, as far as camping went. In celebration of a job well done (as well as their victory over the rock golems) a feast only seemed suitable, and rock lizard was what they had—excepting, of course, the enormous store of food Mile had stashed away in her loot box.

Besides, the rock lizard meat they'd eaten that morning was *so* delicious. And the price of meat that had been burnt to a crisp on the outside would be considerably lower. Saving it to sell was a fool's errand. It was a no-brainer that they should just eat it themselves. Rock lizard was a mildly luxurious ingredient and would cost a pretty penny in any normal restaurant.

But the meat of even one lizard was still an immense amount, and no matter how diligently they tried, they could only manage small portions. Still, they should be able to sell some cheaply to the inn—or even offer it as a gift. They had plenty of other lizards that were still completely intact. Either way, Mile couldn't keep taking the meat in and out of the time-static loot box if she wanted to hide her abilities from her companions.

Unlike their unintended lunch, this time they had plenty of time to prepare. Therefore Mile didn't merely roast the meat, but tried her hand at a number of different cooking techniques. It was not often that you got a chance to have a leisurely meal of rock lizard in the great outdoors, and she desperately wanted to find out more about what kind of ingredient they'd collected. More than anything, she wanted to eat some delicious food.

Reina and Mavis could not cook. Mavis was the daughter of a noble family, so that was one thing, but it was curious that

Reina had never cooked much—neither while traveling with her father on his peddling ventures, nor as a member of the Crimson Lightning, the party where she had been the only girl.

When Mile had asked about this, Reina's reaction made it very clear that they should not broach the subject again. And so Pauline was in charge of the main course, while Mile experimented.

A while later, dinner was ready. Mile and Pauline laid the food out before the others.

Pauline's dish was just standard roasted meat. The only seasonings were rock salt and various herbs. Mile's dishes, meanwhile, were rock lizard *au vin* and fried rock lizard.

Since Mile couldn't drink alcohol, the red wine she used for the *au vin* was only a cheap cooking wine that she'd stored away in the loot box. To that she added salt, garlic, onions, shimeji-like mushrooms, whole wheat flour, high quality spices, and a number of other ingredients, including vegetable oil which Mile had pressed herself, creating an enjoyable, complex flavor. It hurt not to have soy sauce available, but she made do as well as she could under the circumstances.

And then there was the fried lizard. To the flour, she added salt, seasonings, and garlic, as well as leeks and egg whites that she'd freeze-dried and powdered using magic. She mixed those and various other things together into a breading mix, then dredged bite-sized pieces of the meat, using wind magic to mist them with a small amount of oil. If it were chicken, the fat in the meat would have been enough, but somehow she could tell that there wasn't much fat in the rock lizard.

Finally she fried it, without oil or a pan.

In Mile's previous life, her father had been given a hot air fryer for his thirtieth work anniversary. It was a useful cooking gadget that could make fried foods with just heated air, not oil. In that life, Mile—then Misato—used it now and then to make fried potatoes and gyoza as a snack. Mainly, though, her mother used it to make fried chicken. Now, imitating its principles, Mile whipped up a hot wind.

180° C for 12 minutes. Half the work was just preparing the breading—the cooking itself went fairly quickly.

Afterward, she took some vegetables out of the loot box, chopped them up, drizzled the dressing she had prepared, and added the fruit. Her dish was complete.

"Th-th-this is delicious!"

The outside was crunchy, but when you bit into the rock lizard, the inside was soft, juicy, and flavorful. It had the savory nature of meat and the tang of spices, as well as the warm fragrance of garlic. Together, these flavors satisfied the whole palate.

"What is this?! Mile, have you always been such a talented chef?"

With just one bite of Mile's experimental fried lizard, Reina and Mavis were raving.

The praise put Mile at ease. She was lacking certain seasonings, so she hadn't been very confident. Pauline, however, appeared rather uninterested—Reina and Mavis hadn't said a word about the dish she'd prepared. But the moment Pauline tasted the *au vin* and fried lizard, her eyes opened wide, too.

"It's delicious..."

Mile hurriedly set aside a portion for herself so that she would not miss out.

"Mile, you've got to handle the cooking from now on—at least sometimes!"

"Yes, yes, please!"

"You have to show me how to cook like that! I'm begging you..."

However, there was something they didn't know. The seasonings she'd used were incredibly expensive, and it would be difficult to recreate the process without Mile's magic...

Eventually, they had all more or less eaten their fill, and their bellies were stuffed.

"So, are we actually strong?" Mavis asked quietly. "Or are we weak?"

"I guess it's best to say that it depends on the situation."

"Such as?"

Mile and Pauline listened as Mavis and Reina talked.

"In terms of swordsmanship, we're probably a low-level B-rank. In terms of magical ability, when we aren't limited it's a high-level C-rank. When our powers are limited by restrictions, like being unable to use fire magic in the forest, we're probably a mid-level C-rank. We rely on magic for defense, so we're weak against physical attacks that can't be staved off with a sword..."

They didn't have a dedicated shield bearer, and given the size of their party, this couldn't be helped. Still, it was a clear weakness...or it would be, if they didn't have Mile.

Though Mile had, to some degree, demonstrated her magical knowledge to the others, she hadn't shown them her full strength. Nevertheless, the other three recognized her magical knowledge was considerable—comparable to a court magician—and her actual power was at least two levels above Reina's. In terms of swordsmanship, she vehemently insisted: "Gren was just playing around, lowering himself down to my level," but it was clear that she was still at least a B-rank.

"If you include the value added by Mile's storage magic, as well as factoring in our dearth of experience, our weak points, and whatever else, I'd say that we're still a solid mid-level C-rank. Wouldn't you? For novices we're incredibly strong, but we're still average as hunters. That's about our current level."

"You don't think our magic's any higher than that?"

"Only in terms of raw power. If you factor in our maneuvers and experience in magical battles as well as our various weaknesses, taking one-on-one combat into account, I think that's about right. Hubris is forbidden here!"

There was still one thing that Mavis couldn't grasp. "But didn't we just topple some rock golems like it was nothing—with only four people?"

"That was just because we had an advantage," Reina said, stopping Mavis's objections in their tracks. "Rock golems are known for their sturdiness, not their speed, so against you two—with your god-like speed, and those 'cheap swords'—they didn't stand a chance. But what if it were something like a wyvern? Attacking from the air where your swords couldn't reach? Or an iron golem that those swords couldn't pierce? What if it were a toxic mouse, which is much smaller and quicker than you both? Can you really say that you have any special qualities beyond the strength of your sword?"

"Er..."

"I guess that's how it is, then."

"That's how it is."

Mavis seemed to have accepted this, but Reina continued to speak.

"Actually, there is one more weakness in our party."

"What? What's that?" asked Mavis.

Reina looked all of them over slowly. "Well, have any of you ever killed a man?"

"Uh..."

"Those faces tell me all I need to know... when the time comes, if you can't kill another person without hesitation, you'll be the one to die. Even if they're an acquaintance or a friend..."

As Reina spoke, her eyes were fixed not on the others, but on her own hand, gripping a small stick pierced through a piece of meat.

Late that night, a small form slipped out of their camp.

It was Mile.

A worry had taken hold of her, and she couldn't shake it. She crept through the night back toward the place where they'd fought the rock golems.

When she arrived, she approached the rock golem's lifeless body and sliced off the pierced head with her sword.

Were this any other monster it would have been grotesque, but thankfully, rock golems were nothing like other living things, so blood and guts were not a concern.

"Hm..."

The head was fixed solidly to the body, four eyes evenly spaced around the perimeter so there was no need for it to turn around.

She cut the head into four parts and peered inside, scooping out one of the eyes...

"I see... The head is just a sensor. In that case, destroying the cranium isn't necessarily needed to stop its—"

"What are you doing?"

"Gaaaaaah!!!"

Mile screamed as a voice emerged out of the night.

Reina, Mavis, and Pauline stepped out of the shadow of a tree.

"Wh-what are you all doing here?"

"You went sneaking off in the middle of the night! We followed you so that you wouldn't get snatched up by a monster!"

"Huh? But you said we were coming to see what she was up to—"

"So, what did you come here for?!"

Reina took no heed of Pauline's confusion.

"Um, er, well, I was, picking flowers...?"

"Oh? Picking *flowers*, hm...?" said Reina, staring at the extracted golem eye in Mile's hand. "Well, it looks like you have an eye there. I suppose a tooth will be next, and then perhaps a nose to add to your bouquet?"

Mavis let out a snort.

Eventually, Mile confessed that she was so curious about the inner workings of a rock golem that she couldn't help herself and came to investigate—thinking that perhaps she might discover a weakness that would help them defeat other golems in the future.

"That's stupid. You should have just told us. Wouldn't it be better if we all came to investigate together?" Reina asked.

As the night wore on, the girls dissected the rock golem's body, searching for weak points. But the golem was stone through and through, without a weak spot to be found. All they found inside was a round object—a bit like a gold coin—which Mile stored away in her loot box.

Despite their late-night excursion, the three girls got to bed at a reasonable hour and had plenty of sleep. They greeted the next morning with vim and vigor.

All except for Mile.

Something else had weighed on her mind the previous night, and she had barely slept a wink. In fact, it was because she couldn't sleep that she'd gone to investigate the golem in the first place.

What concerned her was the question:

Am I...invincible?

Until now, she'd avoided getting hit as much as possible, even in practice battles. She hated pain, so even when she lost on purpose, Mile made sure to take only weak blows on the thickest parts of her armor. It was probably why her opponent always saw right through her ruse.

In any case, thanks to all this effort and scheming she hadn't really known pain up until now... no, in fact, she had never known it.

Never? Even when we were deep in physical combat training? Did I ever once feel pain?

In the battle with the rock lizard the previous morning, she was struck by its tail and dashed against the rocks. But, despite the clever excuse she gave her teammates, she had not blocked with her sword. She hadn't leapt back to neutralize the attack, and she hadn't cushioned herself on impact with wind magic. She had taken all of that damage, full force.

And yet, she was uninjured. It had barely even hurt. It was similar to getting local anesthesia, a feeling like: *I know something is touching me, but it doesn't hurt a bit.*

Did that mean all the effort she'd made to avoid pain had been for nothing?

No, that wasn't the problem.

Just how durable is my body? I'm going to guess it's at least half as impervious as an elder dragon. But then again, if there was something even sturdier, then...

Mile couldn't recall taking even a scratch since the day of that fateful migraine. Her mind began to race. If she revealed this fact to others, would they treat her as inhuman? Would they use her as a test subject? Or would they try to use her as a weapon that could smash even a rock golem? One after another, terrifying scenarios cycled through her head until she could not sleep at all.

That morning, the four enjoyed a breakfast soup made of the now-customary roasted rock lizard. Then they packed up their camp. All that really meant was stowing their bags in Mile's storage space and extinguishing their campfire.

Eating meal after meal of roasted rock lizard probably didn't make for the most balanced diet, but no one ever said that camping meant enjoying a variety of cuisines. Besides, the lizard meat was delicious. *Incredibly* delicious. And it wasn't as though they would always acquire goods that they couldn't sell—at least if they could avoid it. It was possible they might never get a chance to eat lizard meat again.

Certainly, they could seek it out on purpose or pay money to eat it at a restaurant in the capital. However anything they caught that could be sold, they would sell. For the price of even a single plate of rock lizard meat at a restaurant, they could order a small feast of more affordable dishes.

Poverty. That single word could quash all of their dreams.

"All right! Back to the capital!"

"Yeah!!!"

Everyone cheered Reina's decree, and finally, they were back on the road again.

A lot had happened, but all four of them were beaming. They had safely completed their first job away from the capital and hunted enough to earn far beyond what the job had promised. It was decided: they would no longer take jobs for novice C-rankers, but those for mid-level C-rank hunters. Jobs that would test their mettle.

Mavis was thrilled at the prospect of finally facing real battles.

Pauline grinned at the idea of boosting their earning potential.

Reina seemed deep in thought, but in a good mood.

And Mile's head swirled as she tried to decide what to say to the others about her impervious nature—or the times that she accidentally used something beyond ordinary magic...

The capital was still two long days away.

They made camp in the same spot they'd used on the way out. There was still some time until sundown, but it was better to rest in a place they were already familiar with—to increase their chances of survival if something dire occurred.

Even the littlest things could become a matter of life and death, so they avoided anything that would lower their chances of survival. Even if the possibility of dire injury fell just one percent every time they encountered a dangerous circumstance, if it happened ten times then that was ten percent, and if it happened a hundred times...

After they ate, Reina kicked off the discussion, as always.

"About what I was saying last night... I want you all to get some experience in interpersonal combat—and soon. I don't just mean practice. I mean real battles, to the finish."

"Wh...?"

The other three were stunned, but Reina continued.

"From now on, we're going to start taking escort jobs. Even if we don't, there's still a chance that, as a party of young women, we could be targeted and attacked by bandits, disgraced hunters, or even fellow active hunters—some of whom are more than happy to break the law. Should that happen, even a moment's hesitation could mean death.

"This is not just about you. Are you prepared to leave others to fend off an attacker if you get captured or cut down?"

The other three were silent as she spoke.

"B-but," Pauline piped up, "can't we just incapacitate our opponents without killing them?"

"The only times you'll have that kind of luxury is when there's an immense difference in power between you and your opponent. For example, if you were a B-rank and your opponent a D-rank or lower. Even then there's still a chance that something could go wrong and cause a humiliating defeat. Isn't that so, Mavis?" Reina asked.

"Yes. In a normal contest, there's a pretty strong chance that you'll be able to win if you're stronger. But if an opponent comes with the intent to kill, and you meet that with the intent to incapacitate, then no matter what your strength difference is, it'll be a difficult fight. And if your enemy can sense that, you've already lost. Once he knows his opponent has no intention of killing him, he'll attack at leisure—fighting recklessly without any attention to defense. Once it comes to that, there isn't really much you can do.

"I have no intention of sacrificing my own life, that of my friends, or that of someone I'm meant to protect, just to honor the life of a criminal."

"......"

At Mavis's words, Pauline fell silent.

Mile merely watched, but inside she agreed with Mavis.

"I'm surprised..." said Reina, looking Mile's way.

Mile tilted her head.

"Huh? About what?"

"I would've expected you to start shouting, 'We can't hurt people!' right away..."

"What are you talking about?" Mile laughed. "My motto is, 'No mercy for villains!'"

In truth, Mile had a very straightforward manner of thinking.

In her previous life, when people showed her good will (or at least no particularly ill will) she was always as kind as she could be. She didn't bother herself with people who showed spite or animosity, but she wouldn't do them any favors. And when it came to people who meant her harm, she would respond in turn—within the bounds of the law, but in such a way that they would never dare touch her again.

She was an attractive honors student, and plenty of people had tried to entangle Misato in their schemes. She'd had no choice but to devise coping methods.

Of course, in this world she'd decided to live a carefree life unfettered by the worries of her previous existence. But she had been unable to shake her old philosophy. *There's nothing you can do about bad people, so it's best not to worry.* That was what she told herself.

Besides, the "bad people" in this world killed others without a second thought, for petty cash or just for kicks—and given that the laws were far less strict than those in her past life, reacting "within the bounds of the law" gave Mile more options than she had previously. That was just how it was.

Anyway, Mile thought, *if you let bad people escape, then they might kill tens or even hundreds of innocent people in the future. And they might even attack again for vengeance. Not just you—but your allies and your friends...*

Such an outcome would be truly regrettable, so it was prudent to nip those possibilities in the bud. Then you could rest easy. Nevertheless, Mile was not certain whether she would be able to kill another human if it came down to it. For now, she could only guess.

"I want us to take on an escort job as soon as we can," said Reina. "If we're acting as guards, we'll fight to defend our employer from any bandits who come calling, and there won't be any time to negotiate. We'll have no choice but to face them, whether we like it or not. If you don't have this experience at least once, you might hesitate when suddenly attacked, and it will be the death of you."

"That's true," said Mavis. "We'll leave it to you, then."

"I'll follow whatever you say," Mile added.

After a brief pause, Pauline finally agreed too, looking somewhat grim.

"...I-I guess I'm fine with that..."

Mile assumed Pauline would have answered happily, but she stopped for a moment, reflecting on her three friends. Glancing over at Reina and Mavis, she was a little bit relieved to see their faces.

Ah! It looks like I wasn't the only one thinking it...

The following evening, the Crimson Vow arrived safely in the capital and headed for the guildhall. If nothing else, they had to show that worried clerk they hadn't died.

When they entered, she was at one of the counters.

"We made it back safe!" Mile shouted, waving her hand.

Everyone gathered on the first floor of the guildhall turned to look at them.

"Eeek!" The four girls shrieked at suddenly being the center of attention.

"Aha! You all came back safely!!!" the clerk shouted from the counter. "That job was in a dangerous place—just after you all left, some merchants were attacked by orcs along that same road, and we were extremely worried. I'm so glad to see you back."

"A merchant was attacked by orcs?" asked Reina, a mite concerned.

The receptionist laughed softly. "Yes, a merchant we've been keeping an eye on because he has a history of parasitic traveling.

His party was attacked by a horde of orcs while he was camping, and he lost his wagons—goods and all. One of his guards was injured, but it seems that the whole group managed to get away safely.

"Apparently they complained that some nearby hunters ran off without coming to their aid, but a hunter who isn't on their payroll has no obligation to assist. This man's a known offender as far as parasites go. According to the hunters who were serving as his guards, by the time they were attacked, the other hunters had already moved on.

"The guild master investigated their claim and warned that if they tried to slander other hunters they would be stripped of their qualifications. When he asked for the truth again, they panicked and spilled the beans!"

Judging by the way she was snickering, the clerk had no idea that those other hunters were Reina's party.

The girls were relieved to hear the situation was resolved with no loss of life. The only thing that pained Mile was that something might have happened to the horses.

"Well," said Reina, "Let's turn these in and get someone to sign the job completion certificate."

The girls left the guildhall behind. They'd only stopped there to let everyone know they were back, anyway.

Once they delivered the rock lizards, their client would inspect the goods and decide on a rate of pay. They'd record that amount on the job completion certificate and sign at the bottom. Then, the girls could take the certificate back to the guildhall and withdraw their earnings.

To prevent anyone from skipping out, the guild handled all the money. If they didn't get a signature, they wouldn't hand over the goods.

The girls' other catches would be inspected by the guild officials when they came to exchange the certificate. With no fewer than five rock lizards in good condition, they'd earn at least 75 half-gold pieces—three quarters of their monthly goal. And they had a ton of other catches stored away in Mile's storage space. At this rate, they'd be able to relocate to an inn with a bath soon.

They faced the client's shop, smiles bursting at the seams.

"When we see the client, please don't tell them we have tons of rock lizards. Let's bring out the first one and have them inspect it before we get the other four. And wait until we find out what they will pay for the first five before you let them know that we have even more available."

Mile tilted her head at Pauline's request, but she trusted Pauline when it came to matters of business just as she trusted Reina when it came to battle, and she nodded in reply.

CHAPTER 14 |

The Client

THE CRIMSON VOW ARRIVED at the Abbot Company, the client that had posted the rock lizard job.

"Pardon me. We're the hunters who accepted the rock lizard job. We've come to deliver our goods."

Mavis, their leader in all official exchanges, called an employee over.

"Oh, hello! I'll fetch the owner straight away. Please wait a moment."

The employee went into the back, and after a short while, a man in his forties emerged. His rotund physique was very much that of a merchant.

"Oh, you're the hunters who took on my request, are you? You sure look young..."

He spoke with a smile, but there was a suspicious glint in his eyes. For better or worse, they were also very much the eyes of a merchant.

"Yes, we are the Crimson Vow, a C-rank party. We would like to deliver the requested goods and have you sign the job completion certifi—"

"Yes, yes. Where are the goods?"

"Bring it out, Mile."

"Okay!"

At Mavis's direction, Mile pulled one of the nicely intact rock lizards out of her loot box.

In this case, "nicely intact" meant the head, body, and tail of the rock lizard, neatly separated into three pieces.

"Oh? Storage magic? I see. That's how you did it with so few... never mind, that's impressive!"

It was rare for a merchant to let his true feelings show, but the man showed a hint of real surprise that someone as young as Mile could pull an entire rock lizard out of storage. But just a hint.

He scrutinized the rock lizard, glanced at the four girls and, after some thought, gave his assessment:

"Twelve half-gold."

"Huh????"

The Crimson Vow shouted in surprise. Mavis was the first to protest.

"B-but why? It's in almost perfect condition. Why would you subtract so much from the standard reward of fifteen half-gold?"

"Now, look. The head and tail are detached, so you can't get as big a hide off of it. Plus it's been, what, at least three days since you hunted it? So the pieces are probably a bit bruised..."

Mavis protested again. "Don't you chop it up for processing before you skin it anyway?! And it hasn't even been a full two days since we killed it!"

"Even so, that's our assessment criteria..." replied the owner calmly.

Mavis protested again, but Pauline reached out and tapped her hand near the wrist. This was another of their signals.

"Um, that isn't the only lizard we hunted. Is that the price you'll be offering for each of them?"

"Oh, you've got another, do you? Might I see it?"

"Certainly. Mile, please bring out the other two."

At Pauline's direction, Mile brought only two more of the lizards out of storage. Their condition was almost exactly the same as the first.

"Oh my! You can hold three of them?!"

This time, the shock on the owner's face was clear. He gave the lizards a quick once-over and delivered his assessment.

"I'll give you nine half-gold a piece for these, so thirty altogether. I'd say that's a pretty good salary for just a few days' work, wouldn't you? So, let's go ahead and get that certificate signed. By the by, I couldn't persuade you all to join my staff, could I? If you're on our payroll, you'll never have to worry about work. You'd be earning a steady salary and could live without a care."

It was clear that what he was after was Mile's storage magic, but seeing the way that his glistening eyes roved over their figures, it surely wasn't the only thing on his mind.

"And the reason that the prices of the second and third one were lower is...?" Pauline asked, straight-faced and ignoring the merchant's words.

"Ah, well, to tell you the truth, I was being generous with the first one, giving you a good price and taking a loss myself as congratulations for doing such a good job as novices. However, I can't afford to pay that for the other two..."

It was a lie.

He underestimated them, assumed that because they were young he'd be able to bargain them down. However, if the four of them traveled for days and earned little, they were unlikely to take the job again. So, there was a limit to how far he would go. Now that he knew they had caught *three* of them, he must have thought he could safely undercut them further, knowing that they'd still earn a decent wage and might come back again in the future.

"I understand," said Pauline.

The owner's face beamed brightly.

"Mile, please put all three away."

"On it!"

At Pauline's command, Mile stored all three of the lizards away in the blink of an eye.

"Huh...?"

The owner was taken aback. He didn't understand what was happening.

"It seems that the goods were not in the condition that you desired, so we will consider this job a failure. Now, we shall take our leave."

As Pauline pressed them all to leave, the owner raised his voice in a panic.

"H-hold it! We're the ones who requested those, so I can't allow you to just take them and leave!"

"Oh? You're only offering 60 percent of the pay promised on the posting, so surely these are no good. Getting a reputation for returning such inferior goods would be an embarrassment for us. Thankfully, since the job completion certificate hasn't been signed, the contract isn't complete. We can simply count this job as a loss...

"We deposited the proper two half-gold penalty fee at the guild, so don't worry about that. Come girls, let's go home."

"W-wait! Please wait! Let's talk this over!"

Ignoring the owner's shouts behind them, the four girls left the shop.

"I'm sorry I acted on my own in there... we went through all that effort to complete the job, but now we've failed it thanks to my indiscretion."

"What are you saying, Pauline? If you hadn't refused, I would have. And probably a bit less politely."

"Exactly! How are we supposed to do business with someone who disrespects us? If we let a guy like him get the jump on us once, then it will keep happening. Good hunters never let someone take advantage of them."

Pauline tried to apologize again, but Reina and Mavis answered her with smiles.

As for Mile...

"I bet you have another idea, don't you Pauline?"

Pauline wasn't the type to ruin a business deal on pride alone. Reina and Mavis should have realized this, too.

Pauline grinned shrewdly.

"Here's the new plan..."

"There it is!"

Though they meant to say it only in their heads, the three girls spoke aloud, sighing with relief.

✧◈✧

"Please process this!"

The four girls returned to the hunters' guild and approached the clerk.

"Nice work, hunters. Let's see, we'll process the... huh?"

The certificate had no signature with the assessment fee. The clerk puzzled over the form.

"Ah, yes. It's incomplete. We failed the request. Please, go ahead and take the two half-gold penalty."

"Wait... didn't you say earlier that you'd completed the job?"

Other hunters began to gather around, noticing the rookie party was having trouble. Guild officials began to cluster on the other side of the counter as well.

"To tell you the truth," Mile explained pitifully, "when the client assessed the goods, he only wanted to pay us nine half-gold, even though the job promised fifteen. We couldn't in good conscience hand over any goods that were in that poor a condition, so we just took them and left."

Mile was the perfect actor for this role, although her casting had nothing to do with her acting abilities. As the youngest, she would garner the most sympathy.

"What?! That's only 60 percent! Miss Reina, did you burn them up with your fire magic?"

"No, though I can see why you might think that..."

As they spoke they motioned the gathered hunters back, and Mile pulled one of the rock lizards out of her loot box, placing it in the space before the counter.

"Wh-what is that?!"

"I've never seen such a pristine-looking rock lizard—other than one that was still alive!"

"How on earth did you hunt this thing? And just the two of you with swords...?"

"What? Isn't taking down a rock lizard pretty simple for two or three C-rank hunters...?" Seeing the hunters' stunned looks, Mile asked the first question that popped into her head.

"Don't be ridiculous! That's just a matter of *taking one down*. You can fire attack spells from far away, shoot it with arrows and spears from mid-range and then, once it's weakened, you can approach it close up and hit it with swords. If you approach when it's lively, the tail poses a serious threat... even a standard-priced rock lizard should be full of holes. This should have garnered a bonus reward for its condition.

"The standard market price is twenty half-gold, but for a premium specimen like this, you should get at least four or five more. Or, if you find a particularly generous buyer, maybe seven or eight more!"

"Wh..."

The girls were flabbergasted. The promised reward was already well below market value...and they were crestfallen to learn that they could have used magic and spared themselves some trouble.

"Honestly, to tell you that the market value was fifteen, and then to assess it for nine! Who was this merchant?!"

"Um, he was with the Abbot Company..."

"Unbelievable! He thought he could take advantage of you girls just because you're rookies!"

"Underestimating hunters... he made a big mistake!"

The veterans clapped the girls on the shoulders, and both sides of the counter—hunters and guild staff alike—echoed with voices crying out against the Abbot Company.

Everything's going according to plan...

Inside, the members of the Crimson Vow were laughing.

"Anyway, we do still want to sell this lizard, so..."

"Oh, the guild will take care of that. When the client goes AWOL, the guild exchange normally handles the goods. If you don't sell it through us, we won't get a commission, see? If that happens, it won't contribute to your guild participation points, which you need to get promotions!"

All that went without saying—even little things like jackalopes and herbs earned the guild a commission. If they didn't, the hall would never have any income. It was difficult for hunters to find a buyer for every item, and so the guild took care of it—in addition to shouldering the risk of unsold merchandise. It was only natural that it should take a commission. The guild wasn't doing all this out of the goodness of its heart, after all.

The clerk wasn't about to let the chance of extra money slip out from under her nose. Rock lizards could bring in a nice profit.

Mile and the others looked at each other and nodded.

"We'll do it. Do you want all of them?"

"Huh? 'All,' you say?" the receptionist asked, puzzled.

Mile replied, "Um, yes, well, we have five of them, so..."

"WHAAAAAAAAAAAAAAAAAAAAAAAT?!?!"

Mile covered her ears to shield herself from the shouts of the gathered hunters. Perhaps that was too many. On hearing these girls had brought in five rock lizards, the guild erupted into a ruckus.

"S-seriously? There's no way you girls have five of those things in there, is there?" a veteran hunter asked, trembling.

"Um, yes. We do," Mile answered, staring blankly. "Is that bad?"

"............"

"J-just a moment, please!"

The clerk rose from her seat. She had to consult with the guild master.

Even if the prey was unexpected and outside of their normal purview, the guild would normally buy it, so long as they could sell it for a profit.

Rock lizards were popular for cooking, and their claws and hides made good raw material, but since they lived so far away and they were difficult to transport, the guild never received very many. They could definitely sell them. Two or three, at least.

However for *five* of them, the payout would be huge. The clerk wasn't sure if the guild could even sell them all before they started going bad. If they could, this would be too great an opportunity to pass up.

It was too big a responsibility for the clerk to make on her own, so she consulted with her superiors. As it turned out, this was a wise decision.

"Right this way, please."

The clerk returned and guided the members of the Crimson Vow up to a meeting room. There, they were greeted by the master and submaster of the capital's guildhall.

"Please sit."

As the four entered the room, the guild master indicated several chairs. The clerk, the guild master, and the submaster sat on the opposite side from them.

"So, Laylia already told me your story, but I must ask—is it true? Do you really have five rock lizards?"

Faced with the guild master, Mile had no choice but to tell the truth.

"No. That was a lie. We don't actually have five..."

"I-I thought as much. That would be impossible... that number would never fit in storage space," the submaster said, relieved.

But Mile had not finished speaking.

"Actually, we have twenty-six."

Bang!

The submaster's head hit the table.

"You really have that many lizards in there?"

"Yes..."

The guild master, the submaster (who had eventually recovered), and Laylia faced the four girls of the Crimson Vow. Mile, as the holder of the storage magic, was the one to reply.

"Do you have any idea what it means, if you really have that many rock lizards in there?"

"Y-yes. We want to exchange these right away, but you're not sure whether or not you'll be able to sell them all, and if you sell them all at once, then the price will go down..."

"That's not it, you idiot!"

Mile flinched.

"If you can store that much, everyone and their mother is going to be after you! I don't know if you'd call it luck, but you're all already famous for what you did at the graduation exam. After seeing the power you displayed battling the Roaring Mithrils, you've not only caught the eye of their leader, but also His Majesty the king himself! Even Her Highness the princess is enchanted. I don't think it's hard to believe there are more sinister sorts who want to get their hands on you..."

Mavis was the only one not to notice how his gaze flitted her way when he mentioned the princess.

"On top of that, word has spread of how you saved the prep school from being shut down. And so all the graduates of the school, and all the hunters who believed in it, will want to be your allies. Your existence, and all you're doing now, is proof of just how necessary the school is."

Mavis, Reina, and Pauline beamed with pride, but Mile just looked on dully.

"The problem here is dishonest folks. That is: idiots, people who don't know about the graduation exam, and those from other countries. Since your conversation downstairs in front of all those people, it'll be common knowledge that you can hold at least five rock lizards in your storage. How could you—no, no, it's fine, I understand. If you didn't say you had so many, you wouldn't have been able to exchange them, and it would have been inconvenient later. So, to obscure your true capacity somewhat, you said you had just five. I do understand, but..."

Mile tried to make an excuse, but the guild master pre-empted her.

Even just five rock lizards weighed around two tons—as much as two or three wagons could carry. But that alone wouldn't be extraordinary enough to attract the attention of nobles and royals. Although not many people in any one country were able to use storage magic, the number of those who could was at least in the double digits. Or so Mile thought.

However, there were also a number of other factors—keywords, if you will. These were words like "secretly," "impassible by wagons," "quickly," "escaping," "resupplying," "military," "four or five hundred kilos, while others carried only a few," "exclusive," and "attractive young girl"...

She could travel alone on a fast horse, changing mounts along the way, and two tons of goods would come with her. All without standing out. There wasn't an aristocrat, royal, or general around who wouldn't want to make use of that.

"Well anyway, it's too late for that. Just be careful and, if anything happens, ask for help right away. Do you hear me?!"

"Yes, sir."

"All right then, that's all for now. Please, please try not to overdo it!"

"............"

"Why aren't you responding?!"

Reina, Mavis, and Pauline all turned to Mile.

"Wh-why is everyone looking at me?!"

The three looked away again, and Mile turned to the guild master.

"U-um, there's one more thing I'd like to ask..."

"What?"

"Would you consider buying five of the lizards from us at a time, every few days?"

"Huh...?"

Indeed, that matter had yet to be settled.

And so the guild decided to buy five lizards at a time, one batch every week. Buying all of them at once was out of the question: they wouldn't be able to sell the meat before it spoiled. Besides, flooding the market would cause the price to drop, and the guild would be hard-pressed to explain where so many rock lizards had come from. As one trip should take five days, the interval was more easily explicable.

The guild had no intention of publicizing who brought the lizards in. They had a backup plan in case an explanation was required. Without this, the Crimson Vow wouldn't be able to show their faces in the capital more than once a week.

The rock lizards came with the stipulation that they absolutely must not go to the Abbot Company, nor any of its affiliates—nor even to anyone who might possibly resell them to the Abbot Company. Each lizard fetched 20 half-gold, or two gold pieces. Selling five at a time, they earned 10 gold a week, and 50 gold altogether—the party's minimum monthly earning goal for five months combined. It was possible that the price would drop eventually due to oversupply, but this was unavoidable. It would all depend on their negotiations with the guild.

And there was still one lizard that couldn't be sold, due to its blackened condition. The girls took the tail, which was relatively unscathed, and gave it to the inn as a gift—keeping the rest for themselves.

In less than four weeks, they had exhausted their stock of lizards, but earned their living for the next five months. Even if they overspent a bit on food and clothes, they could still live comfortably for at least three. Only if they got carried away purchasing luxury armor and goods could it could be frittered away in an instant...

To make sure she didn't have to betray the existence of her loot box, Mile invented a "continuous cooling magic" that kept her storage space insulated. Even this was clearly out of the ordinary, but by this time, everyone was numb to the strangeness of the whole situation and could only shrug it off with a "Why not?"

"I forgot something. We can't count this job as a loss for you all. It's clear that the client failed to uphold the terms of the job posting, so you may consider the request cancelled. It will still count as an achievement on your record, and we'll return your deposit. Furthermore, the client's deposit will be forfeited to the guild. After we pay out the maximum reward on the request for five lizards, the rest will become guild property. Any objections?"

"None!"

The Crimson Vow raised their voices in assent, but then Pauline interjected.

"Um, isn't there some other punishment we can give the company? They tried to swindle the guild by submitting a false job request. Is there nothing more that can be done?"

Pauline was asking whether the merchant's actions had been unforgiveable, but the guild master just laughed, shaking his head.

"No, there's nothing else we can do. This was a simple failure to uphold a bargain, and we can only deal with it under existing rules. Although it is a breach of contract, it isn't as if they committed a particularly grave crime..."

Isn't there such a thing as criminal fraud? Mile wondered, but it occurred to her that, in this world, the one who let herself be cheated might be in the wrong, so she said nothing.

Still, Pauline looked frustrated.

"However..."

The guild master was not yet finished.

"Do you really think that anyone is going to accept a job from a merchant who tried to swindle the guild and their fellow hunters? Would anyone accept a job from an untrustworthy client?"

"Ah..."

"Even if they are barred from making individual requests, they can still purchase things from the guild and other merchants. Still, that means they can only get their hands on whatever the guild has in stock at the time, which will probably increase their stock prices. And I wouldn't be surprised if other hunters offered their goods to the guild with conditions like, 'Don't sell this to those guys,' or 'Only sell it at double the price,' just as you did. The company will still be able to order, but it's not going to be easy for them."

The guild master laughed.

The girls finally left the meeting room and descended to the first floor, but just as they were leaving the hall, another clerk called after them in a panic.

"Oh! The Crimson Vow, just a moment! Some letters came for you!"

Letters? They returned to the reception counter skeptically, only to be handed two sealed missives.

"My apologies. I meant to give you these earlier, but with all the commotion..."

Since they had been the cause of said commotion, they couldn't very well complain.

Mavis looked over the addresses on the letters, she found one addressed to her and the other to Pauline. She handed Pauline's letter over silently and looked over her own, trying to identify the sender.

"Oh..."

Of course, she'd known before she saw it. There was only one person who could possibly be writing to her.

When she was still at home it would have been different, but now?

Yes, it should go without saying. It was a letter from her family.

They'd finally sniffed out her whereabouts... in fact, it would have been strange if they hadn't.

There had been scores of people watching at the graduation exam—who knew how many were nobles?

Mavis grimaced and looked at Pauline, only to see her clutching her own letter tightly, face pale. Everyone already knew who her letter was from. There was no point in asking.

"What are you going to do?" asked Reina.

"Ignore it," Mavis answered with a wry smile. "No matter how many letters they send. Eventually they'll just get tired of waiting and send one of my brothers to check on me. Until then, it's whatever. There's no need to kick up a fuss. It will only speed up the process."

"What about you, Pauline?"

"I'll do the same. I already decided I'm never going back, so there's no need to reply."

Clearly Pauline was not longing for home, but her expression was dark—perhaps out of worry for her mother and younger brother.

"If you're worried, then maybe we should all go back to your hometowns..."

"No, that won't be necessary. If nothing else, they're his mistress and her child, so nothing bad will happen to them. Probably."

"I see. But, if anything does happen, please tell us. Because we're..."

"Eternal allies, bound by our souls to the Crimson Vow!"

Reina smiled ruefully as Mile butted in on their motto.

"Now then, let's take a nice few days' rest!"

"Yeah!!!"

"Ah..." On the way home, Mile stopped suddenly in her tracks.

"What's wrong?" Reina asked.

"We forgot to exchange anything besides the rock lizards."

"Oh..."

In the end, to avoid causing another scene, they decided to portion out the sales of their other catches. Since they were already selling rock lizards, it wouldn't be unusual to think that they might have other beasts of the "rock" type to sell as well. After all, they had Mile's premium refrigerated storage magic (though, of course, it was actually the time-static loot box).

"We're back!"

"Welcome!"

Lenny greeted them from behind the reception desk.

"Here! We brought you a souvenir!"

As she spoke, Mile produced the only-slightly-singed rock lizard tail from her loot box, placing it on the floor with a thud.

"Wh-what is that?!"

It was the first time Lenny had seen a rock lizard tail still in its original form.

"Can we really have this? Daaaaaaad, come heeeeeere!!!"

Lenny's father (the chef), and her mother (the matron of the inn), both appeared. They thanked the girls over and over before dragging the tail back to the kitchens with a clamor. It seemed like they'd be enjoying rock lizard dishes for some time.

"That should earn us a lot of brownie points. We might even be able to avoid playing hostess," said Reina triumphantly.

Yet Pauline, who knew the ways of merchants, and Mile, who knew little Lenny, just shook their heads sadly.

CHAPTER 15

Escort Mission

A FTER THREE DAYS' REST, the Crimson Vow found themselves back at the guildhall, ready to take on another job.

During their break, they'd received message after message from the Abbot Company, begging them to sell the rock lizards. The girls turned them all down, protesting that they had only "inferior goods worth less than sixty percent of the market value." When, after several of these exchanges, the courier finally told them that the merchant would buy the lizards for 15 half-gold, the girls responded that the guild had offered them 20. Finally, the owner himself paid them a visit.

"I'll pay you 21 half-gold," he pleaded.

"Unfortunately, we already sold them to the guild for 20. Even though we would have sold them to you for 15 at the start. I suppose it wasn't meant to be..." Pauline replied.

The man gritted his teeth, returning back home empty-handed.

An average merchant would be able to buy rock lizards at 25 to 28 half-gold apiece. If they were divided up and sold piecemeal as a luxury good, they could sell for 40 or more. If they managed to buy the lizards at 15—an already discounted price from the market value of 20 half-gold—then they could turn a profit of 25 half-gold each, which was about 250,000 yen, in Japanese terms. If the merchant had known the girls didn't have just three rock lizards, but many many more, he would have fallen even farther into despair.

But, he reaped what he'd sowed.

When the merchant learned that the guild was selling heaps of rock lizards every week, and stood in line to discover that his company alone was prohibited from buying them, his face was a sight to behold.

"All right, let's find our next job," said Reina.

Everyone nodded and began scanning the board.

After several minutes, Reina's eyes paused on one of the postings. "Hmm..."

"Is something wrong?" Mile asked Reina, who appeared deep in thought.

"The pay on this job seems a little too high for what they're requesting. I wonder if there's some extra condition..."

Escort request. 9 days' round trip to Amroth, including 1 day's rest. C-rank or higher, 12 units requested. Reward: 24 half-gold each. Bonus for B-rank or higher.

It was a job of eight days, one that might put their lives in danger, and it would earn them twenty-four half-gold a piece. That was three half-gold a day. Compared to the value of one's life, it seemed rather low.

However, it was also unlikely that they would see combat daily. On the contrary, there was an overwhelmingly high chance that they might travel the entire distance without a single incident at all. If the road were so dangerous that you could be attacked every time you traveled on it, no sensible merchant would take that route.

But without an escort, the possibility of being assailed by bandits rose steeply. There was also a chance that, with only merchants and drivers, they would be injured by monsters that hunters could have kept at bay. Because of that possibility, it was a matter of course to hire an escort guard in proportion to the size of the merchant party.

However, normally the pay was lower: just two half-gold pieces a day.

"I wonder if we should look into this..." murmured Reina, already heading toward the reception counter. Mile followed hurriedly behind.

"Oh yes, *that* escort job..." said the receptionist, Laylia, scrunching her nose at Reina's inquiry. "To tell you the truth, the road to Amroth is haunted..."

"By g-g-ghosts?!" Mile interjected from beside her.

Reina smacked her on the head.

"D-don't be stupid! What is it actually haunted by?"

Reina looked a bit queasy.

Huh? Don't tell me that Reina's...

"A-actually, yes. Ghosts..."

"Eeeek!!"

"...are nowhere to be seen! Er, oh no, I'm so sorry!"

Laylia had meant it as a joke, but seeing that Reina and Pauline appeared genuinely frightened, she hurried to apologize.

"I-It's bandits! Bandits! Apparently they've been appearing in greater numbers lately, coming in from another country. Because of that, it's hard to recruit people without raising the reward, and the standard rate has gone up a bit. Also, because merchants have been avoiding the road and there are fewer wagons traveling on it, inevitably there are fewer guards on it as well. There's a strong possibility that you *will* be attacked, and I would recommend you all leave this one alone. Even five times the reward wouldn't be worth the danger."

Taking Laylia's information to heart, the girls moved away from the counter.

Bandits rarely appeared in large groups.

If they traveled in large numbers, attacking just a single wagon wouldn't make them enough profit to share. Then they'd have no choice but to increase their attacks, launching more assaults, or attacking larger merchant bands. And if they did that, they were sure to encounter a great number of escorting hunters, meaning that their group would suffer many casualties.

If the bandits killed too many merchants, commerce would grind to a halt, and the crown (or the local lords) would be forced to take action and mount a large-scale opposition to root the bandits out.

Because of that, bandit groups tended to be small and well spread out.

Only those who skimped on their escorts, or had particularly bad luck, would suffer from occasional attacks. As long as a merchant was properly prepared, they normally passed unharried. Most bandits would overlook a more formidable target in favor of easy prey.

Even if you were attacked, while the guards might be killed in combat, those who didn't take part in the fight—the merchants, the drivers, and any passengers—could generally give up their possessions and escape unharmed. After all, if you were likely to be killed even if you surrendered, you'd fight to the very last and set fire to your cargo in one final act of retaliation. The bandits' casualties would increase, and their profit would amount to nothing.

For the escorting hunters, sparing any bandits that surrendered reduced casualties on both sides. As for the merchants, if they worked hard they could earn back the cost of a lost wagon, provided they escaped with their lives.

Therefore if the client consented, and the hunters in charge of an escort decided to surrender, then the hunters still received their proper pay, without penalties. While the escort might not have been a success, they had performed their duty to the best of their abilities.

But in this case, it seemed that the bandits—operating in large-scale groups and moving in from other countries—were migratory. Raiding without setting up a permanent base. This meant they killed everyone: merchants, drivers, and guards alike. It was likely they planned to make as much as they could, then move on to some other land before a suppression force could be organized. After all, it took time for the local governments, or even the crown, to mobilize.

"Let's take the job."

"Huh?"

"If we dress Mile up in something cute and have her sit up by the driver, I bet we can attract even more bandits."

The other three were stunned at Reina's proposal.

"B-but, that sounds dangerous..."

"Yes! And it's not even worth the pay."

"If we're away for nine days, that's a waste of our inn fees..."

At Pauline, Mavis, and Mile's grumbling, Reina raised her voice, sounding angry.

"Did you all not agree to take on an escort job?! You said you would leave it to me."

"We did, but we thought it would be a *normal* escort job. It wouldn't be so bad to take on an escort request one day, and if we took one a little sooner then we'd get used to the process. Gain some experience fighting other people. But the possibility of getting attacked on this job is *way* higher than usual, the pay is too low to be worth it, and the bandits are traveling in huge groups. There's no need for us to stick our necks out just for kicks. There are other escort requests. I don't think we need to go leaping into such a big job."

Mavis voiced her opposition, followed by Pauline.

"I-I agree."

"What's more," Mavis continued, "I'm sure the day will come when we'll have to kill someone. But when that time comes, we have to make our own decisions. How can we do that if we can't say, 'We made the judgment, and I know it was the right one. I have no regrets'?

"Are you even interested in the guard duty, Reina? Or do you want us to take this job just so we can kill bandits? You want to force us into our 'first time killing a man' rather than let it come around when it does. And on top of that..."

Pausing only to take a breath, Mavis continued.

"What on earth was that 'dress Mile in cute clothes and put

her up by the driver' thing about? Fighting the bandits should be our last resort. We should use the power of intimidation to keep the bandits from attacking in the first place. And you're suggesting that we *ask* to be attacked by showing that there are no guards around and a little girl present?

"Besides, what are you going to do if the wagons or cargo are lost or damaged? What if the client or the drivers are injured or killed? Why the hell do you *want* to do something that would purposely put everyone in danger? It's the exact opposite of our goal. What about Mile, dressed like that, having to fight a swarm of bandits without any armor? Did you even think about that?"

Reina stood silently, hanging her head, as Mavis threw one last jab.

"Why are you being such a fool?"

Reina stood quietly for several more seconds, then turned on her heel and ran.

"Reina..."

In a corner of the guildhall, the three remaining members of the Crimson Vow stood still as statues.

Reina returned sometime before dinner.

A hunter's body was her bread and butter, and she wouldn't allow her own ego to cheat her out of a meal. Eating elsewhere would be a breach of loyalty toward the inn, and Reina was most definitely the type to worry over such details.

"......"

Reina ate her meal without talking. Finally, Mavis spoke up.

"Reina..."

"......"

Reina ignored her, and continued to eat.

"We took the job. We leave tomorrow morning, so try not to oversleep."

Reina spat out her food.

"Gaaaaah!! Reina, that's disgusting!"

"Aaaah, my food!!!"

Mile and Mavis squealed. Pauline had somehow managed to hold her plate far enough away to escape being sprayed.

"I thought you all said we couldn't take that job!"

"*Wahaha*! It wasn't true!"

As Reina glared at her, Mile quickly ducked behind Mavis.

"I was just raising a few concerns for you to consider—but I don't recall ever saying we wouldn't take the job. And then, you disappeared before we could talk about it, so the three of us thought it over and came to the conclusion that we may as well take it... what's that look for?"

Reina glared as Mavis breezily waved off her earlier concerns.

"S-so you were just badmouthing me...? Then, what happened to all those objections of yours?!"

"Oh, it's fine. We took everything into account and decided that the job was still within the realm of possibility for us."

"What is with you guys?"

Reina grumbled and fussed, and someone tapped her on the shoulder from behind. She turned to see little Lenny, who grinned before shoving a water bucket and rag her way.

"Sorry..."

✧◈✧

After Reina had rushed out of the guildhall, the other three were greatly troubled.

It was clear that she was obsessing over something. However, they couldn't do whatever Reina wanted just to make her happy. That might put their party on an unthinkable path, and if Reina wouldn't listen to their concerns then they weren't truly friends, much less the Crimson Vow.

After thinking for a while, Mavis spoke.

"We should find out more about that request."

She went back to Laylia, the clerk, and asked to meet with the client so that she could hear more about it for herself.

Luckily, the day was still young, and there was plenty of time.

"I see. So that's how it is then. Are you sure you're all right with this?"

"Huh? No, actually it would be a big help for us, as long as you're sure it's okay."

"On the other hand, this place..."

"Huh?! But the budget..."

"If we fail then we won't get anything, right?"

"Hrm, you've got me there..."

"Well, then. How about this?"

"What?! What is that?! Are you serious?"

"Yes, it's fine."

"In that case... we had planned to delay our departure until we gathered more guards, but now I suppose we can head out right away. Is that acceptable?"

"No problems here. We are the Crimson Vow, and we're ready to leave at a moment's notice."

Later that morning, the three girls borrowed the guild meeting room to have a chat with the two men and talked until they reached an arrangement that satisfied both parties.

✧◈✧

"I want to thank you most sincerely for taking on this request. I know that it does not come under the best of circumstances."

Early the following morning, the merchant party made their introductions in the city square. There were six wagons in the caravan with one driver for each, and four merchants altogether.

The merchants seemed to be long-time companions, and the meet-and-greet was more for the benefit of the escorting hunters. There was no need for the guards to get too friendly with the merchants, but it was necessary for the hunters to get to know one another's strengths and skills—for assigning and coordinating roles. Even if it only slightly increased their chances of making it safely through the next nine days, it was worth taking the time to do it before their departure.

"Some of you weren't present when the request was accepted. You may have heard some of the details from your leaders, but allow me to give a brief overview."

It seemed Reina wasn't the only one yet to receive a direct explanation. Clearly there were other parties where only a few representatives had gone to negotiate.

"Amroth," the merchant continued, "is four days away, making for an eight-day round trip. Upon arrival, we'll be stopping for one day, during which you'll be free to do as you like. Now, as you all may have noticed, the reward for this job is 50 percent higher than standard. The reason for this, as I'm sure you've already heard from your companions, is that this route has recently been plagued by a rather large-scale bandit operation."

Here, the head of the merchant group paused to look over the group of hunters, but no one appeared to be surprised. They'd all heard about the situation from their leaders. The Crimson Vow had filled Reina in the previous night.

"That's not all. A number of people are suffering because of the decrease in the number of merchants, thanks to the bandits. For their sake, our group is not carrying expensive luxury items, but absolute necessities, including critical medical supplies and specialty tools for craftsmen. In addition to transporting these goods, we have one more important goal. That is..."

The client looked over the group again.

"We aim to wipe out the bandits."

That was the merchant group's true aim, just as Mile and company had heard last night.

"It is going to take some time before either the national or regional governments are prepared to do anything about this. If we wait, business in Amroth will be completely cut off. We've mobilized this group with the assumption that we *will* come under attack. If nothing happens, we'll proceed with our business as usual. However, if we *do* come under attack, we intend to fight to the end.

"Though we've yet to confirm the numbers, estimates say there are at least twenty bandits. I have faith that our group of twelve hunters—one B-rank and eleven C-ranks, including four magic users—will be more than enough to take these scoundrels down.

"This information wasn't included in the job posting because we assumed that the bandits might very well have allies passing through the guildhall. Therefore, we requested that the details be given only at the clerk's discretion, to hunters who approached them about the job. There were four other parties who inquired and were turned away, as well as one more that we had to decline when we judged they were lacking in power.

"We understand that, considering our true aim, the promised reward is relatively low. However, the requested goods promise a very low return, meaning that we couldn't set aside more even if we wished to. For merchants, it is a point of pride not to engage in business that we know from the outset will put us in the red. We kindly beg your forgiveness."

The client cast a glance at his fellow merchants, who nodded in agreement. Then he turned his attention back to the hunters.

"On the other hand, should a battle arise, there is no need for you to focus on protecting us. We will simply barricade ourselves inside the cargo wagons and ready our swords. It's an advantageous position, so if any bandits try to lift the cargo from the wagon, we can probably take them. Besides, it's more likely that they won't be interested in stealing during a battle. They can see to that once all their opponents are gone.

"Therefore, you may keep all of your focus on annihilating our opponents. Even if we're taken hostage, pay us no mind. If we surrender, I'm confident—based on what I've heard—that they will still kill us.

"That's all for now. Does anyone have any questions?"

The guards gaped. The client's request—to prioritize slaying the bandits over protecting the merchants—was completely unprecedented. Moreover, this was the first time that any of them had heard about this aspect of the job.

"Why would you go this far?"

The question came from one of the three parties that had accepted the job, a trio of young men in their late teens.

"Er, well, the reason is... if I may be so bold as to say, it's just that, well... we're merchants, and Amroth has always been a prosperous place for us..."

"That's ridiculous! You're all idiots!"

This was the fellow who appeared to be the leader of the third party, a group consisting of three men and two women somewhere in their late twenties or early thirties. He guffawed loudly, but the woman standing beside him cut in.

"Well then, what does that make you, the one who accepted this job?"

"Isn't it obvious? A *big fat* idiot!"

The five members of the party laughed uproariously. It seemed like they were always this way.

The leader of the third party turned serious, looking to the rest of the hunters.

"Now then, how about we introduce ourselves? I'm Bart, the leader of Dragonbreath. I'm a swordsman, B-rank. Seems like I'm the only B-rank here. And since it appears that we're also the biggest party here, I'd like it if you left the escort planning and battle tactics to me. Any objections?"

Heads shook, and seeing there were no dissenters, Bart continued.

"Our other members are Callum, the swordsman; Fargus, the lancer; Vera, the bow-and-short-sword wielder; and Jeanie, the

magic user. Jeanie specializes in combat magic, but don't expect too much from her in terms of healing."

Next, the trio of young men introduced themselves.

"I'm Brett, the leader of the Flaming Wolves. Me and Chuck here are both swordsmen. Daryl's our spear guy."

"Er..."

A few of the others cut in. They couldn't help it. No matter how you looked at it, their team balance was horrible.

Generally speaking, a reasonable size for an F to C-rank party was five to seven members. If you were B-rank or above, you might have even more on your roster. With only four people, you could really only take on low-level monsters, but so long as you were skilled, you would be fine. With eight or more you would have to split into two groups, or keep some members as reserves. That is, if they weren't already near retirement and just sticking around to mentor younger hunters.

When it came to parties, it was dangerous to have too few members. But if you had too many, there wasn't enough money to go around and it was easy to fall into interpersonal conflicts. If there was a fixed reward and you had a large group of people, then each individual's share would go down.

And then there was the matter of balance, unrelated to the number of members.

Take two parties. In party A, you have a swordsman, a lancer, an archer, and a mage. In party B, you have a swordsman, a swordsman, a swordsman, and a swordsman. Which of these parties will do better as hunters? The answer should be clear.

Considered from this perspective, the balance of the Flaming Wolves was horrendous. More than that, they had only three members. It was thoroughly puzzling, no matter who you asked.

"We know. Our balance and our numbers are terrible. Up until just a few months ago, we had two girls with us too, an archer and a mage."

"What happened to them?" Mile asked, innocently.

The others looked aghast, but it was too late.

"A party of four handsome guys came calling, and they ran off! The other day they came crawling back, all, 'Let's team up again!' But we refused. We're not interested in dragging pregnant women off to battle, and we have no intention of raising other men's kids!"

"I... *I see...*"

A deep silence fell over the group, but Mavis broke it handily.

"W-we are the Crimson Vow. I am Mavis, a sword-wielder and our leader. These two are Reina and Pauline, our mages. And this is Mile, the magic swordswoman."

"Magic swordswoman?" the Flaming Wolves asked in unison.

Apparently, while Dragonbreath had been present at the graduation exam, the Flaming Wolves had not. It was no surprise that the larger party weren't shocked to see such young girls taking on an escort role.

As it happened, the client had also been watching the exam. If not, he probably would have hesitated, if not outright refused, to let the Crimson Vow take on this request, when only Mavis appeared to be of age.

"Yes," Mile said. "I'm fairly good at magic, and also at using a sword. So don't worry about stopping for water along the way!"

Seeing the haughty looks on the Flaming Wolves' faces, Dragonbreath shared a wry smile.

"Reina does combat magic, and Pauline's specialty is healing. She can also use a decent level of support and combat magic, so she's kind of an all-purpose magician..."

"What? That's amazing! We figured a bunch of little girls would be dead weight, but I guess you could be pretty useful," said the Flaming Wolves' lancer.

His leader gave him a nudge, but Mavis kept smiling. She knew how their party appeared to outsiders.

After exchanging a bit more information about magical specialties and the like, the group departed. From the outset, it was determined the guards would ride in the wagons with the merchants. This way, they could move quickly and save energy to fight if needed. Normally, you'd want the guards to be a bit more conspicuous to ward off danger, but that was hardly a concern in this case.

The first of the six wagons carried three members of Dragonbreath, while the remaining two sat in the second. The three Flaming Wolves sat in the rear wagon, and all four members of the Crimson Vow rode in the fourth.

They were positioned so that, if the caravan were attacked from the side, they could all respond together. Even if they were attacked from the front or back, there were still people who could react right away. In that event, those at the opposite end were instructed not to rush to assist. This wasn't a matter of distance, but of strategy: it was a common bandit tactic to launch a second attack at one end while the fighting force was focused at the other.

It was possible that Bart had placed the Crimson Vow strategically too, positioning the young girls at the center where it was the safest. While he surely knew in his heart that the Flaming

Wolves were probably the weakest link, his paternal instincts demanded that the Crimson Vow were protected.

The Flaming Wolves might be in their teens, but they were most certainly adults, and had not complained at their positioning.

On the first day out of the capital, they weren't assailed by either bandits or monsters, and made it to the spot where they would camp without incident.

The merchants slept wrapped in blankets in the crooks of their wagons. While it was cramped, it was preferable to sleeping outside. The drivers slept on the ground, with one blanket beneath them and one on top. The same was true for the hunters. If it rained, they would sleep beneath the wagons, or under a tree.

As for Mile and the other girls...

"Hey, what the heck is that?"

"Huh? It's just a normal tent and bedroll and blankets..."

"Where on earth were you keeping that?!"

The youths of the Flaming Wolves had questions. The cargo in the wagons was packed in tight with just enough room for the merchants to sleep. Everyone else had disembarked for the night. There was no room for the Crimson Vow to pack such bulky personal items.

After using the last of the light to complete their preparations for the evening, everyone sat down to dinner. The merchants provided meals for the journey, but they were all cheap fare: things that were easily preserved, light, and didn't take up much space. Which is to say, there wasn't much variety. Yes, it was their old pals: hardtack and jerky, with a side of dried vegetables dissolved into hot water as a "soup." The portions were far from filling.

Still not too far from poverty, Mile and company would take whatever they could get. They accepted their hardtack and jerky, but handed it all over to Mile, who placed it inside her loot box. She stumbled away for a moment and returned with two jack-alopes in each hand.

Mavis prepared the meat with a kitchen knife that Mile had produced from somewhere or other, while Reina grilled over a conjured bonfire. A delicious aroma filled the air...

"Would you all like some?"

At Mile's invitation, the other hunters—who had been circling at a distance—rushed over.

(Mavis had switched from her short sword to a kitchen knife for cooking because, somehow, Mile had been able to sense a faint weeping coming from somewhere—asking why such a beautiful blade was being used for basic chores. The noise had made her uneasy.)

When the jackalope meat ran out, it seemed that not everyone had eaten their fill, so Mile pulled a portion of orc meat and some toasted rock lizard out of her loot box.

"What? St-storage magic?"

This time, both the Flaming Wolves and Dragonbreath expressed their amazement. At their initial meeting only Bart, the Dragonbreath leader, had heard about Mile's storage magic. It was a rare skill, and she hadn't shown it off at the graduation exam.

Out of pride, the merchants (who had provided the original meal) had not come for any of the rabbit. However, seeing what came next, they couldn't help themselves. The whole merchant party, drivers included, approached.

"Storage magic sure is handy..."

Their jealousy was evident in their voices. An ability like that was every merchant's dream.

"M-might we have some meat as well?" the merchants asked, and everyone chowed down together.

This time they used magic to round up the scent particles, explaining to the others that the smell wouldn't attract any monsters and they could eat without a care.

Afterward, they provided hot showers to anyone who wanted one.

The two women from Dragonbreath, Vera and Jeanie, gladly accepted.

Finally, Bart uttered the words that so many others had said before:

"What useful girls you all are..."

When they gathered for breakfast the following morning, the merchants' eyes nearly popped out of their heads.

"Wh-wh-what is going on here?"

Brett, the leader of the Flaming Wolves, was trembling violently. Several others were in the same state. Only the lead merchant and Bart, the leader of Dragonbreath, appeared relatively unshaken. They, at least, already understood. The shocking sight they all had seen was...

Mile and Reina wearing Eckland Academy uniforms, and Pauline wearing a gym outfit from the same school.

It was Reina's bandit-fishing plan.

During her time at boarding school, Mile wore her uniforms day in and day out, so they had worn out quickly. Through numerous exchanges, she'd lost possession of one that fit properly, ending up with a uniform that was a little bit too big. This fit Reina perfectly. And, since the person who had proposed the plan was in no position to refuse, the reluctant Reina had been forced into wearing it.

Despite pretending to hate the uniform, Mavis noticed that Reina actually seemed thrilled with it.

Pauline was less than thrilled.

At school, the only times that Mile wasn't wearing her uniform (i.e. when she was sleeping) was when she wore her gym clothes. They were stretchy, and even when the size was a little off, you could still wear them comfortably.

But when Pauline wore it...it was bulging. There, there, and especially *there*...

"Nooooo!"

Mavis, the only one to escape from Mile's school uniform fashion show, thanked her lucky stars she was too big to fit in any of Mile's outfits. Reina's cheeks were a bit pink, while Pauline's face was completely red. Mavis looked on, uncomfortable. Only Mile continued as usual.

After they'd eaten and packed up, the four girls of the Crimson Vow set up beside the drivers of the first four wagons, one on each seat as they set out again.

"Please watch over me!" said Mile, beaming.

The elderly driver of the first wagon smiled back and replied, "Oh, sure thing. And thank ye fer the meat last night!"

Mile chatted with the driver to pass time. He showed her how to drive the wagon, and she asked why someone of his age was still working as a driver.

"Well now, I already done well retired, but I heard they was lookin' fer drivers to take some wagons to Amroth. I thought to myself, well if them folks are goin' down a dangerous road, better it be us old timers who ain't afraid to die. Seems like some of them other folks thought the same. Fer these six wagons, there's four of us old vets like me.

"Plus, my little girl 'n her husband do business out in Amroth. If they stepped outta town to get supplies or what have ye and got attacked, they'd be in a heap of trouble. I ain't got much longer here, so if I got a chance to die fer a cause then... the goddess sure knows how t' grant an old man some peace in style. Bwa-ha-ha!"

"A-ah..."

Mile nodded at the old man's words, thinking that he would *not* be dying on this road. Not if there was anything she could do to prevent it.

There were a number of reasons why this job posting had caused Mavis, Pauline, and Mile some concern. Of course there was the matter of Reina, but that alone wasn't enough to change their minds.

Their first concern was that the reward was far too low for the requested work. In this case, it wasn't because the merchants were crooked, but rather because travel to Amroth was so difficult that only the most necessary goods were requested. These items carried a slim profit margin, so the budget was very tight on the whole. And, no matter how much effort they might go to for valued customers, there was no way a merchant would make a deal that would lose them money. So the girls understood why the pay was so low. It was something else that made them question whether they should take the job.

It was the question of killing bandits.

On a normal escort job, going out intending to kill bandits—and especially going out of your way to attract them—was preposterous. However, if that was the intention, then the task could be viewed as extermination duty on top of guard duty, at 1.5 times the normal pay. If it was truly the clients' desire to attract bandits, this was no issue.

Lastly, there was the matter of taking a job with the strong chance they'd be thrust into combat.

Of course, they could never know with 100 percent certainty that they *would* be attacked. It was possible the bandits had just finished attacking another caravan. Even bandits couldn't possibly work *every* day. And there was a chance that the bandits might have already moved on to another country.

Really, this was a standard escort job with a heightened chance of being ambushed. What happened was completely up to fate. Still, Mile, Mavis, and Pauline had very different opinions on that point, so they tried not to discuss it too deeply.

Mavis was exempted from the "cute clothes plan" because, as an advance guard fighter, her gear took the longest to put on. In addition, she simply couldn't wear Mile's clothing. The magicians required little time to prepare their gear, so they all participated at Mile's insistence—perhaps because she was embarrassed at the prospect of being the only one in school girl's clothes.

As the progenitor of this plan, Reina had no right to object and, dogged by her companions, Pauline couldn't escape either—even if it meant having to wear a tired old gym uniform. Mavis, concerned that the slightest comment might get her sucked into the maelstrom, did her best to remain uninvolved.

And so it was determined that Reina, Pauline, and Mile would wear Mile's clothing from her academy days—along with their own boots, which were a bit awkward to change out of. Their footwear would be the only thing that might mark them as hunters.

They hadn't worn these outfits on the first day because they were still close to the capital, where the chance of bandits appearing was low. But the number one reason was simply ego—if their acquaintances from the city saw them dressed like this, they would never live it down!

They practiced again and again until they were able to don their gear in a matter of moments. As long as they weren't struck by a surprise ambush, they would be prepared to fight.

In any case, the magic users were never meant to be involved in close-range combat. Even their leather armor could not offer total protection against sword and spear. For them, gear was something of an afterthought.

Even as Mile chatted with the driver she secretly cast surveillance spells and, finally, a ping attracted her attention.

Hmm, looks like...orcs, perhaps? Six of them.

Mile leapt from the cab onto the tarp covering the wagon, giving a hand signal to the others behind.

The wagons following her came to a gentle halt. Then, Mile climbed back down to the cab and directed the driver to stop. She jumped down from the wagon and ran ahead.

There they are!

Mile hid behind a big tree and peeked around.

There were six orcs, just as she'd predicted. Perhaps they'd spotted the wagons from an elevated place and were lying in wait—or perhaps they'd simply stumbled upon them. Either way, if the wagons proceeded they would encounter the orcs. She had to fight them here.

There was no point in conveying this to the other hunters. With that in mind, Mile pulled the slingshot from her loot box and gripped it in her left hand, taking out an iron sphere about the size of a pachinko ball.

It's funny to think that these bullets look so much like the balls you use in the game. Perhaps there's some connection? Here, the stakes are somewhat higher...

Pondering this, Mile inserted the metal ball into the pouch of the slingshot. She didn't use pebbles here, worried they might shatter and end up dispersed throughout the orc's thick flesh. If someone were to crunch down on a rock in a piece of orc meat, it wouldn't just be unpleasant. Since this world had no real dentists, you'd be out of luck if you cracked a tooth... unless maybe, it could be restored with healing magic? Or re-grown in place of the old one? Either way, Mile had no desire to find out. Worse, what if you chewed up a rock? Would you absorb the minerals?

Her thoughts grew stranger and stranger, so she decided to stop thinking.

As she wasn't gathering small animals, she held her left hand out as far as she could and moderated her right hand, drawing the carbon nanotubes back to two-thirds of their maximum stretch.

Aim steady...

Whoosh!

...Bang!

Whoosh!

...Bang!

Whoosh!

...Bang!

The sounds of firing rang out three times each before Mile flew out of the shadows, brandishing her sword.

As the remaining orcs puzzled over how their companions were suddenly spewing blood from massive holes in their guts, two more orc heads were blown away and the three remaining orcs were driven into a frenzy.

In truth, when Mile saw the bullet fly into the first orc's gut, she realized that she had mistakenly ruined the best of the meat— so she shifted her aim to the heads. Could she truly be so calm in the face of danger? Perhaps she just had food on the brain...

In any event, Mile flew toward the raging orcs and dashed between them, her sword swinging.

Slash!

Thud! Ka-thunk!

Behind her, the top halves of the three orcs separated from the bottoms and fell to the ground, oozing blood. Not a drop splashed onto Mile's clothing.

"Y-you..."

Hearing a voice behind her, Mile turned to see Dragonbreath— their mouths half-open, staring in awe at Mile, who stood before the corpses of a half dozen orcs.

✦◈✦

"Why would you go out there by yourself?!"

That evening, as they made camp, Mile got a stern lecture from Bart.

"If you spot orcs, you report them to me first! We were right behind you—with just a curtain in between us! Why wouldn't you say something before you jumped out?!"

"I-I'm sorry..."

"I'm not looking for your apologies! Explain yourself!"

Humiliated, Mile had no choice but to tell the truth.

"Well, suppose, Mr. Bart, that you were in the middle of an escort job, and you were walking along at the front of the line, when suddenly you saw some young jackalopes in the middle of the road."

"O-okay..."

Bart was a little perplexed as to why they were suddenly talking in hypotheticals, but he didn't want to interrupt, so he listened.

"What would you do?"

"Well, I would just kick them out of the way, and... wait, don't tell me—!"

"You wouldn't bother making a fuss and calling everyone over, would you?"

"Are you trying to tell me that a horde of six orcs is the same to you as some baby jackalopes?! Honestly, how am I supposed to manage this young C-rank girl, just doing whatever—"

Someone patted Bart on the shoulder, cutting him off.

"I'm not sure you're really getting your point across while you sit there chowing down on the orc chops that kid just hunted all by herself," said Vera, one of his party members.

Reflexively, Bart looked down at the orc bone he was gripping in his left hand. He was already on his third, and his next portion was nearly done roasting.

"Forgive me." Mile said. "I signaled to the wagons behind us, but I forgot about the people in the wagon I was riding in! I'll be more careful in the future."

The group had grown quiet, and Bart decided it was time to back down.

It wasn't that he wanted to pick on the girl. He was simply concerned for Mile, and with the importance of maintaining a strong chain of command while coordinating three separate parties. Mile understood this perfectly, and her apology was sincere.

"As long as you understand that, we're fine. Go ahead and eat. You're the one who hunted these guys, after all."

With Bart's permission, Mile began to eat. But just as she did, the Dragonbreath second-in-command, the swordsman Callum, started on her.

"Oy, where'd you learn to swing a sword like that? How'd you cut three orcs clean in half?"

He hadn't been drinking, but his eyes had a glazed look.

"I-I'm short, and I can't reach their necks, so I just cut at their bodies—"

"That's not what I'm asking! Quit acting like you don't know!"

Mile fretted and Vera, the archer, came to her defense.

"Now, now. Don't bother that girl. No one likes a pushy guy."

Callum grumbled and pulled away, refusing to meet Vera's eye.

"Phew. Thank you so much, Miss Vera!"

Relieved, Mile tried to extend her thanks.

"Whatever. It's no big deal. I was wondering, anyway—when we got there, you were already jumping out with your sword and the first three orcs were already down. Those wounds didn't look like they were caused by magic. What kind of crazy attack did you use?"

Uh-oh.

As Mile backed away, something soft smacked her in the back. She turned around, breaking into a cold sweat. Jeanie, the magic user, had clamped both her hands on Mile's shoulders and was grinning widely.

"Was it magic? Was it some super cool magic?"

"Aaaaaaaahhh!"

It was going to be a little while before Mile could get her hands on that meat.

✧◈✧

It's a good thing I prepared my slingshot...

Hoping to escape from Vera and Jeanie's interrogation, Mile produced her weapon and showed them it was not magic. Merely a simple, almost toy-like, tool. Yet, rather than diverting their interest, this—just like with Reina—made them inquisitive as to how something so simple could produce such power.

And, just like Reina, as soon as they learned they absolutely could not use it themselves, their interest swiftly flagged. As it turned out, Mile's experience with Reina had come in handy. It seemed that this old dog *could* learn new tricks, after all.

It was considered taboo to inquire into another hunter's background and experience, and Callum, Vera, and Jeanie's intensive questioning was clearly against the rules. Enough that Mile, were she so inclined, could request a formal apology from Dragonbreath.

If she and her company were adult men, they probably would have—but then again, if they were adult men, the three hunters likely wouldn't dare to push so hard. If you were generous, you could argue that they were just shooting the breeze with friends. If you were inclined to be harsh, you might say they were taking advantage of both Mile and the Crimson Vow.

Bart and Mavis should have intervened as the leaders of the two groups. However, Bart was interested in the conversation, and like the others, he saw the members of the Crimson Vow as little girls, not to be taken too seriously.

Mavis could not stomach being belittled by veteran C-rank hunters but, at the same time, she knew that the slingshot was merely a disguise. Mile's way of using her wind magic without attracting notice. So, she kept quiet. If she truly wanted to earn the respect of the veterans, it would have been better to intervene, but this was a high hurdle for a new leader.

If the interrogators acted in a forceful or threatening manner, one of the Crimson Vow would have intervened. But Vera had already shut Callum down, and their questions had the air of "just a little chitchat between girls," which made it difficult to step in—even if it was clear this was more than that...

After a few minutes of this, Mile escaped and finally got her hands on some orc meat.

"Time for some grub!"

"Hey, let me see that thing."

It was Bart.

A look of despair crossed Mile's face.

"Never mind," Bart apologized. "You keep eating. I saw when you were showing Vera how to use it, so I think I get the idea..."

No longer able to muster the energy to protest, Mile handed over her slingshot.

Whoosh!

To Mile's surprise, Bart pulled the strap back with slightly more strength than Mile used in her critter-hunting mode, cracking through a tree branch.

If you thought about it, this wasn't all that mysterious. On Earth, even normal people used slingshots for hunting. And with nanotubes instead of rubber you could get a fair bit of power, even if you didn't pull the strap back to its fullest. The difference was that all the others who'd tried didn't have Bart's physical strength.

Still, as an archer, Vera, should have had a fair bit of upper body strength. She should have at least been able to stretch the strap back part of the way...

It seemed that Bart was rather extraordinary. In the way that only a B-rank hunter could be.

Fascinated, he began gathering pebbles, but Mile ignored him and focused on her food. Then she attempted to slip back to her tent unnoticed...

"Mileeeey! If you don't mind?"

"Sure, sure..."

The women of Dragonbreath called for a shower.

The next morning, Mile awoke to a strangely delicious smell.

She dressed herself and went to find Bart roasting meat over the campfire.

Behind him were birds, jackalopes, and foxes.

Whoa...

Apparently, he had been hunting since the crack of dawn.

A swordsman by trade, Bart was in high spirits. He'd quite enjoyed his first experience with long-range hunting.

DIDN'T I SAY TO MAKE MY ABILITIES
AVERAGE IN THE NEXT LIFE?!

"This thing is amazing! It makes it so easy to grab prey! If you had this—"

Noooo! Don't finish that sentence!!!

Ignorant of Mile's plea, Bart grinned and continued.

"—you wouldn't even need bows or combat spells!"

Aaaaaand he said it.

Smack!

Feeling a hand on his shoulder, Bart turned to find the Dragonbreath's archer Vera, and their mage Jeanie, glaring down at him.

"Oh."

The two women dragged him away from the fire, and Mile heard jostling before Bart returned with the borrowed slingshot.

"...Here you go."

His face appeared somewhat swollen.

It was now the third day since they departed from the capital. If nothing out of the ordinary occurred, they would arrive in Amroth by the evening of the following day.

Though they were a fair distance from the capital, they were still quite a way from Amroth. Today held the greatest likelihood of a bandit attack. With that in mind, the Crimson Vow once again took up their places beside the drivers.

The bandits were free to select the location for their assault. So it was only natural that it would happen somewhere they had the advantage due to terrain or fatigue on the part of the merchant party.

Evening, most likely. When we're the most tired and just getting ready to settle in for the night... will they strike while we're still moving? Or when we get to camp?

That was Mile's thinking. In reality, it was late morning when they appeared.

Her surveillance magic revealed seven human figures in the distance.

That's fewer than I thought. Are they just a diversion? Is the main party elsewhere?

Figuring that out was a task for their leader. Mile drew back the curtain and gave her report to Bart, who sat in the luggage compartment.

"There are seven people about 300 meters ahead. And they're not moving."

"How on earth do you know that?!" Bart looked slightly stunned, but recovered quickly. "Let's stop for now and get ready. Then we'll proceed and confirm the group up ahead, keeping an eye on the rear. If they're bandits, we eliminate them. Even if a fight breaks out, the Flaming Wolves will lie in wait in their wagon. That way, if a separate group ambushes us they can fight them off, and if these guys get too close, they can defend the merchants."

Of course, the merchants had told their escort not to worry over their protection, but no one could sit by and listen to that kind of talk. They had to defend their clients as much as the circumstances allowed.

Mile nodded at Bart's instructions, then jumped on top of the tarp and flashed hand signals to the wagons behind. She couldn't relay Bart's instructions word for word, but she could get the main points with this simple sign sequence.

As the wagons came to a stop, Mile moved to the fourth wagon to change clothes.

If there'd been no time, the plan was for the men to look away as they changed—or simply don their leather gear on top of the uniforms. However, since they had a few moments, there was no need to change in front of the other hunters. *That* was by no means a service that Mile was eager to provide.

By the time Mile made it to the fourth wagon, Reina, who had been riding in the third, had already finished changing. Pauline had been in the fourth wagon from the start, and Mavis, who had no need to change, was still in the cab of the second wagon, waiting.

"I guess it's time..." said Mile.

Reina and Pauline nodded silently.

When they were finished, all three headed toward the first wagon, collecting Mavis along the way. The members of Dragonbreath were already waiting on the ground in front.

The guards began advancing, with only the Flaming Wolves lurking behind in the final wagon—their hidden ace. They had received their orders from Dragonbreath while the girls were changing.

"All right, then. Let's go!"

"Ah! Please wait a minute!" Mavis interrupted. "Could I persuade you all to let us take care of this part?"

"What?"

"At the moment, it seems like there are only seven bandits up ahead. And we'd like to try get some combat experience. Of course, we'd welcome an assist if it looks like we're at a disadvantage or if more reinforcements appear... with just us going out at the start, the bandits may get careless. And then, perhaps, the rest of the bandits might be convinced to show themselves as well..."

Bart thought a moment, then agreed.

"Yes. Go on ahead. But if it looks like you're in danger, we're going to step in. And if reinforcements appear, then we can't guarantee you backup. Do you understand?"

"Yes. And please forgive my rudeness. Let's go!"

The other three nodded at Mavis's direction. This was the moment they were waiting for.

It was time for the Crimson Vow to have their first real fight.

The six wagons trundled along at a far more leisurely pace than usual. And four young girls walked at the head of the procession.

The five members of Dragonbreath hid in the first and second wagons, ready to mobilize on Bart's signal.

As they advanced, they came across a log rolled out to block the road. It made it impossible for a wagon to pass, and with such a narrow road, it would be hard to get around it. As the caravan came to a halt, the bandits showed themselves.

"Well, well. You all had better—wha?"

Seeing the Crimson Vow, the bandits froze in place.

"Y'all are *hunters*? We thought you were some bratty little academy students. Damn. What the hell were those lookouts even spying for?"

The bandits must have been watching from somewhere along the road and selected these wagons as their targets. Normally, the presence of an escort acted as a deterrent, so hiding guards away was unheard of. The bandits simply assumed that their lookouts had made a mistake.

"Whatever. Seeing how young you are, I bet y'all just graduated to D-rank, huh? And there ain't much you can do with so few. Better surrender now and save yer skins. If you just go ahead and hand over yer gear and yer weapons, along with whatever you get from those merchants, we'll take that as payment and leave ya alone."

The man appeared to be the one in charge, but it was clear from his face that the girls would be wise not to trust him.

"That's what you say," said Reina, glaring. "But the moment we hand over our weapons, you'll just capture us and use us for your own amusement—or sell us off as slaves!"

The head bandit gave a thin smile.

"Oh? Well, in that case, we'll just have to take you by force. Gonna end up the same either way."

At their leader's signal, the bandits surrounded the party.

Mavis and Mile readied their swords, while Reina and Pauline began casting their spells.

"Get 'em!"

Several bandits rushed at Reina and Pauline, hoping to stop their incantations, while two more moved on Mile and Mavis to make sure they wouldn't intervene.

From the bandits' viewpoint, it made far more sense to be wary of a spell, which had unknown power, compared to a couple of little girls with swords. It would take time for such inexperienced magic users to cast their spells. So long as the bandits moved quickly, they should be able to overwhelm the girls easily.

"Gah!!"

Pauline jabbed her staff into a bandit's gut, while Reina smashed another in the chin.

"You idiots! If the back-line magicians are in the front, then—guh!!"

"Wh—?!"

The chief bandit took several steps back in a panic, looking at the two bandits who'd been meant to keep Mavis and Mile in check. They were lying on the ground in agony. That left only three bandits—including the chief—standing.

"H-bomb!"

Pauline, who had continued casting through the ruckus, fired her spell.

While it had a rather unsettling name, the spell was nothing more than water, striking with explosive force—nothing involving nuclear fusion.

Obviously Mile had been the one to name it.

She had in mind the kind of bomb she'd seen in comic strips: a round ball with a fuse that had been historically used back on Earth. If such a thing ever made an appearance here, Mile had decided she would call it a "medieval bomb." Really, it was a particularly primitive thing, so she probably could have called it a "basic bomb" or better yet, just a "bomb." And one that she'd devised for blowing away groups of kobolds could be called a "kobold bomb."

In any event, Pauline's "H-bomb" sent two more of the bandits flying, tossing them into a tree and to the ground respectively. The only bandit left now was the chief. Reina stared him down.

"Hellfi—"

"Stop it!!"

As Mile and Pauline screamed, Mavis jumped over to clamp a hand over Reina's mouth.

It was *that* spell. The spell that her opponent in the graduation exam had used. The spell that, if not properly moderated, would burn any opponent to ash.

Judging the situation based on the state of his companions, the chief bandit dropped to the ground, bowing his head.

"Well. It looks like there's been a mix-up." Seeing the fight was over, Bart descended from the wagon. "There aren't any reinforcements, and honestly, these don't seem like the bandits we were after. They're probably just a normal raiding party..."

"I guess so." Mile and Pauline replied, but Reina and Mavis were still scuffling.

"I'm gonna destroy him! Let me destroy him!"

"Stop!!!"

CHAPTER 16 |

The Past

THE BANDITS SUFFERED some bruising and broken bones, but thankfully there were no life-threatening injuries. In just a few short minutes, the whole group was restrained.

Interrogating them, the hunters found that these bandits had no ties to the large brigade they were after. They explained that the number of wagons traveling through their territory had greatly decreased, and since most of the wagons that still came were larger caravans and armed to the teeth with guards, they had leapt at the chance to strike a smaller caravan that was apparently unguarded, with rich-looking little girls in tow.

"We should kill them!"

"Hmm..."

A debate raged over the fate of the bandits.

"We still have at least a day and a half's journey to Amroth, and we can't bring them all that way," Reina argued passionately. "There's no room for them to ride in the wagons, and if they're on foot, they'll slow us down and we won't make it to Amroth before night-fall. Besides, they could escape from their ropes and slit our throats while we're sleeping. If we bring them to the city, we could collect a reward—or fetch a nice sum selling them off as forced labor—but right now we're in the middle of an important job! Isn't it better to just bring in their heads and claim the reward that way?!"

The bandits trembled at her words.

"Yeah, but...while killing them in the midst of battle is one thing, it's another to murder them when they're beaten and help-less. If any of their friends show up, we can kill them, no question, but for now..."

Bart seemed far more inclined to bring the bandits along with them. It wasn't clear if that was because he was uninterested in wanton murder, or just because he was unwilling to give up the money they would get by selling them off.

In the end, it was determined that this was a matter to be decided by majority, and they held a vote for the twelve hunters and four merchants. The drivers were excluded.

The result was a 9-to-7 decision to bring the bandits along with them—alive.

Mile was surprised that the merchants, who seemed relatively gentle, had all raised their hands in favor of killing the bandits, but then again, perhaps it was to be expected. The bulk of the hunters had voted in favor of bringing them along—not because they were kind, but because it was a chance to increase their prof-its with relatively little danger to themselves. The Flaming Wolves in particular seemed strapped for cash and were in favor of any plan that involved making money.

Pauline and Mile used magic to heal the bandits just enough that they'd be able to walk and left the rest of their injuries to decrease the danger of them escaping. They'd provide more healing before turning them over to the authorities in Amroth. That way, after the bandits were sentenced they'd be healthy enough for forced labor, and the Crimson Vow might even be able to receive payment for their healing work.

As they moved out, only the bandit chief rode inside the wagon, bound. The other six had their arms tied and ropes around their necks, each attached to the wagons. If they chose not to walk, they'd be strangled. It was up to them whether they'd walk or be dragged along as a corpse. That also prevented them from wasting the merchants' time by walking slowly. Naturally, they were separated so that they could neither conspire with their companions, nor collaborate on a story they might tell the authorities when they stood trial. It was Pauline who'd proposed that system.

By now, the Crimson Vow had given up on sitting by the drivers, instead assembling in the fourth wagon just as they had upon their departure from the capital. They were all wearing their hunter's garb.

However, the atmosphere amongst them was not a cheerful one.

"Reina, what were you thinking back there, trying such a lethal spell?" asked Mavis. "The other bandits were already incapacitated, and we were almost in the clear. Besides, we still needed to press them for information. There was no need to kill their leader. I'm sure you have plenty of spells you could have used just to capture them, don't you?"

"There was no reason to leave him alive. If you take pity on a bandit, who knows when he'll stab you in the back? Plus, I'm sure they've murdered countless innocent people. Who are they to complain when their number's up?" Reina's face was sullen.

"Still, it's one thing to kill them in battle. After they've been incapacitated, that's another matter. Their punishment is something for the authorities to decide. You don't want our 'first time killing someone' to be the one-sided slaughter of a helpless opponent! Do you?"

Reina was silent.

"It's not like you to fixate on something like this, Reina!" said Pauline. "Did something happen with you...and bandits...?"

Reina was silent a little while longer before she nodded, her voice quiet.

"...them..."

"Hmm?"

"They killed them! My father, my friends—everyone! The bandits killed them all!"

And so, Reina told the rest of the party about her past...

✧◈✧

Reina was a merchant's daughter.

Ever since she could remember, her days were spent traveling with her father in a modest cart from town to town and village to village, peddling their wares. She had no recollection of her mother.

Reina's magic was just enough to make life a little easier. At a level akin to that of a sorcerer's assistant, she could produce water for humans and horses, and light small fires to cook by.

"I don't know what I'd do without you, Reina."

"*Hehehe!*"

They were not wealthy, but not destitute either, and their peddling days were easy and free. They imagined their journeying would only end if they saved up enough to settle down somewhere and open a shop, or perhaps Reina's eventual marriage...

But that wasn't to be.

Reina was ten years old when it happened. They were making their way between towns. She was napping happily in the front of the wagon when her father, who was driving, cried out.

"Bandits! Hurry! Hide yourself between the crates!"

Reina climbed quickly into the tightly packed cart and slipped between the wares. In all their long days on the road, this was not the first time they'd been assailed by bandits.

Of course, bandits knew that a peddler with a single cart, who could not even afford an escort, was unlikely to have much money. Even if they stole their peasant pots and pans and gardening tools, they were bulky and unlikely to yield much profit. Normally, bandits would let such a wagon pass by unmolested, holding out for a more profitable prey.

However, now and then, you found bandits who were especially strapped for cash. Who'd snap at any scrap of profit. In these cases, Reina's father would merely hand over any coin he had on hand and leave with cart and cargo intact. The more folks who were injured by bandits, the more likely it was that the region might form a bandit-hunting brigade. Rather than snatching unprofitable goods, it was better for bandits to allow the poorer merchants to continue on their way. If they lost their money but still had the cart and goods, it wasn't so hard for a merchant to get back on his feet, meaning he might provide a target for these same bandits in the future.

And so Reina's father stayed calm in the face of the attack. They had encountered countless misfortunes in the past, so what was one more?

Yet, perhaps because the bandits they encountered were in particularly dire straits, this turned out to be the greatest misfortune.

"Quit yanking us around! Is this all you've got?!"

"W-well, you see, I used my earnings in the last town to restock my wares... most of my humble profits go into maintenance, so I don't have very much to—"

"You think I care, old man?! We need money! It looks like we just have to take what you've got. Oy!"

At their leader's command, his three underlings descended on the cargo.

"P-please don't! If you spoil the goods, then I won't be able to..."

Thinking of his daughter hiding amongst his wares, Reina's father tried desperately to stop them, but of course, the bandits refused to listen. Instead, they climbed onto the cart and began rummaging for valuables, and after a short while there came a scream.

"No! Let me gooo!!!"

They dragged Reina from the cart.

"Oh, she's a feisty one, ain't she?!"

Seeing Reina, the leader of the bandits gave a sinister grin.

"So you did have some 'valuables' in there..."

"P-please, stop! She's only ten years old!"

"Don't you worry. We'll take good care of her... and afterwards, she can live a happy life as the slave to some rich gentleman. Ha ha ha ha ha!"

"B-boss! O-over there!" one of the bandits shouted in a panic.

"What is it?"

The chief looked in the direction the man was pointing, wondering what could be dampening his good mood.

"Wh—a hunter?!"

Four hunters were running toward them at top speed, coming to the wagon's defense.

There was no way that these bandits—who had fallen into thievery after failing to become hunters themselves—could possibly stand up to an active party. Worse, there appeared to be a magic user amongst the approaching group.

Whether the hunters were acting out of chivalry or whether they simply aimed to collect the reward for the bandits' heads, they would fight with their all. The bandits, having been caught up with the merchant, his daughter, and their cargo, had been too slow to escape.

"Damn it! We gotta go! Take the girl!"

At the man's orders, the bandits tried to pull Reina up.

Yet Reina knew that if she could stall for just a moment longer, she would be rescued. Slipping out of the bandits' hands, she rolled beneath the cart.

"Damn you! You little brat!"

The underlings hurried to drag her back out, but she wrapped her arms and legs firmly around the axles, so that even with their greater strength, they couldn't dislodge her. As they struggled, the hunters drew nearer.

"Little girl! Don't you care about what happens to your father?!"

She could hear the lead bandit shouting. From her position

beneath the cart, Reina couldn't see, but she could well imagine the scene above. The bandit was holding a sword to her father's throat.

"If you don't come out, then... how do you like this?!"

Reina heard no sound.

"You piece of filth! Your little girl can't hear you... how do you like *this*?!"

"G...Gwaaah..."

This time, it was too much for Reina's father to bear. He let out a moan of pain.

"St-stop! I'll come out! I'm coming out right now!"

"No, Reina! Don't come out! You can't—"

Hearing her father's anguished voice, Reina could no longer resist. She crawled out from under the wagon, only to be snatched up in the arms of the bandits.

"Father!" Reina screamed.

Her father was collapsed on the ground, gripping his right shoulder where the sword had struck.

"All right." The chief drew his sword from the merchant's shoulder and pierced him through the stomach.

"Guhh..." With a sharp twitch, Reina's father doubled in half. The strength rushed out of his body.

"Looks like we're all through with this guy. Let's make sure that magic man wastes his time on him... oh my, was that too much? Looks like he's gone and died... oh well! Let's get outta here!"

"Faaaaatheeerrr!!!!!!"

Reina pounded her arms and legs with all her strength, clawing at the bandits' faces.

"Oww, hey, settle down there. Quit fighti—eurgh!!"

Her foot flew into the bandit's guts.

"Gaahh!"

Her toes ground into his abdomen.

"What the hell are you doing?! Hurry, those guys are... wahh!"

Fwoosh!

An arrow grazed the chief's cheek.

He broke away from his underlings and ran as fast as he could.

"B-boss?"

The moment the others realized, they let go of Reina and made their escape.

"Father! Father!!"

Reina clung to her father as he mustered his last breath. He gripped Reina's hand and forced out a few words.

"Reina, be happy... your father...and mother...will always..."

And with that his hand went limp, falling to the ground.

"FAAAAAATHEEEEEEEERRRRRRRR!!!"

The hunters, who had finally arrived at the cart, showered the fleeing bandits with arrows and attack spells. Three ran in pursuit, while one remained with Reina.

"Are you all right?! Are you hurt?!"

"My father! My father is—!"

The man who'd stopped appeared to be a mage. He quickly checked her father's condition, then shook his head.

"Father...!!"

After a while, the other hunters returned.

They had managed to bring down two of the four bandits, the chief among them. Yet while the hunters' spells and arrows had slowed them, the other two had gotten away.

"If I hadn't been there...or if I could have stayed under the wagon and stalled...just a few more minutes..."

Reina sobbed, repeating these words. The four hunters of the Crimson Lightning took turns stroking her head in silence.

The Crimson Lightning was a party of four men. There was Braun, the swordsman of 38. Ari, a swordsman of 27. Gordon, the archer, was 22. And then there was Erik, the jack-of-all-trades, a twenty-eight-year-old mage-archer. Erik didn't have an immense amount of magical power, but he could use every type of magic without any strengths or weaknesses. To keep from taxing his magic, he could also use a bow so, while he was not especially skilled in either area, he was quite useful to have around.

Certain that their approach was one of the reasons Reina's father had been killed, the men felt no small sense of responsibility, although that was unfair: the situation had been hopeless from the start, and their presence had only helped matters.

Still, as far as hunters went, they were rather softhearted. Upon learning that Reina had no family besides her departed father and that, thanks to their lives as wandering peddlers, there were no other acquaintances who might take her in, the hunters discussed things for a bit before asking Reina, "Would you like to come with us?"

"Huh...?"

Things would be certainly be difficult for a ten-year-old girl living on her own.

Her best bet would be to go to an orphanage, but even finding one would be a challenge.

She could work herself to the bone as a servant in exchange

for crumbs, only to be tossed out the moment she fell ill—or she could simply resign herself to the slums, where she might find other orphans. After that, since she was good-looking, there was the chance that someone might try to sell her as a slave, or worse.

With all that in mind, any dangers she might face living with hunters paled in comparison.

She was only ten years old, but she was still a peddler's daughter and had observed many things along their journey. So Reina thought for a while, and then gave her reply.

"I would. If you'll have me."

The men of the Crimson Lightning dug a hole to bury Reina's father, then loaded the fallen bandits onto the peddler's horse and headed toward town. If they didn't have a wagon, it would have been much easier just to bring the heads of their victims, but if they had the option of bringing the whole corpse it was simpler to claim the reward.

With Reina's consent, they sold the wagon and goods upon arrival. Though having a wagon would have been a boon when traveling the highway, they couldn't use it in the forest or the mountains, and the cost of maintaining both wagon and the horse would be dear. For hunters below C-rank, these were luxuries they couldn't afford.

Naturally, all the proceeds from these sales were Reina's alone.

That was how Reina, at ten years old, began her life with the Crimson Lightning.

She had only ever studied magic independently, focusing on things that would help her and her father along their journeys. That meant she was only capable of a bit of water magic to provide for both them and the horses, some earth magic to pre-vent the wheels of the wagon from getting stuck in muddy roads, and some basic fire magic—enough to light a bonfire. After join-ing the Crimson Lightning, Erik, the party's jack-of-all-trades, started to teach her many things. Although her magical abilities were even more modest than his, she began steady progress to-ward the proud status of jack-of-all-trades #2.

As she was small, with magical abilities far weaker than those of any full-fledged mage and neither strength nor combat prowess, the Crimson Lightning encouraged her not to register as a hunter.

Perhaps they imagined that one day, when she was older, she could settle down in some town and get a normal job. Still, there was no harm in teaching her a few useful things. Even if Reina did not have the strength to become a full-fledged hunter, she could still practice with her weak magic, as well as train with a staff for self-defense.

Indeed, Reina trained diligently, hoping that she might be useful to the others—in magic, in wielding her staff, and as a hunter—even if only just a little bit.

So among these grown men in their early twenties to late thir-ties, there traveled a single little girl, ten years old, not even regis-tered as a hunter. And while fellow hunters mocked the Crimson Lightning mercilessly, they all knew that they had taken Reina in for her own protection. As Reina grew older the teasing con-tinued, although soon, half were jealous of the party for having a cute girl in their midst.

Time went by. One day, when Reina was thirteen, the Crimson Lightning took on an escort job.

There were four guards in the two-wagon train, an appropriate number. Reina was yet to learn much combat magic, but she could summon their drinking water as well as handle small-scale healing and recovery spells. Since that allowed Erik to conserve his magic, there was no need to train her in the ways of war.

Apart from the Crimson Lightning, their group consisted of a single merchant and a driver for each wagon. The fact that the procession was guarded made it clear that these were not simply carts loaded with various sundries, but vehicles carrying something of value from town to town. It was unclear whether the presence of guards would cause bandits to overlook them or whether it would make them a more desirable target—bringing danger into their midst. It depended on the bandits' outlook, and their finances.

That day, the bandits' scales tipped in favor of an attack.

"Bandits! Forward right side! They're blocking the road! Ten of them!"

"And six from behind! It's too many!"

Even with guards present, the bandits could attack with ease. There were sixteen bandits. Without at least seven or eight hunters, there would be no contest. They'd be forced to surrender before the battle even began, and the bandits would escape without injury. Even bandits were not interested in killing hunters on a whim, so if they could do their job without fighting, all the better.

"We have to surrender."

"No, I want you to fight them!"

"What?"

The merchant, their employer, directed them to fight.

As leader of the Crimson Lightning, Braun protested. "B-but

it's sixteen versus four! There's no way we can win! We'd just be throwing our lives away!"

"Isn't that a guard's job?! Besides the fact that I'll lose my money and my cargo, do you expect me to pay a guard that abandons their job?! Now, get out there and fight them off!"

"..........."

After several moments of silence, Braun declared, "We'll surrender."

"Roger that!!!"

"H-how dare you disobey a command from your employer?! This is a breach of contract!" the merchant cried.

Braun's voice was cold. "Perhaps you're hoping to surrender after your guard is all wiped out, so that you don't have to pay our fee? There is a rule in place for such malicious clients: *Surrender is allowed by the consent of the client or when deemed necessary by the escorting party. If the circumstances are accepted as valid, then the escort is considered to have performed their duty, and the fee must be paid.* In any case, the guild will run an official inquiry. As no rules have been broken, judging by the circumstances here, I don't think there will be a problem."

"Wh-what are you saying?!"

Ignoring the still-shrieking merchant, Braun loudly announced their surrender. The bandits, seemingly relieved, approached at a leisurely pace.

Even if there were few guards, fighting against hunters who were most certainly stronger than they were was likely to see some of the bandits injured or killed. If they could complete their job and avoid that, things would go far smoother. In fact, the bandits had gathered together this group of weaker, less experienced men just to bolster their numbers, hoping for such an outcome.

"We surrender. Please leave us with our lives. You may confer with our employer about the money and goods."

"Roger that. Yer free to go, as is the custom. Just give us that wagon and yer coins and we're square."

After the exchange with the hunters was complete, the bandit leader moved to speak with the merchant.

"So what'cha got in there?"

"Salt and dried meat. Pickled meat, flour and other foodstuffs. And liquor."

"Yahoooo!!!!"

A great cheer rose from the bandits.

"All right! We'll take all of it!"

"Wait! I'd like to negotiate!" said the merchant.

"Negotiate what?"

The bandits' leader looked dubious. Naturally so. What was there to negotiate with a bunch of bandits who had just decided to take all of your cargo?

"What's yer angle? You got somethin' else to offer us?" the chief asked, with a vulgar laugh.

The merchant continued, "I request that you leave me one empty wagon and half my salt. As payment, I'll offer you a girl. She can produce water and light fires—she's useful for all sorts of things. All *sorts* of things..."

The words sent a chill down Reina's spine.

"What are you doing?!"

"This wasn't part of the deal!" The members of the Crimson Lightning bellowed in rage.

"Aha!"

It was clear from the bandit's face that he was suddenly very interested, though his words conveyed the opposite.

"Yer a pretty funny guy, aren't ya?" said the bandits' leader. "Trying to sell off yer own guards... however, that'd be against the terms of the surrender. If we go around breakin' our promises, eventually the hunters are gonna stop surrendering, and that means more of our guys get hurt. This ain't just a problem for us, ya see. It'd make life harder fer all the guys out there who don't have no choice but to start banditing. And that ain't somethin' I can abide."

"But that's only if people found out...isn't it?" the merchant replied, with a grin. "What if we had a bunch of foolish hunters with their eyes on the reward, refusing to surrender despite their employer's orders? And a little girl who abandoned her fallen friends to run off with the bandits... it's a likely story, isn't it? So long as I can say that's the honest truth, the matter should be settled.

"I don't have to pay a wage to guards who disobeyed my command to surrender, and I keep one of my wagons and half my salt. You didn't break any promises, and you get your hands on a useful little slave girl. I'd say it works out pretty well for both sides, don't you think?"

"Wh..."

The Crimson Lightning was dumbstruck. Reina could barely breathe.

"Hehehehe! What a snake! Yer a disgrace to mer—no wait, I guess that's just like a merchant!" the chief laughed.

His roving eyes fell over Reina. He thought for a moment, then issued his command.

"...Kill 'em."

In a flash, a thought crossed Reina's mind: if she could kill the merchant with magic, this exchange would never take place.

Killing a bunch of bandits would change nothing but, if the merchant died, it would look as though the bandits made a kill despite agreeing on a surrender. That would be exactly the outcome they'd been trying to avoid. It would be a matter of hunters killing a merchant who tried to betray them, in which case perhaps the bandits would think it best to simply take the cargo, release the hunters, and call it a day. Since he was not a bandit, but merely a defenseless merchant, perhaps even someone with relatively weak magic abilities could...

Yet Reina had never even considered killing a person, let alone done so in the heat of the moment. It was all she could do to even squeeze out a word of protest.

"St—"

Before even that single word was spoken, the bandits' swords and spears rained down on the Crimson Lightning.

Surrounded by bandits, Braun, Ari, Gordon, and Erik had no means to resist, and fell to the ground, crying out.

"A-aah!"

Reina crumbled to her knees.

"Ah... Aah... Aaaaaaaaaaaahhhhhh!!!"

"Now then, let's unload that cart there, and move the salt..."

Ba-dump.

"Man, you really are a snake in the grass, huh?"

"Ha ha ha, same goes for you, doesn't it?"

Cr-crack...

Cr-runch...

She didn't have the magical strength to become a mage.

She wasn't a hunter—just a civilian who could summon a few puddles.

That's what the merchant had been told about Reina when they were introduced, and what he had related to the bandits.

Though she was still weak, Reina could use some combat magic. It was something the Crimson Lightning always told their employers. It was close to the truth, that even if her magic was modest it showed battle potential—belaying the misgivings many had about bringing a young girl along on a mission. On the off chance that it convinced their enemies to drop their guard, then all the better.

Reina's true specialty was water magic, but with her abilities so weak, she could not produce anything particularly impressive. Or so you'd think.

"Man, if we don't gotta worry about water we can spread out a lot farther. Guess Lady Luck's on our side..."

Szzzzzzzz...

What was this thing, bubbling up hot inside her chest...?

Was it sadness? Despair? Anger? Or perhaps...hatred?

The bandits laughed wickedly and leered at Reina, who was still on her hands and knees on the ground, muttering.

"Well then, let's hurry up and collect our..."

A warm breeze rushed past the bandit leader and the merchant, who were still deep in conversation. When they turned to see what was causing it, they were faced with—

"Gaaaaaaaaah!!!!"

About half of the bandits had become torches, each one enveloped in raging crimson flame.

"Wh-wh-wh-what is..."

The merchant couldn't believe his eyes, and the lead bandit

was petrified, his mouth hanging dumbly. Dazed, the other bandits could only watch as their companions burned.

And then, from the midst of the flames, a small silhouette emerged.

"Th-that's impossible! You can only summon water! You're just a half-baked..."

"Oh, yes. That girl?" Reina interrupted. "She's dead."

"Huh...?"

Seeing that the merchant did not understand, she continued.

"Reina, the merchant's daughter, wielder of only weak water magic? She died just a short time ago, along with her dearest companions. Now I am the embodiment of the Crimson Lightning's dying wishes.

"I am Crimson Reina, the Bandit Slayer!"

"Kill her!!!"

The chief screamed, his body still paralyzed. But the bandits had yet to draw their swords, and Reina was very close. There was no time to even swing before the spell was complete.

Reina's words flowed. Words that boiled up from the bottom of her heart.

"O flames of Hell, blaze! Reduce them to ash and bone!"

✧◆✧

A large-scale merchant caravan of thirty wagons and a great number of guards passed by a scorched field. They saw what appeared to be the corpses of four hunters, seventeen piles of ash and two wagons, their drivers trembling within.

And one little girl standing still as a statue, with a blank expression.

Didn't I Say
to Make My Abilities
Average in the
——— Next Life?!

CHAPTER 17

The Fight

"**I** DON'T REMEMBER MUCH about what happened after, but the two drivers testified on my behalf. They had seen something so terrifying that they were certain they'd be killed if they lied. So they told the whole truth, and I was found innocent.

"The merchant's assets were seized and distributed to the families of the Crimson Lightning. But the money that I had from selling my father's wagon and wares was considered part of the party's property as well. It was all handed over, and I was penniless.

"Apparently, awakening to such magical ability in the face of mortal danger is fairly rare. I suppose most of the time you end up dead, which means it would be rare to find out even if it did happen... anyway, they wanted to study me closely.

"They found that I didn't have the enormous power the drivers described, but I did now possess a fair amount of magical ability. It was concluded that the drivers, in their fear and awe, had overestimated the power of the magic. And I, having cast a series of fire spells well beyond my magical limits, had suffered a kind of power deficiency that clouded my recollection of that day.

"After that I registered as a hunter and, a year and a half later, after I was promoted to E-rank, I was encouraged to take the prep school entrance exam."

"Hmm..."

"Hmm? That's all?"

Reina seemed dissatisfied at her party members' relatively subdued reaction.

"Did you want us to say something?" Mavis asked bluntly. "Like, 'Ah, so that's why you're so interested in killing bandits,' or, 'No good can be born from hatred!' or..."

"Wh-wha?!"

Reina's face turned bright red.

"Anyway," said Mavis, "now that we understand why you're so obsessed with bandits, let's just leave it there. You're free to think or feel however you like. That said, you still can't pull the other members of your party into your affairs. Got it?"

"Let's put an end to this business of 'killing practice,'" Mile chimed in.

"Wh..."

Reina looked displeased.

"We thought *you* were supposed to be showing us the right way to do things, as the senior hunter!" Mile continued. "But, you were just being selfish, weren't you?"

"Uh..."

Reina couldn't reply.

"I'm sure there will be a 'first time' someday, against someone and for some reason. But I don't think it's necessary to make that day come any sooner. Even just preparing oneself for such a time would be..."

"......"

Reina had no words to reply to Pauline, either.

"Anyway," Pauline continued, "if you killed them, they'd only be in pain for an instant, right? I think it would be much more satisfying to draw out their suffering and make them *really* regret their actions..."

There went another perfectly ethical argument.

"Until the time inevitably comes, let's try not to kill our opponents in vain. However, if our friends or allies—or even strangers—should ever be threatened, then I for one will not hesitate to slay the enemy. The life of my allies is far more important to me than those of any foe. Still, that doesn't mean that an opponent's life is worthless, just that an ally's life is so much dearer. And also..." Mavis continued. "I said it already, didn't I? If you're facing an opponent who aims to kill you, if you only aim to capture him then the battle will be a difficult one, regardless of your strength. But it's only a difficult fight if there's a small power gap—for if the difference in power is great enough, then the battle is already over."

"Wh..." Reina gaped at Mavis's words. "I-I'm not stupid! I already..."

When she looked at Mile, who appeared not to have a worry in her mind, she realized that this much was clear already.

"It doesn't mean you can't wound an enemy. We have recovery magic, and even if they lose a few limbs, there are plenty of places for a criminal laborer to be put to work. If they die, then they

die—that just means that it *was* 'that time.' But just as there's no need to go around killing on purpose, there's no reason to go to such lengths to avoid it that you put *yourself* in danger.

"If you capture an enemy alive, you'll get a bigger financial return and they'll suffer for a nice long time. Therefore, capturing should always be our primary policy—but not to the point of obsession. It's a little different when you need to make them talk..."

Pauline was Pauline, as always.

Reina kept silent for a little while longer, then uttered a single word.

"Understood."

The wagons stopped, and they ate lunch.

The merchants and drivers ate as normal, but the hunters barely touched a thing. Today they'd reach the climax of the journey, meaning that it was time to ready themselves for battle. Except Mile...

"Mile?"

As Mile ate with her usual enthusiasm, Reina looked on, exasperated.

"If you eat like that, your body's going to cramp up! And no one can help you if you swallow a bone!"

"Oh, really? They never taught us that at the school..."

"Because even a child knows that!"

"Oh. Well then, I'll just hurry up and digest it!"

"Just what kind of a body do you have?" Reina huffed.

"You look tired, Reina."

"And whose fault is *that*?!"

"Um, might we butt in?"

As Reina stewed, the three men of the Flaming Wolves approached.

"After this job is over, would you like to—"

"Absolutely not!" Reina refused without even hearing the rest of the sentence.

"Wh—a-at least let us finish! Anyway, we'd like to hear the opinions of the other thr—"

"Absolutely not!"

"Absolutely not!"

"Absolutely not!"

Having heard the other three's opinions loud and clear, the Flaming Wolves slunk back.

Their stations were fairly far apart during travel, and that evening they wouldn't have much opportunity, so perhaps they'd figured that this was their only chance to ask. But it truly didn't matter if they did it now or at any other time. The girls' reply would always be the same.

Overhearing this exchange, the men of Dragonbreath all felt rather sorry for the boys. As far as Vera and Jeanie were concerned, the Flaming Wolves were better off knowing their place.

After lunch and a long rest, the caravan set off again.

From a distance, the captured bandits probably looked no different from guards. Of course, that was only true if you were a fair distance away. If you saw the ropes the jig was up, but no bandit scout would ever come so close—preferring to confirm the numbers from the distance of a nearby peak.

Although these were not the bandits they had been aiming for, it was quite likely that they had attacked plenty of parties traveling along this road and, depending on the circumstances, killed not only guards, but merchants as well. Considering their clients' desire to wipe the bandits out, capturing even these criminals could be considered a part of the job.

But it would be a bother to encounter any others besides their true targets. Therefore, they put a stop to the girls' overly effective "lure" tactic. Instead, the Crimson Vow remained on standby in the fourth wagon, just as they had upon leaving the capital.

Inside the wagon, Reina hugged her knees, thinking.

Bandits were the enemy. Villains who preyed on those who followed honest paths and snatched their lives away. Just like goblins and orcs, they were dangerous predators and should be killed.

Even if bandits remained alive at the end of a fight, that didn't mean they should be allowed to live. How many people had they already killed? How many families had they sent into the depths of despair?

If they were allowed to run, they would continue to inflict pain. If they ran, they would try to kill those who'd captured them or return for revenge later, even after they'd made their escape. And if they couldn't pursue their captors, they might even target their captors' friends or family...

The danger was too great.

Killing them was the safest route. It kept you safe and unharried, and it put your mind at ease. The others were all far too optimistic: Mile, Mavis, and even Pauline.

Mavis was an aspiring knight. Wasn't felling evil-doers her sacred duty?

Wasn't Pauline more cynical than she'd shown?

Reina had killed people.

Yet her recollection of that time was hazy. Why couldn't she remember?

She'd killed the foes who had murdered her friends. Shouldn't that have been an exhilarating memory? Why couldn't she recall it clearly?

Or...was it something she *didn't* want to remember?

Did she *regret* killing those bandits?

That was stupid. She'd slain the Crimson Lightning's enemies. How could she regret that?! But there was some truth to what Pauline had said.

"If you kill them, their pain is over in an instant." Perhaps it wouldn't have been so bad if they'd suffered, repenting their crimes as they labored in a mine until they perished of accident or illness...

Perhaps it was true that their deaths could have been deferred...

Regardless, there was no reason why they couldn't each act as they pleased. Just as their opponents were free to choose whether they lived or died.

Reina looked toward her companions.

At Mavis, sword drawn, polishing her blade.

At Pauline, grinning strangely as she wrote something in her notebook.

And at Mile, fast asleep, drool running from her open mouth.

Looking at them, it suddenly seemed ridiculous for Reina to be sitting there and worrying. And yet...

No, stop that! These people are the reason *I have to be strong! This time, I won't let anyone die! No one!*

Reina's worries never ceased.

Twitch!

Mile was sleeping soundly when her body spasmed. That sort of thing was wont to happen now and then.

Her eyes flashed wide open. "The enemy's here."

"And just how do you know that?!"

Ignoring Reina's shout, Mile climbed from the back of the cart onto the top of the tarp, and whistled through her fingers.

Piiiiiiiiiiii!!!

The six wagons stopped, and the leaders of Dragonbreath and the Flaming Wolves rushed over. The others remained in their wagons, watchful and ready.

"What's wrong? Is it the enemy?"

"Yes! There's about twenty of them up ahead."

"How do you know that?!"

It seemed that the leader of the Flaming Wolves was still not accustomed to Mile.

"Around twenty, huh? Can you be any more precise?" Bart asked, ignoring him.

"Umm, there are nineteen. They're in two lines of nine, with one in the front."

"I'm asking you again: *just how do you know that*?!"

"What did you say?!"

"Are you ignoring me?!"

They were, in fact, ignoring him.

"Gather everyone. This is a Code Red!"

Once all the hunters were gathered, Bart explained.

"We're in a pinch. According to Mile's magic... it's magic, right? According to her magic, there are nineteen bandits up ahead, lying in wait. They're in lines of nine, nine, and one..."

"That's about what we expected, isn't it? We'd heard there

could be more than twenty, so with less than that, it should be a cakewalk, right?"

Chuck, one of the swordsmen of the Flaming Wolves, was optimistic. Even if there had been twice as many bandits as hunters, it still wouldn't be a huge problem, he thought.

Fargus, the Dragonbreath lancer, shook his head.

"It makes sense that there would be fewer than were reported at the time of the posting. You might overlook people who are there, or hallucinate people who aren't. If you think you see about twenty people in the forest, it's natural that there might be more, and just as likely that there are fewer. The fact that they are standing in line is bad."

"What's so bad about that?"

The Flaming Wolves failed to catch Fargus's drift. The Crimson Vow had no idea what he meant, either.

"The reason that there are so few is probably because they've split into two parties to form a pincer attack. So, it's possible that there are actually twice as many. And furthermore..." Bart said slowly, looking over everyone's faces. "Bandits don't stand in neat little lines. The only people who stand in nice lines while waiting for their prey are knights and soldiers. That is to say, armies."

"............"

Bart continued: "Most countries' armies organize their fighters nine to a squad. Those eight soldiers are split into four groups of two, or two groups of four, with one more to direct them. Four of those squads together make up a platoon. The platoon will have a commanding officer, an aide, and two more lower-ranking officers. Forty in total, with each of those lower officers in charge of two of the squads. And so, the fact that there are nineteen people in lines means..."

Several people gulped at once.

"Indeed. Just a little farther ahead are twenty-one more, including the commander and their aide. I did think it rather strange that, in the absence of any war or famine, such a large group of bandits would remain in an area like this without either establishing a base or moving on. Without some means of resupply, they wouldn't have been able to maintain their food stores."

"It's hopeless! We heard that there were twenty-ish bandits at best, so we thought that this amount of firepower would be enough! But twice as many, and soldiers, no less?! There's no way we can win!" A cry of despair rose from the Flaming Wolves. To be fair, the reaction was only natural.

"What's an army doing here in the first place?! Why would they suddenly decide to turn to banditry?! Are we sure they're not simply here to wipe the bandits out?!" The Flaming Wolves continued to cry out.

Mile spoke softly. "A trading blockade?"

Bart looked surprised.

"Oh! Aren't you the one who's supposed to be a bit dim?"

"Who said that I was?!"

"Anyway," Bart ignored Mile's protests, instead looking over the uneasy faces before him. "For now, this is all just speculation. It's not that I can't think of any countries that might do such a thing—but there's still a chance that these are just plain old bandits, and that this might be all of them."

An air of relief washed over them.

"But," he finished, "we had better prepare ourselves for the worst."

"What's the probability that this is a worst-case scenario?" asked Brett, leader of the Flaming Wolves.

Bart replied with a calm expression. "About eighty percent, perhaps?"

"............"

He turned to consult with the merchants, who had yet to speak up.

"So what do you, our clients, feel is the best course of action?"

"Hmm well then... if they're soldiers, with three times our fighting strength, there's no way that we can win against them in an honest fight, is there? We don't have much choice but to simply confirm their identity and numbers and retreat, do we? Then, we can report our information to the palace, and they can return with their own troops.

"However, these enemies might move on before our own army has a chance to mobilize. Plus, the fact that they've slaughtered every caravan they've encountered up until now means that they're probably hoping to conceal their true identities. No matter how good their disguises are, leaving survivors means there's a chance they could be discovered.

"If we turn back, the enemy will realize that we've spotted them, won't they? They'll get worried, wondering how much of their true identity we've uncovered, and they may pursue us. Even if we'd already disposed of the prisoners, they'd quickly catch up to our wagons. And there's a chance that they've also prepared some cavalry for the chase. Rather than running, not knowing when or where we'll be attacked, we have at least a slightly better chance if we choose the place to face them head-on."

Bart gazed over the hunters and grinned.

"What? All each of you has to do is kill three or four apiece! That's no big deal."

"Are you saying they've got no choice in this?!"

"That's what I'm saying."

Bart and the merchants laughed together.

The other members of Dragonbreath shrugged, exasperated. For Bart, this was probably normal behavior. The Flaming Wolves had gone a bit green in the gills but kept their silence, perhaps as a matter of hunters' pride. As for the Crimson Vow...

What is with these people???

They were stunned at the nerve of the other hunters. And also...

"They don't seem very bandit-like, do they? I guess there wouldn't be much use talking to them...?"

"No. Even if they're soldiers, they've invaded another country and are looting without a formal declaration of war, which means that this can't be a sanctioned operation. We should consider them like bandits, which means that there's no problem with killing them. We'll deal with them accordingly."

"If we can capture their commander and press him for information, I bet we'll fetch a nice big reward."

"You guys...?"

Normally they would be able to travel a little farther. This time however, they decided to make camp for the night where they were. The highway wound into the mountains, a steep cliff face to their right and on their left a rocky plain with no trees or water. It was not a place where you'd normally choose to camp. Especially since a grassy field stood just beyond the mountain.

However, this place was convenient for their true purpose—not camping, but fighting.

On a rocky field, free of trees, you could use as much fire magic as you liked.

Fighting with a sharp cliff face behind them helped to avoid being ambushed.

Of course, any foe who came to investigate their prey might be suspicious of a merchant caravan setting up camp so early and in such a strange place, but there was nothing the hunters could do about that.

They didn't expect to wait until morning, only a few hundred meters from the bandits. They knew that they would be attacked.

The wagons were parked close to the cliff wall in two lines of three, making the lines that the hunters had to defend as short as possible. The captured bandits were bound tightly—not just by their arms, but by their legs as well—and it was agreed that, if possible, they would be knocked unconscious before the battle. Should the battle turn against them, or the enemy draw too near, the merchants gave strict orders to kill their prisoners immediately. It would be a small task to kill seven people who were tied up and unconscious, the merchants argued—but then, these world-weary men had little reservations about killing bandits in the first place.

After securing the wagons and binding the bandits, the hunters prepared for an all-out counterattack.

They didn't eat. Any idiot who stuffed his face right before a melee battle would not live very long.

All there was left to do was wait for their enemies to move.

Around an hour passed.

"They're here."

The archer Vera, with her keen eyesight, was the first to spot the first enemy.

Because they'd prepared their camp so early, there was still time until sunset, and the sky was bright. No doubt the bandits had judged it would be more advantageous to strike while it was light, surrounding their enemies with overwhelming force. When it got dark, there was too great a chance of people slipping away unnoticed.

There was no need for the attackers to divide their forces, for the cliff wall behind the merchants blocked any possibility of retreat. Therefore it was about forty enemies who surrounded the caravan in a semi-circle—likely the entirety of their force. Just as Bart had predicted.

"We are bandits! Forfeit your weapons and capitulate!"

The man who seemed to be the leader gave a rather abrupt introduction, "We are bandits." Furthermore, he did not command them to "surrender," but rather to "capitulate."

"Since it looks like we've got a fight either way, it doesn't matter what we say, right?" Bart asked. "I want to try to get some information out of them. All right if I lob a few comments their way?"

The merchants nodded. The Flaming Wolves and Crimson Vow, who had no idea what was going on, bobbed their heads in unison.

"Well, if that ain't the voice of the commander! Just what are y'all doing all the way out here?"

"Uh..."

Bart's bluff hit the bull's eye, and the commander began to stammer.

"It's me! From the shop in the capital!"

"I-I don't know what you're talking about! W-we are mere bandits! Quit speaking nonsense. Forfeit your weapons and capitulate, immediately!"

"What d'you think?" Bart asked the others.

"Ha ha!" Mile gave a wry laugh in reply.

"Well, I didn't get a straight response, but I think that about settles it. If we surrender, they'll certainly kill us all. Are you all ready?"

Everyone nodded silently.

"All right. Noncombatants, retreat to the second wagon, as planned. Guards, take your positions!"

Everyone took their places as per Bart's instructions, the merchants slipping into the second wagon, which they had already unloaded the goods from. Now they were in the very middle of wagons parked tight against the cliffs. Any arrows or magic to come flying their way would be blocked by the other two wagons first.

Mile accompanied them as they'd decided earlier, casting magic over the prisoners, bound like silkworms in the wagon.

"Beings of ether, steal consciousness away! Until dawn breaks, cover the noses and mouths of these bandits!"

It was appropriate—a sort of magic spell, if a somewhat silly one. Anyway, the nanomachines caught Mile's meaning, and the bandits lost consciousness. This eliminated even the distant chance of them launching a counterattack. Should the time come, it would be up to the merchants to "handle" them. At the very least, Mile had absolutely no intention of doing such a thing herself.

"All right. Now, please just wait here!" Mile smiled at the merchants, before climbing down from the cart.

Before she left the wagon behind, she whispered a few more words: "Lattice power barrier with transparency!"

There was a small *shing,* and for just a moment, the air seemed to sparkle with reflected light.

Mile returned to where the others were waiting just as the enemy began to advance, moving in orderly formation.

Although at first they had been at least a bit bandit-like, their movements and their weaponry were uncomfortably stiff. Everything was far too efficient, far too uniform. Some of them even wore metal armor underneath their rags.

As they got within firing range, Jeanie fired off a spell in accordance with Bart's instructions. It was not unusual for a force with inferior numbers to make a pre-emptive strike in an attempt to reduce enemy numbers, rather than waiting until they were close enough to strike with more power and accuracy. This time, Bart hoped to test the waters.

"Firebomb!"

The flames that Jeanie fired toward the enemy's front line dissipated before they could strike.

"Well, of course a force that seems to include special ops fighters would have one or two magic users in their squads..."

In war, a standard fighting force would not include mages. Instead, magic would be concentrated into a separate, special force. Their effectiveness was far higher this way. However, a special ops squad—one that would move independently on the battlefield—had no such limitations.

It seemed that Bart had quite a detailed knowledge of armies, though it was unclear whether this was thanks to his many years as a hunter or because he had once served as a soldier himself.

"They've got some pretty skilled guys in there. We have four magic users on our side, but the question is, how many do they have?"

As Bart spoke, Reina began to incant a combat spell.

"Firebomb!"

Another flame bomb went flying.

"They're just going to block that ag—" Jeanie started.

Reina's firebomb was consumed by the enemy's protection magic, shattering into embers. But a single foe fell.

The soldier who had taken the direct hit was blown backwards and the men to his left and right, who'd also been caught in the blast, rolled on the ground trying to extinguish the flames. The first soldier was now incapacitated—alive only by the grace of the squad's protection magic, (which had deflected some of the power) as well as the metal armor he was wearing underneath his cheap bandit clothing.

"Huh...?"

"What?" asked Reina, as she turned around to see Jeanie staring speechlessly.

Reina had not gotten a chance to show off her combat magic at the graduation exam. The match was called before she had the opportunity. And so Jeanie was stunned. Judging by her appearance, she'd assumed that Reina was around twelve years old, the same age as Mile. Now, she discovered that Reina not only had the stalwart protection magic that she *had* shown at the exam, but also combat magic with a power that surpassed even Jeanie's. She'd been certain that Reina was a support-focused magic user, with protection magic as her specialty.

"Boiling Water Ball!"

Pauline fired off the spell that she'd begun casting just after Reina. Two softball-sized globes of water whooshed through the air at a leisurely pace, looking somewhat less than menacing.

Having judged that it was not worth using their magic to intercept these jiggling water balls, the enemies stood back and watched Pauline's spell approach, stepping back to avoid it. But the moment the spell reached them, the balls suddenly changed course, striking the soldiers on the backs of their necks as they moved away.

"Gaaaaaaaaaaahhhh!!"

Scalding water, well past its boiling point, spread across the soldiers' bodies, seeping beneath their armor and clothing.

As it squeezed and compressed, the water had grown hotter and hotter due to diffusion. The moment the water moved through its pressurized loop into a space with lower air pressure, the results were explosive.

No matter how much they flailed and rolled, the boiling water blistered their skin—even their clothing wouldn't absorb it. As the seconds passed, their burns grew deeper and more severe. Others, who'd taken the water balls—no, *boiling* water balls—to the face, were screaming.

Mile waited patiently.

A number of soldiers from the back line rushed to those who were wounded.

Okay, now!

Just for the sake of appearances, Mile uttered a quick spell so that she wouldn't appear to be casting silently. Then, she closed one eye clumsily, her expression calm.

"O little eye of mine, strike electric bolts into these bumblers!"

There was a crackling noise, and the line of enemy soldiers fell in place.

It was lightning magic, and Mile had held back just enough to avoid killing them. Thus was born one of Mile's seven special techniques, which she would later dub the "Winking Angel Shot."

Those who had been rushing across the battlefield to the aid of the injured were most certainly magic users, attempting to use healing. And this was exactly the reason that Mile had chosen them as her target. As the mages were wearing bandit garb like the others, there was no way to tell them apart—except by their movements.

Now the number of enemy magic users should have been greatly reduced, assuming that Mile's thinking was correct. The injured soldiers had taken the shock as well, losing consciousness—a mercy for many of the casualties, and especially those burned by Pauline's spell, who writhed on the ground in agony.

"Wh..."

The three Flaming Wolves had taken their eyes off of the enemy to stare at Mile.

Fortunately, the enemy had stopped in their tracks, but this was still not particularly advisable.

Dragonbreath, of course, were not as foolish, and though they were surprised, they remained vigilant of the enemies' movements.

"They're coming!" Bart called out to the distracted Flaming Wolves.

There were only six guards with one or two mages at best. That's what the "bandits" thought. The guards would simply surrender and then, once they'd given up all their weapons, the cargo from the wagons would be up for grabs.

They assumed it was a simple job, just like many others. Then suddenly, they were on the receiving end of a magical onslaught. In an instant, they had lost about 20 percent of their fighting force. Furthermore, half of their most valuable magic users had fallen. Their forces halted for a moment, then advanced again at their commander's direction. This was not the leisurely pace of earlier, but a full-on rush.

If they walked slowly they'd be picked off one at a time by magical attacks. They had no choice but to attack all at once to stave off the possibility of a counterattack.

A few soldiers didn't approach, but instead stopped some distance away. These were the archers and remaining mages. Now they were within effective range. The spear-throwers would have to continue approaching.

During Mile's attack, Reina, Pauline, and Jeanie had prepared their next spells, and they sent them flying toward the swordsmen and lancers at the head of the assault.

Boom! Whoosh! Ka-splash!

Reina let off another firebomb, but she did not aim directly at their foes this time. Instead, she let it crash to the ground and explode, lighting several enemy soldiers ablaze.

Pauline's attack consisted of two bursts of the condensed fireball spell she'd demonstrated at the graduation exam. One of the bursts pierced a soldier's right shoulder, while the other struck a man in the gut. His abdomen was well guarded by armor, but the direct strike combined with the heat and the fire spreading across the soldier's body left him writhing on the ground.

Jeanie's spell was an ice spear. Unlike fire-type spells, that were constantly combusting with magical energy, ice spears were solid and would strike even if they were blocked by magical means.

This time, the mages did not use protection magic, prioritizing attacks over preventing casualties to their already-reduced numbers. The ice spear pierced the soldiers, and the three casters began preparing their next spells.

Mile observed the movement of the soldiers in the farther formation.

Whoosh!

The enemy archers sent a wave of arrows flying. Mile, in turn, sent a protective gust of wind in the direction of the arrows.

"Wind-ow! Wind-ow! Wind-ooooow!"

Swept off course by the wind, the enemies' arrows crashed to the ground.

This, naturally, was because *windows always crash*.

The spell was not particularly shocking, though it was slightly stronger than the typical wind casting.

The barrage of arrows continued, and soon attack magic came flying toward them as well: a coordinated storm of firebombs. Not precisely targeted shots, but a large quantity aimed at causing harm over the widest possible area.

The swarm of firebombs was timed to coincide with the exact moment Mile should have been busy deflecting the archers' previous attack. Fire rained down on the merchants' party.

"Magic Shot!"

As Mile let off her "spell," several intercepting bursts went flying.

The shots—each one guided by the nanomachines—struck the enemy's firebombs, causing them to explore in midair.

"Incredible..."
The platoon commander, certain that his enemy's back line would be easily crushed, was stunned to see their attack power.

Still, he was confident as his close-range forces entered the fray. Though their attack power was inferior to the mages, they had the superiority of numbers. Besides, there was no way that a lowly hunter could stand up to a soldier when it came to close-range combat with spears and swords.

If a melee began to rage, mixing friends and foes, magic use would be difficult. They could deal with the mages after they'd felled the front line. There were a number of tactics they could use to deal with the magic users, particularly since they too had mages on their side. True, they'd sustained a number of casualties during their approach, but these could be healed with magic afterwards... shaking himself back to reality, the commander shouted.

"Attaaaaaaaack!"

Hmm... I wonder if I could fire off one more round before we get into close quarters combat?
Mile had no intention of crushing all the enemies by herself.

If she did, there would be nothing else for the other guards to do, and besides, it would attract too much attention. No matter what, she was just a *normal, average* C-rank hunter, after all. It was unwise to draw too much notice to herself.

Yet at this rate, if they entered melee combat then the

casualties among her own allies would increase. And while magic could heal most injuries, death was another matter.

For now, she had to focus on doing everything she could to decrease the enemy's fighting strength.

Some way to make the enemies weaker without standing out... Ah! That's it!

Mile chanted a spell.

"Shave off the soles of their shoes and fill the insides with pointy rocks!"

"Gaaah!!!"

"Owwwwwww!!!"

Some groaned and grabbed their ankles, while others, feeling the pain on the bottom of their feet, cried out in a very unsoldier-like manner.

"What's wrong with them?"

Bart was perplexed by the enemy's sudden stop.

"What's going on? It looks like they've all got gravel in their shoes or something." Seeing the strange way that the enemies wobbled from side to side, Vera gave an extraordinarily precise analysis.

The soldiers' shoes were the broken-in combat boots worn by most fighters. Mile knew that it took a lot of time to change in and out of this kind of footwear. In order to alleviate their pain, they would have to unlace their boots, remove the gravel, and then put the boots back on. Naturally, there was no way that they could do such a thing right under their enemies' noses.

The soldiers would have to withstand the pain and overcome the difficulty of walking to resume their assault—running in a strange, faltering way.

This wasn't just thanks to the pebbles in their shoes. There were also a number of soldiers whose ankles had started to ache terribly.

"All right, vanguard, roll out! Mages and Vera, please support them from here!"

They were on the verge of melee. The rear guard remained where they were, while the forward guard started to advance. The Flaming Wolves were stunned to see Mile calmly join the advance guard, having assumed that she was primarily a mage and carried a sword only for self-defense. But they said nothing about it. There was no time to waste.

A volley of powerful attack spells flew at each of the front lines. Without Mile, however, the mages on the merchants' side were working at about half their normal efficiency, their spells dissipating on the enemies' protection magic. Still, Mile blocked every shot from the enemy. Once the melee began, they would only be able to use precise, short-range spells, or else fire long-range magic at the opposition's back line.

And so the true battle began.

Dragonbreath's three vanguard fighters were strong. Bart, their leader, was a B-rank, and the other two were quite close to earning that distinction. Their promotion was near, and their power could be relied upon in all normal circumstances. They didn't bother chasing the enemy, but instead skillfully fended off any attackers who came near.

On the other hand, the Flaming Wolves were quite flustered.

For a group of middle-of-the-road C-rank hunters, fighting against numerous soldiers was a challenge. However not long after they began fighting, the Wolves got into the swing of things, realizing that they were more capable in battle than they had thought.

A big part of this was because, for some reason, the enemies' movements were unsteady and they were unable to put their backs into either attack or defense. The precision support that the front-line fighters received from the mages and Vera's archery also helped. They were not striking men down in a single blow, but still managed to handle the attacks, landing a few blows themselves. Fighting like that against soldiers who greatly out-numbered them was highly commendable.

Among the mages, Reina exchanged long-range fire with the enemy back line, while Pauline and Jeanie were in charge of attack and support for those within the fray.

Only three enemy mages remained. With two of those focused on protecting against Reina's spells, their attack reserves were quite slim. If they took even one direct hit, it would all be over. They had no choice but to focus on defense.

The one remaining attack mage sent spells toward the front line, working between shots to guard against Pauline and Jeanie. Indeed, Pauline and Jeanie had an advantage in this, as the fighting was taking place was closer to the merchants' side than the enemies'.

Two enemy mages blocked Reina's shots, and one fired at the Dragonbreath members fighting in the melee. Meanwhile, Pauline intercepted an attack, then joined Reina and Jeanie in incanting another attack spell. They fired the three attacks all at once, targeting each one of the enemy mages.

The enemies hastily prepared a defense spell, but whereas before they'd only been guarding against Reina, now they were facing three magic users. Furthermore, one enemy mage was still in the midst of casting, without enough time to change tack.

Booom!

The girls' spells struck, and the enemy's magical assault fell silent.

"I think you did it!" Mile cried as she swung her sword.

As she deflected the enemies' magical attacks, her allies added to their support from behind.

Fighting nearby, Bart grinned. This was no time for chitchat.

If an opponent wore leather armor, you struck them with the side of your blade and aimed to break their ribs instead of killing. But with metal armor, you could strike with the blade as normal, denting their armor to accomplish the same. Since many of the "bandits" wore metal breastplates, Mile swung her sword with gusto.

Against the waves of enemy arrows, shot in spite of the danger of friendly fire, Mile merely shook her right hand, chanting a simple spell to deflect them.

Then came the rain of spears.

"Magic Shield!"

Cling clang cling clang!

The spears stopped mid-air as though they had struck a wall and fell to the ground.

Arrows rained down again shortly after...

"Those are fire arrows!"

Just as Bart said, there were fire arrows flying their way, aimed not at the fighting forces, but at the wagons behind.

This was likely a gambit to light the wagons ablaze, distracting the back line and drawing out noncombatants.

Seeing Mile make no move to intercept the arrows, which were just reaching the apex of their smooth arcs, Bart steeled himself for the loss of the wagons. But then—

Clink clink clink clink clink!

The arrows stopped mid-air, just short of the wagons, and fell to the ground like the spears before them.

"……"

Unlike with the spears, Mile didn't appear to have used wind magic. A spell that could render defense without any kind of physical intermediary was simply unheard of.

No use in worrying over that, thought Bart. He had learned not to question the Crimson Vow.

"I'm going to go help the left side, all right?" Mile—her attempts to disguise her magic growing increasingly sloppy—asked to assist the Flaming Wolves.

"Sure. Go!"

The enemies' numbers were steadily decreasing, and they had no magic users left. That finally gave Bart some room to breathe—and worry over the Flaming Wolves' part of the battle. He granted Mile permission immediately. Mavis's abilities had surpassed Bart's expectations, and he was not particularly worried about her.

Mile rushed to the left of Dragonbreath to find the Flaming Wolves fighting a fierce battle.

Callum, one of the Dragonbreath's swordsmen, was the closest by. He was also keeping an eye on the Flaming Wolves. For mid-level C-rank hunters, fighting that many soldiers was a tall order—even if their enemies were clumsy and had difficulty walking. Chuck, the swordsman, had been wounded and gripped his sword with only his right hand, his face twisted in pain. The movements of the other two were limited as they tried to fight while covering their party member.

Just then, an enemy soldier swung down at Chuck, his defenses were already weakened by his injury.

"Ch—"

Shing!

Before Brett, the leader, could even finish his scream, there was a loud clash as the enemy's sword hit Mile's mystery blade.

Shff!

Mile thrust up on the enemy sword, as if to dislodge the blade.

Pushed backwards by Mile's overwhelming force, the soldier lost his balance. And then Chuck's sword struck him. Because Chuck swung with only one hand, the soldier's armor protected him from mortal injury, but even so there was a sound of bones breaking as the man fell back.

"Thanks! You totally saved me!" Chuck said in appreciation to Mile, and Brett bowed his head gently.

Mile nodded and turned to face the next enemy.

By now, the enemy had been reduced by twenty, and without their magic users they took the full brunt of the hunters' magical attacks.

Knowing their arrows would be ineffective, the archers drew their swords and entered the melee rather than standing back, open to magical attacks. However, expert swordsmen were already dropping on all sides, so by the time the archers joined there was nothing they could do to turn the tide. One by one, they too were defeated.

At some point, the back-line mages had moved to the opposite side of the fray, surrounding the soldiers and blocking their path of escape. The enemy, now down to ten, didn't have the luxury of ignoring the fighters in front of them to go after the mages. Even if they'd tried, at such a distance they'd be struck down by a magical attack before they could make their approach.

The enemy commander had already forfeited any possibility of retreat.

Running and leaving behind so many injured soldiers could put him in very hot water later on. No matter how elite his men were, if so many of them were captured and tortured, there was bound to be at least one who'd spill the beans. If they wanted to escape, they'd have to drag the injured along. Unfortunately, if their wounds were too severe, they'd have to silence them.

In any event, with things as they were, escape was hardly an option. Even if they managed to get away, they'd face relentless attacks until they reached the border and they couldn't drag such a persistent force into their own lands.

There was no option but to defeat the hunters any way they could, tie up the merchants and take their wagons, unload the cargo, and then use the vehicles to carry their wounded back home. That way they could transport even those with more serious injuries, bringing the bodies of the fallen to be buried along the road.

There would be time to consider all of that after they had wiped out the hunters. It was still possible that it would not even come to that. After all, the dead had no worries.

With that in mind, the commander swung his sword desperately. With a twisted ankle and boots full of gravel, he couldn't plant his weight and his steps were unsteady. He'd thought that he could ignore the pain because his life depended on it, but found he couldn't summon the fortitude to focus on the battle. His strength had been decimated.

It hurt him greatly to fight his final battle under such circumstances. He wanted to rage, but knew that lamenting would help nothing.

Strangely, it seemed that his subordinates were in the same situation. He knew that no matter how far they had fallen behind in the magic battle, these were not the sort of soldiers to come to a cowardly end.

Why? How had it ended this way?

In the end, there was not such an enormous difference in power after all.

Before they even reached the melee, eleven of the enemy combatants had been incapacitated by just three mages. After that, eleven more—three mages, four archers, and four lancers—had been halted along the way. By the time the soldiers clashed with the merchant group's front line, no more than eighteen remained. The three members of Dragonbreath, the strongest of the hunters, defended the center. Each of them took three soldiers, while the three Flaming Wolves took two apiece. Mavis took two and Mile one more, even though with such uneven numbers they were certain they'd be killed in an instant.

Yet Mavis's special "Godspeed Blade" could kill a man in the blink of an eye. Used seriously, one slash would slice an opponent's body through the middle, so she had only to strike the soldiers in the gut with the side of her blade. It was a lucky thing that she possessed a sword that wouldn't break, even if used recklessly.

Mile dealt with her opponent quickly and then, with a little time on her hands, took care of one of Bart's beside her. After that, thinking it would be rude to steal from anyone else's plate, she moved to intercept incoming arrows. That is, until it occurred to her to aid the Flaming Wolves.

It wasn't hard for each of the members of Dragonbreath to handle three soldiers, especially since all of them were unable to fight at full strength. Even the Flaming Wolves—including Chuck, who'd taken a blow—were fairly evenly matched against their pairs of soldiers.

By the time the archers and lancers entered the field with their swords, Bart and the two fighters from the Crimson Vow already had their hands free. They took turns, taking down one after another.

In the end only five men remained to surrender, and the commander and his captains were not among that group. They hadn't run away. They were probably either groaning on the ground somewhere or, if their luck was particularly bad, among the corpses.

"Fargus! Loose one of the horses and take a message. Go to the guildhall in Amroth and then the local lord. Tell them to send escorted wagons and soldiers straight away! Got it? To the guild first, don't forget!"

Bart made sure to emphasize the final order.

If the local lord knew about their enemies, there was a chance he'd try to hide it from the capital for some political reason. It was best to have insurance.

"After that, pen a letter with a summary of today's events and send it to the capital. Write six more of the same, addressing three each to the guild and the palace, and send them all by different routes. And tell no one. Understood?"

Fargus nodded, heading straight for the horses. He was trust-worthy and quick—the ideal candidate for the job.

Though the animals were really workhorses, they were trained to carry a person for a short time. They had no saddles but, even so, on horseback Fargus would be able to reach town faster than on foot. There was starlight overhead, and as long as he proceeded along the main highway, he shouldn't have any trouble making it to Amroth by the morning.

"That was surprisingly prudent. You really don't *seem* like the sort of person to take a job like this," quipped Mile.

"I'm an oxymoron," Bart replied tartly. "Now, let's go collect the prisoners and the corpses."

"...All right."

Thankfully, while some of their party had been injured, none of the hunters had died.

Soon enough all the injuries—including Chuck's right arm and a few other more minor wounds—were healed with the help of Pauline and Mile's magic.

The Flaming Wolves were stunned to see how Chuck's arm healed without so much as a bruise. Dragonbreath, however, hav-ing been present at the graduation exam to see the situation with the broken limb, were not as surprised. Either way, while seeing such wonders might normally cause their eyes to pop from their sockets in shock, by now they were too exhausted to be surprised.

The Crimson Vow had held back against the enemy, and the only soldier who perished from a direct magical attack was the one pierced by Jeanie's ice javelin. Beyond that, there were a num-ber of soldiers who'd sustained serious burns. The worst of them had been the victims of Pauline's scalding attacks, so now, having their gear removed and wounds treated by the same girl was all the more heart-stopping.

Five more enemies had died from non-magical attacks. Between Dragonbreath and the Flaming Wolves, the latter were less capable of restraint, meaning there was more blood on their hands. Truly, it couldn't be helped. The ones who remained alive were the lucky ones. There was nothing more to it.

Mile and Pauline gave emergency first aid to those who'd lost blood from cuts or stab wounds, as well as those who might have sustained internal damage. Those who'd only suffered broken bones and other simple wounds were left as they were.

Their aim was only to keep the soldiers from dying, not to do anything that would raise the danger of a counterattack. Understanding that, the prisoners didn't complain or even make moves to remove the gravel from their shoes.

Even those who were injured were in no position to complain, as they might die without Mile and Pauline's attentions or, at the very least, suffer long-term effects. Really, they ought to be thanking their healers.

In fact, there were a number of soldiers who *did* thank them. They had attacked the merchants not out of hatred but out of sworn duty, and knew that they were the ones in the wrong. Really, the fact that they'd only lost six men was something of a miracle.

Their enemies had held back, and the soldiers were well aware of that.

The guards collected the dead bodies, and prisoners were rounded up and restrained. Now, it was time for questioning.

Once they dragged them to the authorities and turned them over, they'd lose their opportunity. It was best to collect as much information as they could right away. There were no guarantees that justice would be served without irregularities—like all the men *somehow* escaping from the hands of the local lord or *mysteriously* killing themselves before they could go to trial.

Mile quietly lowered her protective barrier, allowing the merchants to emerge and move the unconscious bandits. Though they weren't supposed to awaken until morning, there was always a chance, and the hunters would all rest easier with their foes in sight.

And so the long night began.

Didn't I Say
to Make My Abilities
Average in the
—————— Next Life?!

CHAPTER 18 |

Interrogation

THE CAPTURED SOLDIERS were bound and the mages gagged and blindfolded, then knocked out with Mile's magic. While this greatly reduced the pool of candidates for interrogation, safety was of the foremost importance.

At the outset, the enemy soldiers continued pretending to be bandits, but that meant they wouldn't be judged as prisoners of war. Their fates would then be torture and hanging, or else forced labor in the hellish prison of the mines. There would be no chance of negotiating a return to their home country, and if their identities were discovered, their families and friends would hear only that they were criminals, engaged in banditry in another land.

It wasn't hard to guess who was behind the operation. There was coinage of the Albarn Empire in their purses, and their armor was stamped by a famous manufacturer from that country.

On Earth, no one planning this sort of infiltration would ever carry such things, but this was a primitive world. Either way, such evidence was circumstantial, and even on Earth a criminal could claim that such items had been planted to set them up.

Still, Bart concluded it was unlikely any other country had schemed to place blame upon the Empire.

"Now then," Bart began. "Who should I negotiate with?"

After a long pause, one man volunteered.

"...Me."

It was the platoon commander. He'd sustained serious wounds, but survived thanks to Mile's magic. She had used her powers to stabilize him, and while his ribs and right arm were still broken and blood still leaked from a laceration that would take a while to heal, he had recovered enough to talk.

"All right. First, would you really like for us to treat you like bandits? You'll be handled as the most treacherous criminals, forced to live out the rest of your days as a slave in the mines, with none of the glory or honor of a soldier."

"H-how cruel!"

"Hmm? What's that you say? 'Yes sir, we are bandits'?"

"Gnh..."

The commander was lost for words, his face pained. Pauline tossed him a lifeline.

"I have an idea! If they won't cooperate, we should tell their home country that the 'bandits' participating in the illegal trade blockage confessed everything and received fifty gold each as a reward from our government! That way, everyone will know how brave you were. I'm sure your families will be proud."

"Wh-wha...?"

The commander was speechless.

If that sort of rumor got around, their own government would treat them as traitors. Who knew how their families, friends, and acquaintances would see them after that?

"But if you really *do* tell us everything, we'll say, 'They never told us anything, even under torture. They may have been our enemies, but they were honorable people.' And then, we'll send some personal items to be handed to your families. After that, perhaps you can become informants for our country about matters concerning the Albarn Empire, enlist in our military, or become hunters and go off to another land... you could even arrange to secretly reunite with your families elsewhere. The possibilities are endless!"

"What... are you...?"

Bart nodded. "That's a good idea. Then we can say they were soldiers from the Empire. I mean, you and I know they're just bandits and don't have any families to face the harsh consequences. But this would give our country a good reason to pick a fight with the Albarnians. Yes, it really would be great if we say they squealed in exchange for their own safety and a hefty reward... man, it sure is a good thing you aren't actually soldiers of the Empire with families who live there!"

"Wh-wha...?"

Pauline and Bart talked casually, Pauline speaking as though the men might actually be soldiers of the Empire while Bart feigned ignorance, arguing they were dealing with plain old bandits. While their proposals didn't mesh, it was clear what they were actually saying. The commander was pale as a sheet, and the other captives murmured amongst themselves.

"Anyway, we don't really need this many prisoners, right? We can just keep those who want to cooperate and dispose of the rest. Then when we get the information, we can pin it on all of them and say they spilled the beans before fleeing to another country..." At Pauline's words, the silence returned among the enemies and her allies.

"Y-yes, that's true. Perhaps if we just reduce the numbers a bit..." Naturally, there was a bit of hesitation to Bart's words.

"W-wait, this isn't how you treat prisoners of w—"

"Prisoners? But I thought you were *bandits*! Besides, it wasn't as though you actually surrendered. Even your last five men didn't call for truce, but just begged for mercy. Well, at the very least, we won't kill those five. Unlike you, we honor our promises."

"......"

The enemy commander was silent when a voice rose from the soldiers.

"No! I refuse! I didn't become a soldier just so that I could be killed as a bandit! This assignment is in opposition of our national policies! All of you know this! I don't mind putting my life on the line to fight for my home and country. That's why I became a soldier. But I haven't toiled all this time just to break treaties, murder foreign civilians, and be executed as a bandit! If we go through with this, our wives and children will be ostracized as the families of traitors—perhaps even killed! Is this what our own country has sentenced us to?!"

"............"

Surprisingly, the commander did not chastise the man. Instead, he and the rest of the soldiers all hung their heads, silent. Then...

"I refuse, too."

"Me too."

"The Empire betrayed us. We no longer have any duty to act on its behalf."

The merchant party was stunned at how smoothly this was proceeding.

Please, don't let Pauline ever turn against us... Mile thought, looking to one side and then the other. Judging from their faces, Reina and Mavis were thinking the same thing.

After several of the soldiers voiced their feelings, there was no reason for the rest of them to keep up the front. The truth was going to come out one way or another, and those who did not cooperate would take the brunt of the dishonor, risking hanging or a life in the mines.

"I'll talk!"

"Me too!"

"Me as well!"

One after another the soldiers turned, until even the commander joined in.

In the end, everyone except the unconscious mages agreed to confess, and it was decided that only the six who'd perished would be reported as traitors. It might be hard for their families to hear, but they were in fact, "soldiers who would not turn on their country, who followed the Empire's orders until the very end."

The questioning continued until very late at night. The soldiers told of their current mission, the political and economic situation in Albarn, and even guessed at the reasons they'd been asked to take such a reckless action. Finally, they named merchants the Empire had sponsored to bring them food and other such items.

They would need to repeat all this when they got to the capital, but it was possible they might be silenced along the way, and it was worth getting a full confession immediately.

According to the commander, there were no more traitors in Amroth, but they didn't know if he was telling the truth. Even if he was, there was always the possibility the commander hadn't been informed of other units.

After some time, the mages returned to consciousness. Their earplugs were removed, and the commander told them everything that had been discussed up until that point. After that, they nodded in agreement.

Since the hunters couldn't exactly take away the mages' weapons, they would have to remain blindfolded and gagged for a time. Nothing could be done to prevent them from casting silently, but at least the power of any such spell would be drastically decreased, and with their eyes covered, it was unlikely they'd be able to choose an appropriate magic.

The prisoners were monitored to make sure that they didn't attempt to cut their own ropes, and if any of them made a sudden move they'd be cut down in an instant. Their gags were only removed to allow them to drink water, and even then only for a few seconds under careful supervision.

After the interrogation, it was time for dinner.

The prisoners received none. Human beings could live without food for up to several days. And how could merchants, only a day away from their destination, be expected to offer food to a group of prisoners twice their number? Especially when they were at least a day behind schedule.

It did cross the minds of some in the party that there was

probably more than enough food within Mile's storage space. However, freeing the soldiers' hands would give them the chance to launch a counterattack. On top of that, once the soldiers were handed over, they'd probably be questioned countless times, and the hunters weren't keen to share too much about Mile's abilities.

And so the merchants and their associates were the only ones to eat. The soldiers had had only a light lunch and no dinner, and all their stomachs were rumbling.

Mile pretended to carry supplies from the wagon, while in reality she pulled meats, fruits, and vegetables from her loot box to prepare for the meal. Reina lit the fire, Mavis did the slicing, and Pauline prepared hot drinks.

As always, the four of them were extremely handy.

✦ ◈ ✦

Very late that night the hunters were napping, arranged to protect the six wagons still parked against the cliff.

The merchants slept in the second wagon, while the prisoners and bandits were bound hand and foot under the watchful eye of their guards. They weren't given even a single blanket, mostly because there were none available. Sufficiently fatigued, human beings can sleep under any conditions. Just going a night or two without sleep wouldn't kill them, either.

They had captured every member of both groups—the targeted bandits and the "bonus" bandits—so the chances of being attacked during the night seemed low. But, with all that had occurred, the hunters weren't stupid enough to sleep without leaving someone on watch. Anyone foolish enough to do so would most certainly die, and the gene pool would be the better for it. All the same, capturing the bandits had given them a sense of relief and the mood was light.

To improve their night vision and protect themselves from being spotted, the watchmen could not light a bonfire. Unfortunately this made fatigue more likely—particularly for watchmen who'd just been in a life-threatening battle.

The highway was to one side of the wagons and, beyond that, a rocky plain.

Anyone coming off of the highway would be easy to spot. However, there was still the possibility of enemies hiding in the shadows, approaching without their notice.

And now, exactly six such figures crept close.

Among the group was an individual who appeared to be their leader. At his signal, they stopped and readied their bows. So as not to stand out against the night, each arrow was painted pitch black. Was this a dye? Or were they coated with some sort of poison?

The leader raised his hand. The moment it dropped, half a dozen arrows flew at the watchmen in front of the carts.

Cling! Cling! Cling cling cling!
"Wha?!"

Thoroughly stunned, the leader raised his voice. This was a big mistake. But it was understandable. All the arrows they'd fired at the watchmen had bounced back in mid-air.

That was not the only surprising thing.

Flaaaaash!
"Waaaaaaaaaaah!!!!"

An unthinkably bright flash of light outlined their forms, nearly blinding them. It disappeared again in an instant, but afterward the men could see only darkness. Their night vision was gone.

It was a sign of their good training that, after the unexpected scream, they tried wordlessly to regain their stances. But it was clear there was no point in lowering their voices at this point. Their existence had already been made known, and they wouldn't be sure-footed again until their eyes re-adjusted to the darkness. Under the absolute dark of a clouded sky—without city lights or even stars—eyes exposed to such a bright light would take several minutes to recover.

The panicked men heard a voice. The voice of a very young girl.

"Aha! It looks like the barrier troops have arrived!"

Barrier troops.

Army units that watched over the other units from behind, charged with entering the fray if any of their men attempted to retreat, flee, or surrender without permission. Normally, their job was to compel their men to continue to fight. However, these barrier troops had had a slightly different purpose.

Their duty was to track down survivors from the merchant parties that the blockade troops had attacked and quietly annihilate them. With the merchants' guards wounded and with no means to fight back, they would kill each and every survivor.

Even more than those enacting the blockade, these troops were charged with slaughtering innocent people—something any normal soldier would likely be unable to do. In the end, the deeds were recorded as an action of the blockade units.

The existence of the barrier troops was a shadowy one. They

were nowhere, and they did nothing. That was the sort of fighters they were.

If any of the blockade platoon was taken captive or turned traitor, they would be terminated right along with the enemy. This was the role that they took on today.

They were a specially-trained, elite group, and swore an oath of absolute fealty to the Empire—doing any dirty job without batting an eye. This was the nature of the so-called barrier troops.

This time however, they didn't quite live up to their reputation.

Judging that their opponents were no more than a small-scale caravan with a few guards, the barrier troops had planned to attack the survivors of the blockade on their way to Amroth. Each one of them could take on several guards, so they'd simply move alongside the party to confirm the outcome of the battle and save themselves the trouble of doubling back.

That would have been a sound plan under any normal circumstances.

But this time, the party they were mixed up with was anything but normal—something the barrier troops couldn't have known.

No matter how long they waited, no merchant survivors appeared, and thinking this suspicious, they'd turned back and stumbled upon an unbelievable sight.

Had their troops been vanquished in battle? Or had they betrayed the Empire, hoping to be granted asylum?

Either way, the barrier troops' sworn duty didn't change.

To keep them from talking, they would murder everyone. That was all there was to it.

"I did think it was curious. According to the commander, their instructions were to incapacitate the guards, then steal the cargo and let the survivors go. However, up until now, the number of survivors has been zero. No bandit would bother attacking a merchant who'd already been robbed and was running away on foot..."

Mile's voice was completely flat. It was a strange tone that Reina, Mavis, and Pauline had never heard before—monotonous, without inflection.

Still, it was unmistakable.

...She's angry...

Yes. Angry.

Mile was very, *very* angry.

"Now then, what will you do? Will you surrender, confess everything, and become our prisoners? Or..."

"Kill us!"

It seemed they'd suddenly learned how to talk. Once they had been found and threatened, there was no point in avoiding the matter.

The men's vision had slowly begun to return, a fact that Mile was already well aware of. At the same time, the guards had taken up their weapons and moved into position. Including Mile, there were twelve of them.

The leader of the barrier troops looked stunned.

They had battled forty soldiers. Even if by some miracle they'd managed to win, they should have been in a shambles, on the verge of total ruin. The barrier troops never expected to find all twelve hunters standing before them in good health.

Perhaps, thought the troop leader, *the caravan was a trap from the start, and there are fifty other fighters hidden under the wagons' tarps. Perhaps these twelve are the only ones to make it out unscathed.*

For someone who hadn't actually seen the battle, that would be a reasonable assumption.

Furthermore, for these troops, who were the elite of the elite, it was reasonable to assume that it would require little work to vanquish the hunters, even if the party were twice the size of their own.

For an average C-rank hunter, fighting against a monster was one thing, but against an elite soldier, the difference in power was absolutely overwhelming.

For an *average* C-rank hunter.

"No one lay a hand on them."

"Huh...?"

Everyone was shocked at Mile's sudden command. Everyone except for the other three girls of the Crimson Vow, who all took a step back quietly.

Dragonbreath and the Flaming Wolves hesitated for a moment, but seeing the complete calm of their fellow hunters, realized that there must be some plan. They joined the line behind Mile.

Once she was certain all of her allies were a safe distance away, Mile muttered magic without an incantation—that is to say, one that could be cast simply with the name of the spell.

"Sand Wall."

Though the land was rocky, that didn't mean there was no sand beneath them. Mile knew that even if there wasn't, the nanomachines could break the rocks down into something suitable.

A strong wind circled Mile and the barrier troop leader, creating a sandstorm wall.

This was not a method of attack, but a way of obscuring her companion's view of the battle. This had become the sort of situation where Mile intended that.

"Come," said Mile, holding out her left hand.

Even the barrier troops, accustomed to hardening their hearts against anything and everything, looked suddenly angry.

"Don't provoke us. You'll regret this foolishness!" one of the men shouted, drawing his sword and swinging it down at her.

Mile whipped her sword out and back into its sheath in one smooth movement, cutting the man's blade clean in two.

"Wha...?"

As he stared in disbelief at the remains of his weapon, Mile struck him in the side.

Snap, snap!

Something broke. Obviously, it was not Mile's sword.

She had no interest in a man who would take his eyes off of his enemy in the middle of a battle. The man crumpled to the ground and passed out from pain, and Mile shifted her gaze to the enemy leader. She offered out her hand again.

"Y-you little..."

Whshh!

One of the others stepped in from the side and swung his sword down in a slashing attack. It came without warning. It was weak and cowardly. This was not a game or a practice match.

And yet...

Cling!

Though there should have been no time for her to defend herself, Mile's sword rushed up to block the blade, knocking it from her attacker's hands. He pushed back, but his blade couldn't move hers by even a millimeter—like striking an iron bar at full strength.

"Gaahh!"

The man bent over and wrapped both arms around his body, unable to retrieve his sword. Perhaps he was not merely numbed. Maybe his muscles, ligaments, or bones had been damaged.

With a horrible cracking sound, Mile kicked the man in the shin. He cried out in pain and fell to the ground, and flame came flying toward her.

It was a fireball. They had silently cast the most basic, easy-to-use combat spell of any power. Apparently the caster was wearing the same gear as the swordsman, to hide the fact that there was a magic user in their midst.

Using her empty left hand, Mile plucked the ball of flame out of the air and tossed it away. It was an incredibly flippant gesture, performed without expression.

"I-Impossible!" the leader shouted in utter disbelief.

The mage who had sent the fireball stood stock-still, speechless. All the learning he had cultivated through his decades as a mage had just been thrown out the window.

At last the leader realized that tossing attacks at Mile was hopeless. The remaining soldiers attacked all at once. Mile flipped their swords back easily. At first, the men didn't lose their blades, but their sides were left almost completely open and a blow from the side of Mile's sword sent their weapons flying.

The flustered mage began another combat spell, but Mile was at his side in an instant, knocking him unconscious in a single blow.

The fact that he'd advanced with the melee fighters to hide his identity, instead of staying on the back line, had backfired. Then again, even if he had been on the back line, the results probably would have been the same...

As the sandstorm dissipated, Dragonbreath, the Flaming Wolves, and of course, the Crimson Vow, anxiously rushed over to Mile only to find six enemies writhing on the ground. Now it was their turn to stand stock-still, speechless.

"Come on! If we don't hurry up and interrogate them, we won't have any time to sleep!"

Though it was a very Mile-ish thing to say, her expression was harsh, and her voice still sour.

✧◆✧

It was nearly morning when they finally got back to sleep. In the end, everyone except those assigned to watch slept until almost noon.

When they finally woke and began preparing a meal it was time for lunch, not breakfast. As they cooked, a man on horseback passed by. He appeared to be a hunter, and he was riding from Amroth in the direction of the capital.

"That must be one of Fargus's messengers. We'll probably see another one soon."

Just as Bart predicted, soon enough another horse appeared and passed them by.

"One should be going to the guild, the other to the palace. The rest will be traveling by carriage or on foot so that they don't stand out. We'll have those who are fast, but noticeable, those who are slow, but more subtle, and those in the middle. I wonder which of the three will make it there."

Sending out six messengers, including some on horseback, would be quite the expense, but now was not the time to mention that. The messages absolutely had to be sent, no matter what. That took priority. Besides, the hunters expected that their expenses would be covered in addition to their reward.

Later, twelve riders on horseback approached. The group was split roughly in half between hunters from the guild and soldiers from the local lord.

"Looks like you made it!"

As they arrived, a man in his forties climbed down from the first horse, smiling.

"I'm Connelly of the Amroth Regional Forces. We've been in a bind since the merchants stopped coming though. We've looked for them ourselves, but not been able to catch hide or hair of them. News of your victory comes as quite an embarrassment. Nevertheless, you've saved us! Our lord is normally rather thrifty, but he likes to open his purse for those who do great deeds. You should all expect a nice reward!"

Bart was relieved to hear the lack of resentment in the man's tone. It was not unheard of for situations like this to result in bad blood.

Next, an elderly man approached. "I'm the master of the Amroth guildhall. You've all done excellent work. And although this job wasn't specifically advertised as an extermination task, we're going to treat it as a standard bandit-slaying job and pay you anyhow. Of course, you'll also be getting seventy percent of any profits from forced labor deals.

"Now, the escorting wagons probably won't get here till evening, so we'll head out again tomorrow morning. They've got food and such in the wagons, so don't you worry about going hungry. There's plenty to drink, too. We'll stay sober enough to keep watch. You all should relax a little."

A cheer rose from the Flaming Wolves—over the reward or the promise of a drink, it wasn't clear. At this point, they probably wouldn't have cared if they were never paid a copper so long as they could get their hands on something to drink.

"We're grateful. But there's something I'd better explain..."

Bart filled the riders in on the details.

The rest of the day passed without much else of note, and the support wagons arrived before nightfall. The Flaming Wolves had their fill of food and drink, while Dragonbreath partook only of the food. No matter how many fellow hunters or friendly soldiers were present, they were not foolish enough to get drunk.

Pauline's birthday had passed and she was now fifteen, so besides Mile, all of the Crimson Vow were officially adults—not that this country had any age restrictions for drinking in the first place. Still, the girls did not drink anything beyond a bit of wine with dinner.

The merchant party hadn't slept at all the night before and went promptly to bed after their meal. Dragonbreath seemed to be rotating shifts to keep watch.

The Crimson Vow knew that they'd be fine as long as Mile put up her barrier and alarm magic, so they all climbed into their tent and went to sleep as usual. They were all exhausted, and there'd be no excerpts from the Altered Japanese Folktale series tonight.

The next morning they ate a breakfast prepared by the support forces and headed out, bringing the seven bandits, the corpses, and the soldiers.

No bandits would be stupid enough to challenge such an immense force, so they proceeded at a relaxed pace, reaching Amroth safely by nightfall.

One group headed to the barracks of the regional forces, where the prisoner's would be restrained. This didn't mean they'd continue to be bound hand and foot—their restraint would now be more like a house arrest. The commander and other officers would be confined to individual rooms. The rest were divided into groups, with interaction between them prohibited to stop them conspiring or aligning their stories ahead of time. They might be cooperative turncoats for now, but there was still a chance that they'd try to escape at the first available opportunity. There was no room for negligence.

After handing the prisoners over, delivering the bandits to the guild, and deciding to leave the final calculations until the next day, the hunters and merchants headed to their final destination.

"So sorry to keep you waiting! I'm so glad you arrived safely."

It was the customer who had requested the merchants' services in the first place.

"As promised, I'll be selling these for the standard price. So, I hope that you'll..."

"Of course. We won't be raising the cost on you. We'll exchange them for the standard price."

The merchants clapped their right fists to the left side of their chests in some sort of oath.

"To tell you the truth, we brought along some items beyond the requested goods. Might we persuade you to purchase any of them?"

"Oh? Well, we're short on most stock, so I'd be happy take them off your hands. But isn't what's in the wagons all that you have?" asked the purchasing merchant.

The clients called to Mile.

"Miss Mile, if you would!"

"Ah, of course!"

At the request, Mile produced the goods from her storage, AKA the loot box: about two tons (as per public report) of materials.

"Wh-wh-wh-wha...?"

The merchant took several steps back instinctively, gaping at the mountain of goods that had just appeared from thin air. A mountain of goods that the merchants knew were in dire shortage. The buyer leapt at them.

"Th-these are all at the standard price, yes? I'll buy!!!"

This merchant knew all about the bandit-killing mission. However, even though he was aware there had been efforts to organize merchant parties, he didn't expect them to succeed until well into the future. While he had no intention of raising prices for his own profit—even this amount of merchandise would allow him to make heaps. More than anything, it would make his customers ecstatic. They didn't have any other venues to buy from.

"That's storage magic, right? But, for such a large amount... you've found an incredible person here. I'm jealous!"

A magical storage chamber that held two tons of merchandise and lasted for at least another fifty years. For a merchant, even a thousand gold pieces would not be too dear a price to pay for someone like Mile. He was truly, deeply jealous.

"No, unfortunately, she's not one of ours. She's merely one of the escorting hunters, and she offered to take on the extra weight. So we'll be splitting half of our profits from this portion with Miss Mile..."

Pauline's eyes opened wide. She seized Mile around the chest.

"D-don't listen to them, Miley!"

"D-don't say that, Pauline! It's bad enough already with just Reina..." Mile slapped at Pauline, whose arms were wrung around Mile's neck.

"What about the money?"

"I-It's the party's! Of course!"

Satisfied with this response, Pauline finally released her.

"One more thing, Miley..."

"Yes, what is it?" asked Mile.

Pauline grinned. "Of course, you'll have to transport some goods on the way home, too!"

Didn't I Say
to Make My Abilities
Average in the
####———Next Life?!

CHAPTER 19

Rewards and the Road Home

T HEY WERE SUPPOSED to have the following day to themselves, but in light of all that had happened, they were invited to the local lord's manor that evening.

The Crimson Vow planned to stop by the guild first thing in the morning to collect their pay, after which they would go sightseeing. They had come all this way, so it was worth seeing what sort of city it was, and they wished to buy some souvenirs for little Lenny.

"Uh, so would you girls perhaps like to go sightseeing with—"

"You keep out of this!!"

The Flaming Wolves were barely able to spit out their invitation to Mile and the other girls before Jeanie and Vera chased them away.

"All right, let's get going!"

"A-all right..."

The first stop of the day was the guild, so the Flaming Wolves came along with them.

"You all did well. Here's your payment from the guild. It wasn't part of the listing, so it's not a lot, but there's a standing fee of three gold a head for bandit extermination and a seven gold commission for any who can be sold into labor. Your seven bandits make seventy gold altogether. The fact that the other forty-six weren't actually bandits was only determined afterwards, so for our purposes they're just as good. They still get the standard three gold a piece—no reward for selling them—but there were forty-six so... that's 138 gold anyway. Which makes 208 altogether. Really, it's a bit low for what you all did, but it's what the merchants of this town could afford, so I hope you'll accept it. I think our lord will have a bit more for you too, which will leave you fairly well off..."

When they arrived at the guild, they were guided to the meeting room on the second floor where the guild master laid everything out and handed over 208 gold pieces. That was a bit over seventeen pieces each which, in Japanese money, would be over 1.7 million yen. The job had originally been advertised at only 24 half-gold, or 240,000 yen. Now, the earnings of the Crimson Vow's four members totaled just under seventy gold, or a fortune of almost 7 million yen.

Everyone nodded eagerly.

"Everyone take one gold a piece. Mile, you put the rest away."
Even Reina was not comfortable walking around with such a large sum, and she directed Mile to deposit the bulk of the

earnings in her storage. Safety concerns aside, that much gold was heavy.

Mile was always in charge of the Crimson Vow's money.

All their income and expenditures were drawn from their shared funds, which were also used for necessities such as lodging fees, repairs, and replacing equipment for the front line. If a party didn't operate this way, for example allotting money to the actual person who felled a bandit, then any back-line supporters and healers would start looking for a different career.

Asking the front-line fighters, whose gear wore out more quickly, to take individual responsibility for their equipment expenses would be similarly unfair. Therefore, aside from whatever random funds they might earn in their spare time, the whole party drew from the same wallet.

They all received a flat rate of allowance to cover individual purchases, and whenever they brought in any small sums of money they divided them amongst themselves on the spot.

In some parties, there might be a difference in wages based on rank and tenure, but as the Crimson Vow were equal in that regard, there was no need for a division. Nor did it occur to any of them to change the pay rate based on profession or strength.

Even Mile's commission for carrying the merchants' goods was destined for the party wallet, as it was earned during a party mission.

Although Mile was in charge of holding the money within her storage, it was naturally Pauline who directed the spending. Every night, Pauline had Mile produce the money so she could count the contents of their enormous purse with a maniacal grin across her face...

"Here's one gold for each of us. Let's spend big today!" cried Reina.

"Yeah!!!" the other three happily replied.

That said, none of them planned to drink or visit any particularly shady venues.

Instead, they would eat delicious food and purchase souvenirs. And since they didn't have to worry about carrying their luggage, they were all free to buy whatever they liked.

"All right. Let's go!"

"We didn't even spend a tenth of it..."

Reina looked exhausted.

Other than Mavis, all the girls had come from poverty and had the mindset to match. There was simply no way they could bear to spend money like water. They'd tried eating some expensive things, but their small stomachs could only hold so much and they weren't interested in the local delicacies. When it came to clothing, gear, and foodstuffs, both the quality and variety would be greater in the capital, so there was no point in buying any of that here. Plus, while they had Mile for transportation, their room at the inn was small enough that large or bulky items were out of the question.

In the end, Mile ended up buying only heaps of the dried and smoked fish and other seafood that were the specialty of this town by the sea.

"Guess we should get going..."

The sun was already beginning to descend, and the time to head to the lord's mansion was approaching.

On their way back to the inn to meet up with the others, Mile made a suggestion.

"Um, when we talk about the job, why don't we say that Dragonbreath and the Flaming Wolves did most of the work, while we mostly provided backup?"

"Huh???"

Reina, Mavis, and Pauline were baffled.

"Why would we do that?! We have to promote our name so we can aim for B-rank!"

"As a noble, if I reach an A-rank at a young enough age, there's a possibility that I could even become a knight!"

"Well, I don't really mind either way."

Though Pauline was indifferent, Reina and Mavis weren't inclined to accept Mile's suggestion.

"Um, the thing is, I think it's possible that a lot of troublesome developments will come out of this incident. The palace, the Albarn Empire, other countries, nobles, politics... I don't think we'll be launching into a war anytime soon, but it's not out of the question. Anyway, if people know that four of the soon-to-be-famous 'twelve guards who defeated forty-six soldiers' were still young girls, we might get questioned or drawn into things we don't want to be involved with. It could be a big problem.

"Besides, we only just became C-rank hunters, so rising to B-rank is far in the future, even if we do perform extremely well for newbies..."

As Mile explained, Reina and Mavis thought.

"Hmm, I suppose you're probably right. If we get a reputation beyond our actual abilities, we'll probably just get tripped up. And we should still be focusing on polishing our skills," said Mavis.

"Er, well, I guess that's true..." Reina hastily agreed.

Afterward, they explained their plan to the others. Dragon-breath agreed and, somehow or other, the Flaming Wolves seemed to get it, too.

However, someone would to have to be the center of attention. Who would take the credit for their victory?

Dragonbreath were already close to B-rank, so public attention wouldn't be a problem for them, and they were strong enough to rebuff anyone who bothered them about it. So the three parties decided to submit their official record with Dragonbreath in the spotlight, taking on the bulk of the action along with the Flaming Wolves while the Crimson Vow acted as support and protected the merchants. As the merchants and drivers had been hidden away in the wagons during the battle, they hadn't seen the play-by-play and there was no danger of them accidentally contradicting the hunters' story.

The Flaming Wolves were a little embarrassed to be taking credit for the girls' achievements, but they desperately needed a reputation boost if they wanted to replenish their party's numbers. They grinned at the thought of all the hunters who would come running to join them.

"Don't you know what happens to parties who advertise themselves as bigger than they are? Do you not understand why these girls are choosing to hide their power? You'll die," said Bart.

The Flaming Wolves' shoulders slumped.

"Your reasons aren't bad, so I'll allow it. I do understand the need to attract more recruits. So for now, we'll let everyone know that you did your best and really shone on this mission. Just make sure you tell people the truth about your abilities when you're interviewing them. Lying will bring disaster on your heads."

"Yes, sir..."

Even the Flaming Wolves were well aware that without the unholy power of Dragonbreath and the Crimson Vow, they would have been annihilated. Seeing that they genuinely understood their foolishness, Bart was relieved.

The lord's name was Count Amroth, the same as the town.

"Congratulations on a job well done! With the trade between our territory and the capital blocked, our finances were dwindling, so we thank you for your efforts!"

His subordinate, the soldier by the name of Connelly, had said the lord was normally a bit of a miser, but he seemed to have an honest character as nobles went—giving a proper thank you to even these lowly hunters. Rather than gazing down at them from a dais, he welcomed them to a big table, laden with food and drink. To set the hunters at ease, the food was piled on big dishes in the style of commoners. It seemed that his invitation was not merely for the sake of appearances, but that he was truly giving them a warm welcome.

"I see that there are children in your midst, and yet you defeated forty-six men without a scratch on you. That is no small feat. What do you think? Any interest in staying in this town? We can promise you our hospitality!"

For a middle-of-the-road C-rank hunter, this might be a very attractive offer. They could pass their days in comfort, and once their bodies began to weaken, they could retire and live on their savings. Get married. Open a little shop. Yet for a party that was near B-rank, a party of young men burning with desire to make their name known and recruit some attractive girls, and of course, for the Crimson Vow, this was not an especially appealing prospect.

In the capital, there were more jobs, as well as greater variety. There were more merchants, caravans that traveled out in every direction, and plenty of material-gathering requests. Plus, there were national jobs with high degrees of difficulty and requests from other regions whose guilds could not handle a job alone. In other words, there was more danger, but also more opportunity—plus, the pay was good, and they earned lots of points toward promotion.

The lord was certainly aware of this. His offer was merely a courtesy, one he expected the hunters to refuse.

After that, it was time to talk money. Upon hearing that they would be receiving 300 gold pieces in total, everyone— especially the Flaming Wolves—overflowed with veritable "jars of excitement." (An idiom of this world, suggesting you were so excited you appeared to weave through an arrangement of large pots.)

This reward consisted of 100 gold for each party, and the hunters' excitement swelled at this increase in their individual shares. Even if they replaced all their equipment, they would still have more than enough to live on comfortably. For those who had begun in poverty, it was like a dream.

Of course, if each of those forty-six soldiers had been mere bandits, the hunters would not be treated to such a lavish feast. However, they'd not only stopped a scheme by a foreign country while keeping the number of casualties low, but also gone so far as to take prisoners of war. These achievements were extremely valuable.

Even if the soldiers really had been bandits, by capturing them and selling them all into forced labor, the hunters' profits would be nothing to scoff at, either. It worked out either way, and they should be grateful for the lord's consideration.

Afterward, the lord told them of how he'd gone to speak with the prisoners directly the previous night and penned a letter with his findings to His Majesty the king himself—which had been sent out that morning. At these words, everyone present breathed a sigh of relief that the lord was no traitor.

Then he explained how he'd like those who persuaded the prisoners to cooperate to speak directly with the troops from the capital, so the prisoners knew that their previous agreements would be honored. Finally, he spoke with the hunters' employers, the merchants.

After returning to the inn and conferring with the merchants, they learned that only the Crimson Vow and the Flaming Wolves would be serving as escorts for the homeward trip, while Dragonbreath remained in Amroth to assist with the prisoners.

Based on the messages that Fargus had sent, there would likely be some action from the palace. They expected that things would unfold at least one day ahead of the lord's proposed schedule. No matter how trustworthy he seemed, you could never truly be certain, and they had chosen not to inform the lord of the letters they'd sent beforehand.

"We'll say that we requested this of Dragonbreath and send our confirmation of job completion to the guild, A-grade," the head merchant said.

Bart nodded lightly.

"Thanks. We owe you one."

In reality, no one could claim that a result this fruitful was truly a breach of contract.

The formal meeting of the merchant party dissolved, but the Crimson Vow and Flaming Wolves remained where they were. They needed to discuss their plans for tomorrow, acting as guards on the road home.

"Is everyone fine with me serving as the leader for the return trip?" asked Brett, head of the Flaming Wolves. "I know that your group has more people, but our group does have a bit more experience as C-rank hunters. Also, we have more front-line fighters who will need swift instructions. I'm very aware of how skilled you all are, so you don't have to worry about me underestimating you."

The Crimson Vow nodded in agreement.

"Thank you. Now then, allow me to lay out our strategy. Since Miley can use location magic, we'll have her ride in the front wagon. Little Reina is good with combat magic, so she'll ride at the rear and ward off any enemies who decide to pursue us. Miss Mavis and Miss Pauline will ride in the third wagon, so that they can easily lend support to either end of the train. Our party will be split up—one to each wagon, too—as advance guard and an escort for the magic users. This is going to be a combined effort and should serve as good practice for mingling with other parties and learning other people's ways. Are there any question or objections?"

"I have no issue with this plan, but may I ask one question?"

"Sure. What's up?"

Reina glared at Brett.

"Mile's one thing, but why are you calling *me* 'Little'?! You called Pauline 'Miss,' and as her senior, I'm wondering what, exactly, makes me so 'little'!"

"Er..."

The Flaming Wolves froze.

"Um... we thought you were eleven or twelve..."

This was the first time the girls' ages had come up, and they found themselves thoroughly surprised.

"Now then, let's do our best out there tomorrow," said Brett several minutes later, trying to adjourn the meeting. He softly patted out the embers on his singed hair, attempting to extinguish them.

✧◈✧

"Mile, how did you meet the other three in your party?"

"Ah, well, we were all classmates at the Hunters' Prep School—roommates in fact. And..."

Chuck sat beside the driver of the head wagon and Mile rode atop the tarp, her legs dangling over.

The cab was a bit narrow for all three of them to fit in a row, so Mile, who was light enough to sit on the tarp without warping the roof, was positioned up top. They weren't trying to get attacked on the way home, so it was better to have their guards visible rather than tucked away as before.

Chuck didn't turn his head as they spoke.

Given their positioning and the height difference, and the fact that Mile was wearing a skirt, if he so much as glanced backward, he was bound to see something that he shouldn't.

Mile, guileless as ever, didn't appear worried. The one time Chuck did attempt to turn her way, he got a sharp elbow from the doddering old man sitting beside him. The driver made a terrifying face, completely unlike the vapid grin he'd worn up until then, and whispered quietly enough that Mile couldn't hear him, with a voice that cut like a knife.

"I'll kill ya, ya scoundrel."

After that, Chuck was an absolute gentleman.

Chuck was also under strict orders to make nice with the girls so that when they arrived in the capital, the Flaming Wolves could try again to invite them to their party. So, he talked with Mile about various things.

Without Brett even asking, Mile had already saved Chuck from the soldier's attack and completely healed his left arm—and that was on top of the fact that she was honest, cheerful, and cute. Plus, both her magic and swordsmanship were on par with a B-rank hunter. He most certainly wanted her in their party and wouldn't mind forging an even stronger connection, if he was so lucky. In just another two or three years he'd be twenty, and she'd probably be old enough. If he took his time and got closer to her before then...

Completely unaware of his intentions, Mile talked happily with Chuck—inadvertently feeding his expectations with her pleasant demeanor. If that old woman from so long ago had been there in the wagon, she would have said to Mile yet again:

"Hee hee hee. You really are a wicked girl, Miss Miley..."

A similar scene was unfolding in the third and sixth wagons, too.

Brett had very quickly given up on Pauline, who was furiously writing something in her journal and ignoring him completely. However, he attempted to connect with Mavis as a fellow

swordsman. Meanwhile Daryl, the lancer, had realized that complimenting Reina's appearance and magical abilities would get him nothing but sour responses, whereas stories about the Flaming Wolves' past failures, lessons they learned on the job, and little tricks for monster hunting caught her interest every time. Their conversation was going swimmingly, at least in terms of his ego.

In fact, for the Crimson Vow, getting to speak with hunters who were young but still a bit older than them proved quite beneficial. Mile prepared them a dinner of orc meat in thanks.

Too bad it's always orc... every once in a while it'd be nice to have something with a bit less fat, something a little healthier. I guess you can't eat goblin, but what about ogre? They're less fatty than orcs, and I'm sure they're full of nutrition.

Ogre meat is good for your health...and you could call them "Ogre-nic Meals"!

Realizing that there was not a single person in this world who would understand the pun, Mile hung her head in disappointment.

After dinner that evening...

"It's time for tonight's Japanese Folktale!"

At the mention of Mile's wonderful fairytale series, the eyes of the Crimson Vow sparkled in anticipation. The Flaming Wolves just stared in confusion. Utterly unconcerned, Mile began her tale.

"Tonight's tale is a story of three half-human lady knights, 'The Three Beast Girls.'"

So Mile's story began.

"On her way out of town, the spinster-fox Aramis came across D'arta-nyan, the clingy cat-girl..."

Pfft!

A few people spat out their drinks, but Mile continued.

"D'arta-nyan asked Aramis, 'Meow old might you be, miss?!' And Aramis answered awkwardly, 'Th-three times ten and four years...'"

As they listened, Flaming Wolves' eyes were wide.

Tonight's tale had lost nearly all traces of the original work, and although it had the label "Japanese Folktale," it had nothing to do with Japan at all...

Didn't I Say to Make My Abilities *Average* in the Next Life?!

Home Tutoring

MILE HAD SOME TIME OFF.
After a job that required them to travel some distance, the Crimson Vow were taking a nice long break.

Though they were nearly always together—both during work and their days off—there were things they needed to do on their own once in a while. Sometimes, they just wanted to be alone... or maybe not quite alone. Like when they went on dates with their beaus... *not!* No, sometimes, they wanted to be alone for real.

Mavis and Pauline each had their families to visit, and Reina would go now and then to visit the graves of her father and the Crimson Lightning. On these occasions Mile, who was unable to visit the graves of her mother and grandfather, was left by herself in the capital.

On the first of these free days without Reina's constant chatter, Mile lay around in bed and then spent some time practicing prostrated apologies in case they came in handy someday. By the second day, she'd already run out of things to do. In her previous life, she was used to spending time alone, but now it was strange to have so much time on her hands. She was used to spending all her time with her friends—that was her new normal.

The real problem was that, in this world, there were no TVs or videos or games or comics or books. Not even textbooks or encyclopedias.

In any case, she couldn't spend all her days loafing around the inn until everyone returned. She couldn't stand the boredom and besides, it was embarrassing to have little Lenny treat her like a nuisance every time she came to straighten up the room.

After pondering this for a while, Mile finally had a flash of brilliance.

I should just do a solo job!

And so she went to the capital hunters' guildhall.

The job Mile sought was one that she could do alone, one that sounded like fun, and one that would be finished in twelve days, before the others returned.

"Hmm, something fun... er, hmm..."

After poring over the request board for a few minutes, Mile stopped on one description.

Home Tutor. 10 days. Request details: Help our daughter pass the scholarship exam for August Academy. Payment on completion: 3 Gold.

This was it!

Home tutoring.

Just the sound of it made her heart leap.

Mile had never been taught by a home tutor—even in her previous life.

"This one, please!"

Mile walked up to Laylia's counter. Though she worked with all the hunters, she always seemed to end up handling the girls' requests. Laylia looked over the paper that Mile had handed her. Her jaw dropped.

"Miss Mile, you know that this is a home tutoring request, right? You won't be the student, but the teacher."

"Of course!"

Mile was indignant.

"B-but, this is for a scholarship exam for the August Academy... um, the August Academy is a private school here in the capital, for wealthy commoners and poor—um, nobles who don't have very much room in their budgets. It's an all-girls school. The entrance exam is a written test and a magic practicum. The physical and combat exams are just a practical assessment, so..."

"Wh-what are you implying?! I was an *outstanding* pupil at the academy in my home country!"

"Huh?"

"*Whaaaaaaaaat????*"

Upon overhearing that Mile was trying to take yet another strange job, the other hunters all butted in at once.

"*And just what barbaric country was that?!?!?!?!*"

"What on earth do you think is wrong with me?!?!"

Eventually, an employee from the guild who'd attended the academy in question came to ask Mile a number of questions and discovered that, apart from the history of their country, Mile was far more intelligent than anyone had expected. Finally, she was allowed to take the job.

The hunters and guild staff were utterly stunned. Laylia, who had questioned Mile first, took her leave early, unable to process her surprise.

"There must be some limit to how much you can underestimate me!"

Fuming, Mile left the guildhall behind.

"So this is the place."

Mile had arrived at the mansion of Sir Crady, her latest client and the head of a mid-sized mercantile operation called the Yohnos Company.

Sir Crady seemed to live a rather carefree life, leaving the business to his eldest son except during the busiest periods or especially important negotiations. Perhaps he was thinking of retiring and hoped to prepare his son to inherit his legacy. His children were fairly far apart in age, so his eldest son had already reached adulthood and had a wife and child of his own.

The child his request had been made for was Lady Mariette, Sir Crady's third daughter and youngest child.

"Pardon me! I'm here from the Hunters' Guild!"

Announcing herself like a saleswoman, Mile followed the maid inside.

"...In any case, Mariette absolutely must make it into that school!"

The particulars of Sir Crady's request were extremely straightforward.

Sir Crady had two sons and three daughters. The eldest son was, of course, his heir, and Sir Crady wished for his second son to follow the first into the family business, lest something should happen to either of them. Therefore, the family had stretched their means somewhat and sent the second son to an academy.

He had had no intention of sending his daughters to school, but now his third daughter was growing more beautiful than he and his wife had imagined, and she possessed some magical talent, too. If they sent her to the academy to put a bit of polish on her, it was plausible that she could land the heir of a middle-class merchant or the like—the second son of a high-ranking merchant at worst, and at best the heir of a high-ranking merchant or the third son of a low-ranking noble.

However, it had already cost quite a bit of money to send Sir Crady's two sons to school. If they spent any more money it would start to have an undesirable effect on the company's finances. And so they'd decided to aim for a scholarship rather than regular enrollment.

They would have up to three years after the daughter's graduation to repay the scholarship costs, which should be plenty of time—especially if whoever fell in love with her was able to make the payment as an engagement gift. In the worst case, the girl could simply work for the government until her debt was repaid.

The scholarship was part of a system designed to let particularly talented students attend the academy even if they were too poor to afford the tuition, but you could qualify regardless of your parents' income. As long as you could pass the test, you were in.

Pride prevented the children of wealthy merchants and nobles from aiming for the scholarship, no matter how poor they might be. But for middle-class merchants, particularly if the child was a younger son or daughter, there was no problem. It wasn't such a rare occurrence.

So in Mariette's case there was no problem either, except for one point.

That singular problem was: she had absolutely no hope of passing the exam.

It was a fatal issue.

Thinking he had to do *something* to get his daughter to pass, Sir Crady had hired a home tutor.

Of course, he couldn't afford a regular tutor, and no academy graduate, noble, or merchant would have any interest in tutoring the third daughter of someone of his status. Even if they agreed, they'd request a ridiculously high fee and there was no guarantee that their teaching would have much impact. So, Sir Crady had put in a request at the hunters' guild.

There were a million and one different kinds of hunters. There were former nobles fallen from grace, and the savvy children of merchants among their ranks. In any event, if the hunter in question failed in their task and Mariette didn't pass, he didn't intend to pay them a single copper. That was what he thought as he made the request.

The scholarship exam was administered earlier than the general entrance exam, and so they would know the results much sooner. That was so those who didn't qualify for the scholarship could still sign up for the regular test. If you passed that one then you still had to pay a steep tuition fee, and the idea was to allow plenty of time for families to raise the funds.

Sir Crady's sole miscalculation was assuming that there would be someone to take the job of home tutor.

That was a problem. There were few who fit the requirements in the first place, and since the reward was dependent on success, if their student was an idiot then there was little they could do to stop themselves from failing. The only hunters who'd take that sort of job were fools and softies... just like the girl before him now.

Mile handed over the message from the guild to certify her abilities and provided all the correct answers to the test questions that Sir Crady prepared. Then the job began in earnest.

"Nice to meet you, teacher."

Mariette gently bowed her head.

Mile's pupil Mariette was aiming to enter an academy, which meant that she was ten years old. Since she was of average height and build for her age, she was just a little bit smaller than Mile. Compared to little Lenny (who was the same age) she was a bit small, but that was because Lenny was bigger than average.

Just as Sir Crady had implied, she was growing up well. That is to say, she was a cutie.

She's a rich girl and so cute... what a catch!!!

That was Mile's first thought, though if she had said it out loud she'd have caught looks along the lines of "Look who's talking."

B-but she really is adorable!!

It was true. Mariette was a cutie. It was natural for her father, Sir Crady, to hope that she might be able to find a husband of a higher station in the future.

Mile was enraptured. Not in the future, but now.

How can I make this girl happy? I must!

Mile had always had a weak spot for little girls: in her previous life, it was her younger sister and now there was little Lenny. But while they were both cute, they were also rather stern.

That went without saying for Lenny, but even her sister, when Misato was going out, would ask things like, "Big sister, did you bring your handkerchief? Do you have any tissues? If any strangers talk to you, don't follow them like you did last time!" It was not exactly that she was coddling her elder sister—more like she was certain Misato was going to fall apart.

Mariette was different. Her cuteness was of the sort that called up one's every instinct to protect her. It had an attack strength comparable to a tamed songbird or a three-week-old kitten.

Mile could feel her own courage rise just from looking at the girl—the feeling that she would do anything for her. It was the first time she had ever felt this way.

Mile decided to do everything in her power to help Mariette.

It's like taking Monika and putting her in Aureana's place.

That's how Mile interpreted Mariette's position, and she was more or less correct.

Mile was very familiar with both of those girls' academic abilities, and had a fairly good grasp of the pupils at Eckland Academy overall. Even if this was a different country, the two equivalent academies couldn't be all that different.

Plus, Mile had assisted with the entrance exam for the class after hers as a kind of part-time job. Therefore she had a fairly good grasp of the kind of questions on the entrance exam. Sir Crady couldn't really ask for more than that.

"Pleased to meet you as well. Now then, this might be a little soon, but I'd like to test your abilities, Miss Mariette," said Mile, smiling sweetly before inundating the girl with question after question in the form of an oral exam.

Hmm, I wonder if I was a little too hard on her...

As it turned out, Mariette was not at all stupid. In fact, if anything she was quite bright.

It was simply that the bar set by the scholarship exam was high. Incredibly high. Aureana was quiet and didn't stand out, but her intelligence far surpassed Marcella's. Yet because she used that intelligence mostly to support Marcella, few outside of their class had realized this.

Should I do it...?

Mile didn't often show off knowledge from her previous life. Now and then, she'd use it to make life easier and more enjoyable, but she feared any substantial information might be used for evil or war, put the economy into a tizzy, or worse still, draw attention to Mile herself.

On the other hand, so long as it was only a few small things, perhaps she shouldn't be concerned.

"To start, I'd like you to memorize your times tables. There won't be time to accomplish this during our lessons, so please work on it tonight after I'm gone. Starting tomorrow night and there-after, I'd also like you to memorize some facts about history and law. We'll start with arithmetic tomorrow, after you've memorized the times tables. For today, let's begin with some basic concepts in science in order to learn about the mechanics of our world."

"Wh...?"

No matter how precious Mariette was—no, *because* of how precious she was—Mile's instruction had to be strict. This was all for the sake of Mariette's happiness, after all.

And so, Mariette gaped as Mile rattled off term after term that she'd never heard of before...

The general level of knowledge in this world was very low.

That was not because the people who lived here were stupid. It was simply due to the fact that knowledge was not a priority to most.

Even when it came to study and research there were few books to go around, and they were very expensive. Just making use of the library required a lot of money, textbooks were few, and they were biased when it came to subject matter. Furthermore, their contents were fairly superficial and often included misinformation and conjecture. Most researchers tended to keep their own findings confidential, writing their records in code so that no one could emulate them. As a result, when the researcher died, their findings often died with them.

Even scholars knew little outside of their primary field. Due to their amount of general knowledge and its veracity, they weren't even on the level of Japanese primary schoolers.

There was nothing to be done about this. The amount of information circulated among people was simply far too small. There was no opportunity to reach everyone. Excluding the schools, academies, and research centers, all the knowledge and information that average folk learned came from conversations and tales. This was true for Mariette as well.

And so Mile prepared a tough eight days' worth of lessons.

Her plan covered multiplication tables, arithmetic, diagrams, and the basics of solving equations. There was basic physics, chemistry, sociology, economics, and accounting.

The final two days were for insurance. Of course, Mile didn't intend to study health insurance or life insurance. Rather this was insurance time—in case Mile's teaching methods should fail somewhere.

"Now that we've reached our final two days together, let's study some magic."

"Huh?"

Mariette did have decent magical abilities, but that alone wasn't enough to win her the scholarship. How much better could she possibly get in just two days? Wait, "just" two days?

Mariette thought hard about how much had already been accomplished in "just" eight days.

"Y-yes please!"

And so Mile's special lessons began.

Just like Marcella and the girls, there was no need to actually teach Mariette about the fundamentals of magic. Instead, Mile offered the sort of focused education she had given Reina and the others, without much range of application. As a merchant's daughter, it was probably better to teach Mariette utility magic rather than combat, so Mile decided to focus her lessons on water and healing magic. However...

She's definitely improving, but there haven't been any explosive results yet...

That was to be expected. Reina and Pauline were already among the elite, having made it through the entrance exams of the high-level Hunters' Prep School. It was wrong to expect the same result from lessons covering no more than the basics.

Hmm, hmmmm, what to do?

Fretting, Mile decided to turn to her last resort.

The thing that Mile—the normal, average girl—had decided never to call upon except in great strife and emergencies.

...Hey nanos, you there?

YES, WE ARE HERE!

Addressing them by their full name of "nanomachines" had grown a bit cumbersome, and she'd become quite close to them, so Mile tried this more expedient, friendly title.

Um, so Nanos, is your assistance restricted by an exclusivity clause?

...HUH?

✧◈✧

"Ah, Miss Mile! The Yohnos Company sent over a report of job completion. They gave you an A-grade and even included a special bonus. Would you like to receive your payment?"

About ten days after the completion of the home tutoring job, Mile stopped by the guildhall with the other members of the Crimson Vow. Laylia, the receptionist, called her over. She'd already told her companions that she'd taken a solo job to kill some time while they were away.

"Money is a merchant's lifeblood, and yet they paid you *extra*? That's a considerable amount, too!"

"H-how unusual..."

"What did you do, Mile?"

The three other girls gave Mile a look.

"Wh-what are you saying? I didn't do anything. We simply practiced, just like any tutor and student!"

As Mile dodged Mavis's question, Laylia handed her something that looked like a sealed envelope.

"This is a letter from the client. It came along with the completion report."

Reina snatched it.

"Ah..."

Ignoring Mile's protests, Reina hurriedly opened the envelope and read the contents aloud.

"Blah blah, thanks to you, our daughter placed number one in not only the written exam, but the magic test as well, and was accepted as a scholarship student. Though she has not yet begun school, she is already being called 'Mariette the Goddess,' and 'H-Bomb Princess'... Mile, what did you dooooo?!"

"I'm s-so sorrryyy!!!"

Mile had recruited the nanomachines into her scheme, asking them to stick by Mariette and support her in her magic.

Please, nanos, make Mari's thought pulses and magical affinity strong. Stay by her side and listen to her thoughts always.

In the nanomachines' long lives, even several decades was really only an instant. Perhaps they felt that sticking with a single human for the entirety of that being's life would be an amusing way to pass the time, or perhaps it was simply because it was a request from Mile, with her authorization level five. Perhaps it was a kindness on the part of the nanomachines. Or perhaps they had an interest in the girl. No one could say for sure what caused them to stand by Mariette, increasing her magical ability from that day forward.

For safety's sake, Mile had issued one more instruction to the nanos who'd enlisted in this exclusive contract.

"If Mariette ever attempts to use her magic for evil, please don't allow her to use any more than her original abilities. Of course, being a little naughty or pulling pranks is fine. But if she ever attempts anything clearly wicked—criminal actions—then please void our agreement and leave her immediately."

Normally, the nanomachines would react to requests no matter the type or use of magic. However, they had accepted this agreement at Mile's request, and she had authorization level five, so naturally they agreed to the parameters provided.

The nanomachines weren't allowed to favor anyone of their own accord, not without the instructions of someone with the appropriate authorization. Mile had intended the request as something of a "wish," thinking that the nanomachines could choose whether or not to grant it, but in reality, she had just created their first contract. The nanomachines flung themselves at this chance for a new experience, and the nanomachines who hadn't been nearby at the time of the contract were disappointed to miss out.

Then Mile pressed Mariette, over and over again.

"Okay. I prayed for the blessing of the goddess to aid with your magic, so you must never use your powers for evil, do you understand? If you try to use magic for some horrible crime, that blessing will go away! It's all right to use it for a little mischief, so don't worry too much about that. And it's okay to use it in the defense of justice. However, if you try to commit any serious crime, like the kind that would get you arrested and land you in prison, then we have a problem."

And she could not forget to cover her own behind.

"You must keep this a secret. Please just tell people, 'My powers suddenly awakened with practice!' You don't want anyone to ask how you got better so quickly, after all. It's not as though you can teach them. The blessings of the gods, when it comes to magical power, can be a tricky thing."

Mariette nodded emphatically. She was clever and seemed to understand perfectly.

"If anyone asks about me, tell them I'm just a normal, ordinary, average, C-rank hunter. Now then, I'm sure that you're going to pass the scholarship entrance exam for August Academy... which is to say, if you *don't* pass, then I'll have worked these ten days for free! I'm begging you, truly!"

Mariette, who had looked very meek up until now, giggled.

Though Mile had told Mariette her magic should be fine, she still worried. If Mariette used her magic the wrong way, the god's agents might abandon her.

She must absolutely never do evil.

But Mariette was a smart and beautiful girl, who helped the weak and the needy with her great magic. There was no way that she could avoid becoming famous. In fact, it wasn't long before a myriad of nicknames began to spread. "Mariette the Goddess," "H-Bomb Princess," "Defender of the School," "Number One Most Eligible Bachelorette"...

Perhaps, one day, we shall hear the tale of Mariette, a lovely and misunderstood young girl...

Didn't I Say
to Make My Abilities
Average in the
—— Next Life?!

Afterword

L ONG TIME NO SEE, everyone. FUNA here.
I'm pleased to present *Didn't I Say to Make My Abilities Average in the Next Life?! Volume 2*, the second novel to be published since my commercial debut.

...I'm pretty sure there isn't anyone who's purchased the second volume without buying the first, is there?

Thanks to everyone who purchased Volume 1, the publication of Volume 2 went off without a hitch. Thanks so much to all of you! And perhaps the sales of this volume will even make the publication of Volume 3 a reality! I'm sure of it! ...I'm pretty sure it'll happen... it'd be nice if it did... (*shrinks back*)

So, a-anyway! Somehow, it's been decided that this story will be made into a manga! Starting in August, a manga version by Neko Mint will begin serialization on Earth Star Comics (http://comic-earthstar.jp/)!

This is all thanks to you as well. Thank you so very much!

Next will be the drama CD, and the animated version, and the stage play, and the video game, and the live-action Hollywood movie...

Huh? Give up on that last one? It has a troubled history? It's better to leave it alone? Hmm...

In Volume 1, Mile left school and made a new life and new friends as a hunter. Volume 2 is the story of Mile and her precious friends, and her life as a completely normal, typical average C-rank hunter with no eccentricities whatsoever.

An adventure?

No, no, they just have to make money to get by.

Without standing out, without standing out...

Plus, there's an interlude with Marcella, the other girls, and the royals back in Mile's home country.

As for me, I've been struggling with some health difficulties, but I'm in good spirits.

Volume 3, our next one (assuming it comes out), is one that makes me wonder, "Is it pointless to even try and make a book like this?" It has the problematic combination (as far as the pros and cons of including them) of "Pauline's Home Life" and "Mavis's Home Life," followed by an all-out battle with a wyvern. I'm sure the readers are going to start thinking, "This seems all over the place. Was there some mistake?" It's going to be a very unpopular development!

And if it ever gets released overseas, there's no mistake that whoever has to translate it will be tearing their hair out! I'm so sorry.

Will it be published just as it was online? Or will lots be omitted? Or even tons added?!

Mysteries abound!

For now, just look forward to the next one!

And finally to the chief editor; to Itsuki Akata, the illustrator; to Yoichi Yamakami, the cover designer; to everyone involved in the proofreading, editing, printing, binding, distribution, and selling of this book; to all the reviewers on *Shousetsuka ni Narou* who gave me their impressions, guidance, suggestions, and advice; and most of all, to everyone who's read my stories, both in print and online, I thank you all from the bottom of my heart.

Thank you so very much.

Please continue to look out for these novels, and now the manga, from here on out.

— FUNA

AUGUST 2016